J

WE LIVE INSIDE YOU

"WE LIVE INSIDE YOU is fucking terrific. Jeremy Robert Johnson is dancing to a way different drummer. He loves language, he loves the edge, and he loves us people. These stories have range and style and wit. *This* is entertainment... and literature."—JACK KETCHUM, author of *Off Season*, *The Girl Next Door*, and *The Woman* (w/Lucky McKee)

"A haunting collection from a wildly talented author, WE LIVE INSIDE YOU is composed of nineteen perfectly-wrought nightmares, every one of which will stay with you long after you've finished reading. Jeremy Robert Johnson is one of those rare writers who can see in the dark." —PETER CRAIG, author of *Hot Plastic* and *Blood Father*, co-screenwriter of *The Town*

"One of the first 'rules' of writing you'll hear is that you've got to write compelling characters who a reader can invest in—if not, nobody'll give a shit what happens to them. Jeremy Robert Johnson's stories stand as proof to this maxim: you may not always like the people populating these stories but they're real and vital and you WILL care, deeply, about what becomes of them... and in JRJ's harsh universe, *baaaaad* things happen. Often. Prepare thyself." —CRAIG DAVIDSON, author of *Rust and Bone* and *The Fighter*

"The guy's a genius. Reminds me of William Gibson—the dark interest in altered states of consciousness, the unrelentingly furious forward movement, and the same kind of unlimited imagination."
—BEN LOORY, author of *Stories for Nighttime and Some for the Day*

"Tongue-replacing isopods, brain-raping copepods and body-warping worms are far from the most insidious parasites that infest Jeremy Robert Johnson's hapless literary victims. Though the squirmy bits elegantly pioneer new frontiers of sickness, WE LIVE INSIDE YOU is at its most twisted and mordantly revelatory when it drops the body-horror

metaphors and digs into the real horror of all the parasitic drives that ride us—tapeworms of greed, lust like plagues of crab lice, and the lethal heartworms of true love. So tightly written and so fluidly brutal you'll want to consume this psychosexual demolition derby in one sitting, but you'll spend the rest of the night checking yourself under a microscope. This book should come with a list of side-effects."
—CODY GOODFELLOW, author of *Silent Weapons for Quiet Wars* and *Radiant Dawn/Ravenous Dusk*

"Waaaay out at the deep end of the collective unconscious—where even the bravest of brain cells fear to tread—Jeremy Robert Johnson performs stand-up comedy for the gods. And their laughter is a marvelous, terrible thing. He's the kind of post-Lovecraftian genius berserker who makes the Great Old Ones new again. As with Clive Barker, there is no glorious mutational eruption that Johnson can't nail directly through your gawping mind's eye." —JOHN SKIPP, NY Times Bestselling author of *Spore* (w/ Cody Goodfellow) and *The Bridge* (w/Craig Spector)

"A dazzling writer." —CHUCK PALAHNIUK, NY Times Bestselling author of *Fight Club*

"Johnson weaves vivid and fascinatingly grotesque tales."—Bookgasm

"In its most twisted moments, Johnson's writing is too gleeful to pigeon-hole as strictly horror, and when he steps outside the gross-out game he transcends most other straight literary writers." —Verbicide

"I don't know if Mr. Johnson sold his soul to the devil to give him this gift for nightmare imagery, but by god, this guy can write. Johnson excels at pathology and perversity. A confirmed weirdo and authentic writer of uncommon emotional depth who deserves to be watched."
—Cemetery Dance

"Johnson is probably a few books away from doing for horror what Jonathan Lethem did for science fiction. Plain and simple? Forget horror; this is good fiction."—Girl on Demand

We Live Inside You

Jeremy Robert Johnson

Swallowdown Press
Portland, OR

Swallowdown Press
PO Box 86810
Portland, OR 97286-0810

WWW.SWALLOWDOWNPRESS.COM

ISBN: 1-933929-06-5

"The Oarsman" originally appeared in *Dark Discoveries #17*. "When Susurrus Stirs" originally appeared in *Bare Bone #10*. "The Witness at Dawn" "The Brilliant Idea" "Cortical Reorganization" "The Encore" "Mercy" & "A Flood of Harriers" originally appeared in *Cemetery Dance #'s 56 and 60*. "Consumerism" originally appeared in *Falling From the Sky*. "Trigger Variation" originally appeared in *The Vault of Punk Horror*. "The Gravity of Benham Falls" originally appeared in *Ghosts at the Coast Vol. 2*. "Cathedral Mother" originally appeared in *The Magazine of Bizarro Fiction #4*. "Simple Equations" originally appeared in *A Dark and Deadly Valley*. "Laws of Virulence" originally appeared in *Warmed and Bound*. "The Musty Cow's Teat of Death" originally appeared in *Boneyard Babies*. "The Mars Volta's Descent Into Bedlam" appears here courtesy of Universal Music.

Book design by Carlton Mellick III.

Printed in the USA.

Acknowledgements

Sincere thanks are due to the following folks/entities/collectives for their unending camaraderie, support, inspiration and wisdom: Jessi and Caleb (always), Carlton Mellick III, Rose O'Keefe, Cameron Pierce, Jeff Burk, Mykle Hansen, Alan M. Clark, Cody Goodfellow, J. David Osborne, Brandon Armstrong, John Skipp, Jack Ketchum, Joe R. Lansdale, Craig Davidson, Stephen Graham Jones, Kris Saknussemm, Ben Loory, Peter Craig, David Agranoff, Kevin Sampsell, The Velvet/The Cult/Bizarro Central, The Bizarro Brigade, Sam McCanna, John Roome, Dave Lounsbury, Jackson Ellis, Hernan Ortiz, Viviana Trujillo, Fractal, James Beach, Sam Pool, Powell's Books, the Johnsons, the Wicklunds, Bishop and (most likely) You.

Contents

For Caleb Merrick Johnson

&

Robert Eugene Johnson II

Body of the Host

Collection

The Oarsman

The same space that envelopes my craft surrounds Colony 1, its emptiness floating heavy around two corrupted cells.

A forgotten man in a metal membrane, inevitable death as the nucleus.

Far below—a planet heavy with viral load, perhaps too pregnant to prevent collapse.

Monitor light brings it to me LIVE: The monks on the side of the mountain are still singing, still swaying. But their low-throated hum is tapering. New angles are forming under their red robes, sharp jaunts of bone. A few have collapsed forward, toppled out of lotus position, the metal devices strapped around their necks now useless.

They aren't eating. If they're drinking, I've never caught them. The bastards are starving out, but not fast enough for my liking.

And I just can't stop watching them—the greatest mass murderers of all time, singing themselves to a slow death.

Kurylenko is floating outside of the station. With some despair I noted that his corpse does not spontaneously ignite even when we rotate into the full face of the sun. I pray for a spark.

Shakyamuni. That was the last thing he said, before he shut down.

We were in Sector C, nibbling vacu-packed peas, watching the news, our respective headphones feeding English and Russian language audio.

Everyone was waiting. Me, Kurylenko, the news cameras, the world—we were waiting to watch someone die.

If you would have asked anybody, they would have laid odds on the monks catching bullets. And that's how it would have gone down, if those cameras hadn't been there. Blame China's new media relations policy, promoting cultural events even in disputed territory. *Check out our beautiful history*—monks balancing on thumbs, fireworks shows leaving days of smoky haze—*and don't worry so much about human rights.*

They promised a beautiful display—the Yang-style chanting of a sacred text invoking empathy and oneness, courtesy of the Pan-Chinese

Open Hand Festival, live from the base of the snowy mountains. News helicopters hovered close. Military helicopters hovered just behind them.

I suppose that, to most aside from the Chinese, the assumption was that the circle of white stones and the two great metallic cylinders flanking the monks were part of tradition, perhaps glossed up for the global stage. But when the monitors happened across Chinese soldiers their faces held shimmers of stress and confusion. Tight knit brows. Sweaty foreheads. Something looked *wrong*, but it didn't seem there was any viable order to set things right.

Media speculation filled pre-performance air.

"The purpose of the necklaces is unknown, but they appear to be modern technology, perhaps reflecting China's merger of cutting-edge science and ancient culture."

"… those columns, though un-decorated, do lend a certain regal air to today's proceedings."

"We've been asked, for the duration of the performance, to stay beyond the ring of decorative stones."

"Our best guess is this is all part of the sound design, a way to ensure these beautiful voices are heard both here at the foot of these majestic mountains, and around the world."

This may have all been B-roll station filler if a BBC sound tech hadn't accidentally stumbled across those stones.

Just before it happened, you could see him on a few of the other stations' cameras, barely maintaining his footing over the crumbling shale of the mountainside, body hanging with sound gear ballast, trying to get as close to the white-rocked periphery as possible.

Then his left foot slipped, throwing him into a clumsy shuffle, trying not to drop the boom mic. Two steps to the side and he was in their circle.

His hand raised in apology—*Sorry, guys*.

That same hand ignited like phosphorous, sending out white light. Arcs of radiance flashed down on the sound tech's body from the two silver columns. The tech's mouth opened in a scream, his last breath consumed in the fire that swallowed him whole.

Then there were close-ups of the monks, still seated and ready to sing, their faces flashing something…

Regret?

Did it matter?

Chaos after that. Chinese military tucking ready rifles into their shoulders. News feeds jumping from B-roll to the Global Now. The charcoal husk of a clumsy man sending off smoke from inside the stone circle. Martin Vilkus spotted among the monks, dressed as one of them, the shaggy hair from his FBI photos shaved clean off.

You could have tried to absorb it, to piece together the feed and find a rational response. But Vilkus was barely on the national radar anymore, his history as the Feds' least favorite virologist-turned-terrorist old news. The guy hadn't issued a manifesto in years, and the Boston Subway Massacre, though leaving over seven hundred dead and internally liquefied to the consistency of fast food milkshakes, was long-forgotten in the wake of more popular atrocities.

Even if you knew what was about to happen, from what I've figured, you'd still be dead.

The monks reached up, each one flipping a switch on the tiny box that sat at the hollow of his throat. Blinking LED's registered "On" status.

Kurylenko had sensed it then. He yelled in Russian, the veins popping on his neck, like his urgency might carry the scream through the vacuum of space.

"Fucking shoot them."

His order yielded no response. And why I couldn't stop laughing at him, at his panicked face, I'll never know.

Then the song began. The monks' mouths were open wide, the tone unified and low. It pulled me into a vertiginous state, as if a door had just opened beneath me in the craft and I was flipping back through empty space.

I started to lose my sight, static spreading across my vision. Reaching up through atmospheric quicksand, I tried an old orientation technique. My fingers found purchase on the soft connective tissue and veins under my tongue, and I clasped down as hard as I could.

As it had so many times before, pain brought me into the present. And I was back in the station, and Kurylenko was collapsed on the ground and whispering something. I crouched and leaned in close.

Shakyamuni.

I would have appreciated less obscure last words. He could have told me I was a good friend. He could have told me where he stashed his best pornos.

Nope—fucking "Shakyamuni" was all I got.

Then nothing. His chest shifted slightly, and I could register condensation on a mirror if I held it to his nose. But that breathing and his heartbeat were already slowing and growing fainter.

The look on his face was the worst. His eyes flooded with tears. The corners of his mouth slightly upturned. If I was reading him right, I'd swear he was *smiling*.

I put his body in Bay 2 after his bowels voided. I considered trying some kind of resuscitation, but by then I'd seen enough news feed to know better.

Helicopters, news and otherwise, were earthbound and aflame. The monks' song echoed off the mountain walls and piles of collapsed bodies. Even Martin Vilkus was on the ground, the first red robe to drop. Whatever part he'd had in this, it hadn't guaranteed immunity. At least he looked happy.

A reporter from CNN had fallen right in front of her camera. The channel, for hours, was just her profile, tears running ravines through her beige foundation.

Flipping stations gave me scores of pre-programmed sitcoms and infomercials but I couldn't find any shows that would require a live human being.

No news. No response. Dead air.

There was a certain and lovely sense of permanence to this.

Kurylenko wasn't coming back. I knew that.

Should I have made sure he was actually dead before I tethered his body to the outside of the station? Some would say so.

But rest assured, that son-of-a-bitch was still smiling at nothing when I pushed him into space.

Regular television broadcasts ended days ago, but I've still got my Chinese friends pulled up on the monitor. I suppose this is the saving grace of my job.

Ostensibly this is a way station between Earth—now optimistically referred to as Colony 1—and future homes with nicer things like top-soil and potable water. But if much of the ship's funding came from certain parties in the east and the US that traffic in information, well you might have a better understanding of what we really do. Or *did*, I suppose.

So, for most of my day I tune our cameras in on the monks, watching them sway and starve.

Which contestant is next to be voted out here on Tibetan Idol?

The rest of the time I jerk off, half-sleep, and wonder—*Why am I still alive*?

The broadcast tried to claim me, but it couldn't. It barely effects me, watching it now.

What makes me different? I've been trying hard, so hard for years now, to act like everyone else.

When I was a child Dr. Chodron told me about emulation. I saw him for a few weeks, after the incident with Tommy's cat. Question after question, test after test, hushed conversations with my mother. In the end he sat down with me, wringing his hands, and asked me if I could be a good boy.

The right answer seemed to be, "Yes."

Then he told me I would have less trouble with the other boys if I could learn to make faces like theirs.

Somebody tells you about a naked lady and her dog Free-show; you cough up a few laughs and crinkle your eyes.

Somebody's tells you their mom died; you put your arms around them and pat them on the back. Keep your lower lip pushed up.

I've only gotten better at it since then.

But I've never felt much of anything behind the face.

Two other doctors have tried to label me since, but I shook the name. Fighting, fucking—everybody needs a little of that to stay alive. Doesn't mean some quack can tag me.

One thing you *can* call me—survivor.

But… I'm starting to think I might have to shake that name too.

There are no transport ships coming. My transmissions are reaching exactly no one.

The monk's broadcast couldn't have reached the whole planet, unless it didn't require the television signal as a medium for transmission. Maybe that was just a catalyst. A bonus, zapping Kurylenko up here in the ether, speeding along the process. Maybe those nasty electric columns were sending the song out in worldwide waves.

Whatever those monks did, whatever sonic virus they used to fuck up the human race, it wasn't going to get un-fucked. And, really, I'm okay with that. They sped up the inevitable, and left us all with a song and a smile. It's a downright kind extinction compared to what we've unleashed in the past.

But I'm not okay with the position they've left me in. Shitty, slow death in this metal coffin, watching my murderers slide softly into nirvana.

I've got fourteen hours until the station is directly over their territory.

With the proper use of the ship's boosters, and a sizable chunk of luck, I'm hoping I can ride this thing all the way down. All the way home. And maybe, just for one moment, they'll look up to the sky.

They will see me then, a terrible and fiery God, and I will descend upon them and ram their bad karma right down their fucking low murdering throats.

That is how this song ends.

When Susurrus Stirs

He tells me their life is the best thing going. He says that I need to imagine what it would be like to crawl into the plushest limousine I can imagine, to flop down into a deep, soft leather chair filled with downy feathers from giant geese, to turn the internal weather controls to "Perfect" and have a constantly changing range of scenery and a non-stop supply of food and fluids.

Then he says, imagine that all you have to do is eat and make babies and watch your life roll by in luxuriant comfort. The American dream, but he's a citizen of everywhere—he's just naturally attained what we're all shooting for. And it doesn't matter how big you get, he says, because when you become too large, part of you just breaks off and becomes another you. No dating or mating required. No awkward social moments, never a viscous string of sticky spit running thick from tooth to tongue while you try to talk a woman of vague sexual persuasion into an allowance of simian grinding.

Never a credit card bill in sight.

And his kids, he says proudly, they all turn out just like him. The emergence of a misplaced chromosome is a non-option. Every little him is a perfect chip off the ancient block, and has been for eons.

He doesn't speak to me as an individual; I can feel that in his voice as it creeps through my nervous system and vibrates my tympanic membrane from the inside. The idea of "self" is impossible to him. When he speaks to me as "You" I can tell he's addressing our whole species, every last human representing a potential host.

"You are more fun than the elephants," he says, "They didn't drink enough water and always fed us the same things. You feed us the soft pieces, the animal bits. We spread faster now. We are everywhere. We are growing."

I picture Susurrus as a "him" because I don't get along well with women. Always felt more comfortable around men. Can't truck with the idea of a lady crawling around in my intestines, judging me, saying, "Look at how you've treated yourself here. Too much red meat residue in your upper GI, and your colon could become impacted at a second's notice. How about some bran? Some heavy green tea? Something needs to be done. This place is a mess."

I named Susurrus after the analog "SSSSS" that accompanies his voice as it crawls around in my head. There's always this hissing noise that precedes his speaking and hangs on afterwards, like an itch deep in my ear. Sometimes the echo stays with me for hours. Then I play jazz CD's through my headphones and it sounds like I've got old records running under the needle.

Susurrus wasn't always in my brain, but I've been cultivating him, making him more a part of me. When I meditate I imagine the fibers of my spinal cord stretching out towards him, like feelers. They sway and twitch and burrow into my belly and connect to him, linking us. His hiss slides up through my spine and connects with my slow-chanted mantra, my mumbled OMNAMA's, until it's all white noise and for a moment I'm inside him, inside myself, feeling his contentment as his mouths reach out and slurp away at acidy bits of the day's meal, tiny snippets of sausage and soda pop sugars and oil-soaked ciobatta breads.

He is always at peace, a consumptive strand of nirvana.

According to the last x-ray my radiologist took, he's over fifty feet long, and still growing. My doctors have extracted pieces of him from my stool, pulsing egg sacs waiting to find water or flesh and keep the cycle of expansion in motion.

They say he's not a tapeworm, not a guinea worm, not anything they're used to seeing. He doesn't seem to effect my physiology in any negative way, although my grocery bill has ratcheted ever upwards. Still the doctors think I should have him removed. I tell them I'm a pacifist and it's not in my nature to harm a creature, especially if it poses no threat. That gets me worried glances, furrowed brows. But they don't protest much.

I think they're waiting for this thing to kill me so they can take me apart and extract his coiled body. Get a new species, name it after themselves, get published in the right journals, pull grant money.

I'm a cash cow infestation case. On a ticking clock, they imagine. Especially since this thing is spreading. One end is snaking towards my genitals, they say, and the other is coiling its way around my spine, on the way to my brain. There are more mouths showing up, not just the ones that reside in my belly.

"How did it get out of my stomach?" I ask them, not mentioning my meditation, the way Susurrus and I have bonded now. The way I've encouraged him to become part of me.

"Well, we're not exactly sure. It appears to exit through the duodenum as it heads toward your spine. There's a sort of cystic calcification at the point of exit, where it pushed through the stomach tissue. That's what keeps you from becoming toxic via your own acids. Again, this is all speculation. If you'd let us perform a more invasive..."

"Nope. No can do, Doc. You say this thing's not hurting me. What're the odds that this procedure would kill it?"

They don't know. These guys really don't know anything. Why should I open up my body, *our* bodies, to guesswork with scalpels?

I think I know where he came from, this new part of my life.

Five months ago I was jogging, a beautiful run at dusk through the sloping, rolling green park near my house. I was sucking down deep lung-loads of air when I ran through a floating mire of gnats. They stuck to me, twitching in my sweat, their tiny bodies suddenly swept up in the forward surge of my run. A few were sucked right into my chest, surely now melting to atoms against my alveoli.

But one of them... one of them stuck to the roof of my mouth. There was an itch, so close in sensation to the hiss of Susurrus, and I felt an immediate need to take a nap.

So I did. I collapsed to the ground, mindless of the lactic acidosis that would haunt my muscles, curled there among the duck shit and crawling ants and crushed grass, and I fell into a slumber.

When I awoke there was a tight bubble of tissue on the roof of my mouth, where the gnat had stuck. It hurt when I prodded it with my tongue, so I avoided it.

Later that night the bubble had become even tighter, this small mound of swollen pink tissue with a whitish tip. I stared at it in the mirror, unable to look away from its grotesque new presence.

I could feel my heartbeat inside the bump. There was no way I could sleep with this thing in my mouth. What if it kept expanding until I couldn't breathe?

I rubbed down my tweezers with benzyl alcohol and proceeded to poke and squeeze the bump until it bled. A thin rivulet of blood trickled down from the fleshy stalactite, and the harder I squeezed the more the blood thickened, grew darker. Soon the blood made way for a dense yellow fluid that carried with it the odor of rotten dairy in high heat. I pushed one pointed end of the tweezers directly into the spreading hole at the side of the bump.

Then it ruptured.

The relief of pressure was immediate. My mirror caught the worst of the spray, instantly shellacked with dead-cell soup in a spray pattern near arterial in its arc.

Then the colors came. A thin drip from the open wound on the roof of my mouth, two drops like oil spilling out, swirling with shades I'd never quite seen before, just outside a spectrum my eyes could comprehend. The drops sat there in the curve of my tongue, merged together like quivering mercury.

I'd never felt so intense a need to swallow something in my entire life.

The sensation of the drops was not fluid. It felt as if they were crawling into me, too impatient for my peristaltic process.

And again, almost immediately, I collapsed into slumber, this time dreaming of a sea of human tissue, all of it shifting and turning and surging, soft and hot and wanting to pull me under.

I hadn't had so explosive a wet dream since I was in junior high.

And when I woke up, curled on the floor of my bathroom with my underwear stuck to me like soaked toilet paper, I was hungry as a newborn.

Four month's time passed like nothing, our perception expanded to a broader sense. The human clock thinks small—within seventy-five year death limitations.

We laugh at the idea of death. The upside of being We.

And We are larger now. Eighty pounds heavier, abdomen distended, watermelon tight. One poke with a toothpick just below the bellybutton and we'd tear open like crepe paper. Neck swollen with a circular rash pattern that seeps clear fluids now crusting in the bony pockets of our shoulder-blades. White of the eyes yellowing, thickening. Hair falling out in clumps from soft-scalp surface.

Our penis is heavier. Its skin shifts constantly; there are more veins, white beneath the surface. The head has bloomed from mushroom tip to flower; it is open, flayed, in rose-like petals, red, pulsing. We bandage it to keep it from seeping down our leg.

We have stopped seeing the doctors. They whispered letters last time.

CDC they said.

Our I-brain told us this means trouble. We cannot accept "trouble" so close to the next cycle. We force fed the doctors the bits of us they stole from our excretions. So many of us in each segment that even their testing couldn't ruin all the eggs. Our body was shaking then, sweating hands clutching an oily metal tool, eyes crying. It has stopped struggling since. Its feelings are soft echoes now, little more. Things are quiet.

We are hiding. Hiding ends after the next sun-drop.

Our I-brain is remembering passwords, using fat purpled fingers to stroke language keys.

We are feeling better as we see the screen before us change.

Our tickets have been confirmed. The glowing box has thanked us for our purchase.

"You're welcome," we whisper. The rolling chair squeaks under our ever-shifting weight. We stand up with a grunt and feel that the bandages around our meat-sprout are wet again. Cleaning up is no longer important.

We crawl on four bony-stems towards our meditation mat. Light the incense and try to assume the lotus position. Too much of us; our legs can't fold in to the space filled by our twitching belly.

We lay back and stare at the ceiling. Our mantra has been replaced by a new noise. We push our tongue to the front of our teeth and start leaking air, a steady SSSSSS until our I-brain goes soft and quiet and we lie there in the dark room, shaking slightly from our constant eating and squirming. Much of the old us is empty now. Our new muscles, thousands of them, ropy and squeezing against each other, roll us onto our right side.

At some point we insert our thumbs into our mouth and suck the meat clean from the bones.

Anything to feed the new cycle.

The seat in the theater can barely hold us, but we are here and we are ready. It is after the most recent sun-drop, half-way through the dark period. We are wearing leather gloves (they barely fit except for the thumbs, which drape and look sharp) and a trench-coat at the suggestion of the remnants of the I-brain.

We sit at the rear of the room. No one sits near us but most of the rows in front of us are full. A bright light appears at the front of the room, large, shimmering.

Our I-brain tells us this is a midnight movie, a Spanish film, one of the best. Hasn't been shown in a while. We knew it would be packed. We see a couple of people have brought their children. There is a pained feeling from the old thoughts, but it fades.

There are thin clouds of sweet white smoke floating in this room. We breathe it in deeply, pulling it with a whistling noise into our one un-collapsed lung.

The show on the screen is strange, like the amusing dreams of our I-brain. The humans aren't acting like humans. They are trapped inside a cave lit by a bonfire. They rub each other with burning metal staffs, men and women screaming, skin bubbling and bursting. They paint their eyes with black ashes. They pull a large creature from a cage at the back of the tunnel, many men struggling and falling as they drag the thing in on chains that run through its skin. Some of the fallen men collapse under it as it is dragged forward and it pulls them up into its fluid mass, absorbing them. The space where their bodies merged and melted in begins to ooze a thick white cream. Women ladle this cream from its skin, drinking it and dancing, circles around the fire, ever faster. The women fall to the ground and their chests open up, ribs turned to spongy soft nothing, hearts missing. Slugs ooze out between spread-wide breasts and crawl towards the creature, still just a shape, still cloaked in dark. The men sit before the fire and sweat black oil. Light glows at the top of their foreheads. The slugs turn their stalks to the lights on the men's heads and shift away from the massive beast quivering in the dark. Then the slugs are on the men, long shining trails on shivering skin.

We are touching ourselves while these images glow before us. We have unbuckled and lowered our pants. The leather on our gloved hands is soaking through with seepage. We do not push aside our jacket, but know that the pulsing rose between our legs is emitting a light-red glow. A hissing noise slips from its center.

We are as quiet as we can be. As expected, the audience uproar in the room buries our birthing sounds. The people in this room are laughing, breathing, smoking, fascinated and excited by a world that is not theirs.

We can taste them on our tongues. Two of our heads have emerged, broken through the belly skin, hissing in the flavor of the room.

We slide down to the swollen meat-sprout at our groin and wrap our long bodies around it. Our fanged mouths find each other and lock up, teeth biting into each other's lower jaws. We are a sheath now, squeezing tight, sliding up and down, pulsing, with the blooming rose at our top, its folds now filling with an oil-slick rainbow of wet color.

There is now a desert on the screen. The cave full of revelers has collapsed. A lone man in a cowboy hat has emerged. He walks on crutches made of elephant ivory. He leaves no print in the sand.

We are ready for the next cycle. Hissing at a higher pitch. Our human head lolls back, its now soft skull squelching against the rear wall of the theater, bits of gray garbage draining out.

Our mouths unlatch from each other and we stop stroking between our legs. We bite into the rose-bloom and taste our old warm blood and the oils of our gestation and we pull back and then split the meat-sprout from tip to shaft.

What is left of our I-brain thinks it has gone to a place called Heaven. It feels so good. So alive.

It thinks a word. *Enlightenment.*

Our abdomen muscles contract and push down and a thick, bloody sausage-shaped sac pushes out of the hole we've torn in our crotch, the old flaps of our meat-sprout shaking and slipping against its emergence.

It is rare and lucky to reach this point in the cycle. We are blessed.

We quickly grasp the tube with our man-hands and bring it to our mouth, licking it clean, the taste stirring an old sense memory of the day we swallowed a bug in the park.

One of our new extensions crawls up through our man-throat and slides over the slick, swollen man-tongue. We bite into the sac, spreading it open.

We smile.

Their wings are already drying.

The film on the screen is so strange that when the man in the desert is suddenly eclipsed by the shadow of thousands of tiny flying gnats, the audience gasps in awe, breathing in deep, smiling with surprise, stunned by spectacle.

We ride in on the waves of their exhalation and find soft purchase.

And the people sleep, and dream, and awake to a subtle hissing sound. It is familiar to them. They hear it in their blood.

We are the waves of an ancient ocean crashing to shore, washing everything clean.

Persistence Hunting

Don't act surprised, or shake your bloody fists at the night sky.

You chased this down.

Help is coming—maybe a reality check can keep you seething until it gets here. Better than slipping into shock.

Face it—you're lying there in the evening chill, broken and breathless on the dewy suburban grass because of a basic truth:

You've always been a sucker for love.

And being smart enough to know that isn't the same as being able to do a goddamn thing about it.

You were a mark from the get-go.

Age seven: All Mary Ashford had to do was smile. You kicked over your licorice. She skipped away, shared it with that red-headed oaf Mikey Vinson.

Rube.

Age fourteen: Sarah Miller asked you to the last dance of the year.

Why wouldn't you help her with her algebra homework? An easy down-payment on a guaranteed post-dance make-out session.

You even gave Sarah your final exam answers.

She passed algebra.

She passed on attending the dance.

Stomach flu—very sad. She cried on the phone.

Two weeks later she went to the final dance at the school across town. With Mikey Fucking Vinson. The rumor mill had them crossing fourth base. In a *hot tub*.

You cursed Mikey Vinson, prayed to God for wolves to snuff the bastard, to disembowel him in a hot tub, a steaming red bowl of Vinson soup.

Revenge fantasies waned. You knew the truth. This was on you. You cried yourself to sleep, thinking Sarah Miller would be the last girl you'd ever truly fall for.

Chump.

Age fifteen: Love got blown off the radar.

Was it world-weary resolve? No, you were a mess of hormones and zero savvy charging headlong into the bayonets of the beauties walking your school halls.

Love caught the boot because your parents burned to death on their eighteenth anniversary. Bad electrical blanket wiring and spilled champagne caused a flash-fire.

As with every anniversary weekend since you were born, you were staying at Uncle Joshua's house—a bungalow off Powell on 58th—in South East Portland. The crucial difference that weekend was that at the end of it you had no home to return to.

Uncle Joshua took you in. You didn't speak for three months. You dreamed—your parents screaming with smoke-filled lungs.

Your Uncle did his best. Let you know you were loved. Gave you great pulp novels about druggy detectives and man-eating slugs. Taught you how to swear properly. Let you stay up till any hour, so long as you promised to run with him every morning at seven sharp.

"The morning run blows the morning prayer out of the water," he told you. "Gets you thinking. Breathing deep. It clears out the worry, the garbage, everything."

You ran the city with him—sidewalks, tracks, trails. Portland seemed huge and electric in a way your hometown Salem never did.

He showed you how to run through "the wall"—the utter vacuum of energy that forced you to walk. Soon the wall was pushed further and further out.

You ran to exhaustion—morning jogs with your Uncle and epic evening jaunts that allowed you to collapse far from the reality of your loneliness, from dreams of burning hands reaching for your face.

Five years after the fire, love finally tracked you down.

You were twenty-one. Still a virgin. You'd chased nobility, never exploiting your semi-orphan status for a cheap lay. Besides, that would have meant talking to someone, knowing someone.

You were confident chasing the cat was for suckers anyway. You'd transcended that status because you had a *new* kick, something you'd guessed was better than pussy:

THEFT.

It wasn't for the cash—your parents' trust kept you sound.

You stole because you'd recognized a loophole.

Portland was a runner's city. During daylight it was impossible to hit the waterfront without seeing a jogger, but the nights had their own crews. Doctors or bartenders forced into the late shift. Other running zealots like you.

And Portland's runner omni-presence rendered you a non-threat to the cops. Another fitness freak in fancy gear. You rocked sheer shirts, a Garmin GPS watch, a CamelBak water backpack, a flashy yellow vest, and shorts designed to hug your junk.

You liked to wave at the cops, give them a nod that said, "Here we are, upstanding citizens keeping things safe and healthy."

Sometimes they waved back. Some of those times you ran right by them with a thousand dollars worth of pinched jewelry in your CamelBak.

They never turned around. What self-respecting thief would run by a cop car while rocking reflective gear meant to call attention?

You were just another night runner fading in the rearview.

In fairness to them, you started minor, like some jockey-boxing meth-head.

Your LifeHammer tool was designed for drivers trapped in a submerged vehicle. One side had a hammer specially designed to crack tempered auto glass.

Ostensibly designed for exits, it worked great for entrances.

You trolled the NW hills near the Leif Erickson trail, pulling smash-and-grabs on Suburbans, Jaguars, a smattering of Portland's ubiquitous Subarus and Priuses. You copped cell phones, cameras, MP3 players. You copped hard-ons from the gigs, tracked record runs off the buzz.

You kept the swag in a box in your closet, obsessed over it, deciphering what you could about the people you'd jacked. You fell asleep to stolen play-lists. You studied the smiles of strangers in digital photos.

You soon realized that any tweaker could crack car windows.

The buzz dwindled.

You escalated—houses were the logical progression.

Your first pick was a sharp art-deco joint. You'd done your sidewalk surveying—they had a habit of leaving the sliding glass door on the side of their house open.

You almost bailed. Nerves. Visions of the owners polishing rifles inside.

You decided to hit their car instead—a desperation move.

You got lucky, opened the glove compartment, found a receipt. Franzetti Jewelers—$6,000. Dated that day. Scrambled the car, found zilch.

Was it in the home? A necklace, a ring—they'd fit into your backpack so easily. Something like that was much more intimate than an iPod—it represented history between two people.

The gravity of it pulled you to the side entrance of the house.

You knocked on the door frame. "Hello?"

If anyone answered, you'd feign injury: You'd crunched your ankle coming down from Forest Park. Needed a cab, a hospital.

After your third "Hello" echoed dead, you crossed the threshold.

It took five exhilarating minutes to find the jewelry box. Bedroom dresser, third drawer, under a pile of gold-toe socks. A serious square-cut rock mounted on a platinum setting. An engagement in the cards?

You thought about leaving the stone. But then you remembered Mary Ashford and Sarah Miller, decided to save the guy from becoming another sucker.

You hit the streets, the ring secure in your CamelBak.

Back home, the jewelry went into the swag box. You couldn't sleep, reviewing your plunder, tiny pieces of other lives.

B & E's became *everything*.

One a week at first. Monday through Thursday was casual jog recon. Weekends were break-ins.

Jewels reigned supreme. They spent time close to other people, had sentimental value.

You'd take cash when discovered, but never credit cards.

Once a week quickly became "whenever the coast looked clear." Your record was three break-ins in one night.

You wore thin white runner's gloves, hoping they'd prevent prints.

You carried steak-flavored dog treats but never had the guts to break into a house after you'd heard a dog bark. You petted cats when they'd allow it.

If a whole pack of cigarettes was left out you'd take one smoke, save it for the morning, puff on it at sunrise.

Sometimes you went to hip hop shows before your evening run. It was easy to stay chill, enjoy a show solo, hood up, feeling like an anonymous gangster amidst all the fronting. They could talk up the criminal life; you *lived* it.

You tried to maintain the morning runs with Uncle Joshua. He noticed your owl eyes and lagging pace.

He expressed concern.

You dropped the routine. The nights were just too long.

It was in this state—harried, junkie-hungry for break-ins—that you let love back into your life.

Slow it down. Pay attention. This is where everything fell apart.

You were coming home via Burnside that night, maneuvering around the bum-clusters near the bridge. An alky with a piece of corn in his beard gave you a wave.

You were astronaut high from a twenty minute break-in session. The entire house had smelled like summer lilac. You'd wondered if the owners paid to have that piped in at all hours.

That sweet smell is what you were thinking about at the moment the little black car took a no-look right turn at 10th and Burnside past Union Jack's. You saw a bright flash out of your peripheral, heard a thump that you ID'd as your body hitting the hood of the ride. Then you were rolling on pavement.

Brake lights made the scene run red. You caught the model of the car…couldn't focus on the license plate.

Last-call closeout-boozers were a night run liability. You'd accepted that, but you couldn't accept the fact that you might have been slaughtered by a fucking Jetta with a butterfly sticker on the bumper.

Gorgeous legs in camouflage stockings emerged from the driver's side. The girl stood, giraffe-tall. Five inch heels. Soon she was crouched by your side. You couldn't focus on her face aside from wide hazel eyes, tiny flecks of gold floating in the green.

You sap—you might have been in love before you even lost consciousness.

She danced under the name Avarice. When she told a guy he could call her Ava it guaranteed extra tips. When boys pointed out the fitting nature of her name she called them clever. That pulled more tips, too.

She was insanely irresponsible, taking you to her apartment instead of a hospital, but her license was already suspended for another offense. Ava had bugged at the idea of real jail time and was strong enough to get you into her back seat, then her first floor apartment. She watched you sleep on her couch. You kept breathing. She gave you an ice compress for your head. You asked for Advil; she came back with two Valium and a Xanax, delivered by slender hands, chipped black polish on the fingernails.

She asked why you were out running so late. You told her you worked a day job and preferred to run when it was cooler out. She asked what you did. You said roofing. Seemed tough.

She asked you running questions, caught your excitement about the topic, used it. You could see her game—ingratiate until she knew charges would be dropped—but you didn't want to stop playing. You liked the way she was tending to you. It stirred something you hadn't felt in years.

Plus, she was easy on the eyes. Heart-shaped pale face framed with short black hair. Decent lips made more charming by a crooked smile. Legs that seemed to be two thirds of her frame. She wore grey shorts with pink trim piping, a thin green cotton t-shirt that showed off the curves on each side of her small breasts.

You knew most men didn't get to see her like this—casual, relaxed and gracious. She knew you knew and rode the vibe. She showed you her tattoos—two thin stripes, one running up the back of each leg, meant to mimic the back seam of a pair of pin-up stockings. As she got closer you saw that each seam was actually composed of delicate cursive words.

She bent forward, touched her toes so you could see the entirety of each line.

The right leg said: …I asked him with my eyes to ask again yes and then he asked me would I yes to say yes my mountain flower and first I put my arms around him

The left leg continued: yes and drew him down to me so he could feel my breasts all perfume yes and his heart was going like mad and yes I said yes I will Yes.

"It's from Ulysses," she said.

She admitted that every time she read that last chapter she felt like "rubbing one out." She made a circling motion in the sky with her index finger and closed her eyes. Then she smiled, full blaze.

You were ready to die for this girl, and she hadn't even kissed you.

Your concussion was minor. More disconcerting was the new gimpy sensation in your right leg. When you tried to run the iliotibial band next to your knee registered tight, white-hot pain.

You had to drop running for a week. Better to let it rest than blow it out.

Ava was an Olympic-level tease. When she dropped you off at your Uncle's house she leaned in close, said she wanted to look at your pupils. Be sure you didn't have any brain damage. She locked you in at the eyes. Her lips floated a hair's-breadth from yours, the heat from her face mixing nicely with your Valium/brain damage buzz.

She whispered in your ear, "I think you'll be just fine." Then she told you what nights she worked at which clubs.

She didn't seem surprised that you were there every night. You dipped into the box in your closet, swapped jewels for cash at pawn shops, loved spending ill-gotten gains on Ava.

You bought every lap dance you reasonably could. When anyone else got too close to her they looked like Mikey Vinson.

You turned creepazoid one night, crawled her apartment when you knew she was at the beginning of her dance shifts at Sassy's. You were pro at climbing in through windows. Summer heat had everyone's open. Seemed she barely lived there aside from her disheveled futon and the explosion of clothes scattered throughout. You threw two pairs of her underwear in your CamelBak, rushed home for an epic stroke-fest. You tied her lacy yellow G-string around the base of your cock, huffed the blue cotton pair, and pounded yourself into exhaustion. You never ran short on fantasies—your favorites involved her sneaking into houses with you, violating every room.

If it wasn't obsession, it was pretty damn close.

Things seemed fine, spectacular really, until the night she invited you over for coffee at her place. You accepted, secretly ecstatic, but caught the heebie-jeebies when you noticed she wasn't talking to you on the way, kept looking over her shoulder.

At her apartment she brought you into the loop—She liked you, more than she expected. But she already had a man, on the low, and he was insanely jealous, sometimes to the point where he got rough. She didn't know how to leave him. She didn't want to endanger you. The guy never came down to her clubs, but his friends sometimes did. They'd noticed you. How could they not?

You puffed up your chest. "Who is this guy?"

"Have you ever heard of Stump Lo?"

Shit. You had. You un-puffed your chest.

Stump Lo was a Portland rapper who'd been struggling for years to pimp his pseudo-Cali-gangster-style hip hop to an audience more interested in commercial hits or backpacker rap. He was the dude you sat through while you waited for the good rappers to come on—tolerated but not loved. You could feel his resentment on stage.

Word was he'd shifted to coke sales a year or two back—he wanted the cred and his album sales weren't churning out the royalties—and had worked his way to the upper echelon of Snortland suppliers.

This moment is when you should've jumped ship.

Instead you looked into Ava's eyes and decided to tell her about your hobbies. It was the best sales pitch available, to offer an alternative bad-ass, one who wouldn't trap her in jealousy.

You told her you weren't a roofer, you were a fucking roughneck criminal. At the top of your game you were Portland's best cat burglar.

You also broke your code and exploited your parents' death, saying you'd even had to see their bodies. You told her you hadn't felt fear since that day. If she didn't want to stay with Stump she could roll with you.

You escalated your bravado with each detail. Her eyes sparked.

She wanted to hear more about your break-ins. You told her about all but one of them.

She loved your runner's scheme for evading the law.

She leaned over, put her hand on your face. Said she had an amazing idea.

You were all ears, you sorry Rescue Ronnie Captain Save-a-Ho motherfucker.

You sold the rest of your stolen swag, a whole day of pawn shop hustling.

You liquidated your trust, cashed out your swollen checking account.

Ava found a great place in the Caymans online.

You'd miss your Uncle, but had no other ties and figured that Ava's legs around your back could ease any pain.

Ava told you she'd already bought tickets.

She confirmed she'd found a buyer for Friday night—she knew dealers who liked to show off their cash in the clubs. Now it was just a matter of acquiring the blow.

Stump Lo was going to open a show for Keak da Sneak that night. A small opening, maybe a few hours, but after your score all that remained was a shot up I-5 to meet Ava's connection. Then on to PDX and paradise.

You met up with Ava after her shift on Wednesday night. You wanted her to have your best diamond ring, from your first break-in. You couldn't bring yourself to hock it. You waited near her car, not wanting to risk any of Stump Lo's friends seeing you inside.

She ate it up. Even got a little teary-eyed. She put her hands on your hips, pressed her cheek against yours and said, quietly, "I think I might be falling in love with you."

She smelled like sweat, cigarettes, too much perfume. You loved it. You wanted to kiss her but she was gesturing you towards her car. You got in, thinking she couldn't contain her need anymore. You'd fuck right there in the lot…

Instead she wanted to review details for Friday. She would drop by Stump's place before the show, wishing him luck. She would make sure that his Rottweiler—named Scarface, of course—was kenneled. You'd watch for Stump to leave. Once he did you'd run around back and disconnect the A/C unit running into his office. That's your access point.

After that it was simple—grab the coke/get out. Then a quarter mile jog to your meeting point. You'd roll in her car, make your sale, then get into costume for the airport.

She'd been inspired by your adventures in social camouflage, figured it could work to her advantage too. You'd enter PDX as proud parents-to-be. Her prosthetic belly-bump and draping maternity gear would conceal your collected cash nest egg as well as half a brick.

You questioned the wisdom of bringing drugs. Carrying serious cash was already suspect. The coke made the trip trafficking. Why risk it?

"The US dollar is on the decline. Coke is universal tender. We can turn it into money, connections, favors. I've never seen a pregnant chick getting searched at the airport. Have you?"

You hadn't.

"And now, with this rock on my finger, we'll look like we're engaged. It's perfect."

You considered proposing. Make it real, right then. But it might spook her, and you knew better times were coming. Wouldn't it be cooler to propose at sunset, in the sand, with a buzz kicking from some tropical cocktail?

Besides, you hadn't even kissed yet. For all you knew, though you tried to exterminate the thought, she might still be fucking Stump Lo. But if she was it was just to perfect her cover, keeping things smooth until you could begin your life together, right? You squashed the thoughts.

She pinned you down with her eyes.

"Are you ready for Friday night?"

The version of yourself that you were selling could answer only Yes.

Getting in was simple. You saw those window-mounted A/C units as "Open House" signs. You'd brought your LifeHammer as back-up, but all you'd needed to access Stump's residence was a small screwdriver and the ability to disconnect a plug.

You were halfway up the stairs to the guest bathroom where the stash was supposed to be hidden, feeling like the air had been replaced with a Dexedrine mist. Your mouth was dry, your face a sheet of sweat.

You noticed a drop of perspiration fall from the tip of your nose to the carpeted stair underfoot, and wondered if it could pop up as evidence.

You were bent over using your runner's glove to swab up the droplet when Scarface caught your left calf in his jaws.

At first you thought it was a severe cramp. Maybe you'd been favoring your left leg to protect your fragile right and the imbalance caught up with you.

Even when you heard the growl and felt teeth sinking in you couldn't quite believe it. After all, you'd received Ava's text: DG KNNLD, STMP LVG 1 HR.

What neither of you'd considered was that Stump might extract Scarface prior to leaving.

Call it an oversight.

An oversight that was quickly turning your left leg into shredded meat.

You collapsed forward on the staircase. Scarface dug in deeper, swung his head.

Agony.

You'd stopped thinking. You tried to kick out at him with your other foot but couldn't land more than a glancing blow. You wished you'd started running in steel-shanked boots instead of sneaks.

You tried to say, "Good doggy let go doggy" but when you opened your mouth to assuage, all that came out was, "AAAAAAA! SHITSHITSHIT! JESUS!" It riled him; he clamped deeper.

You found the beefy treats you always carried in your pocket for just such an occasion. You tried to extend your arms backwards with the snacks so Scarface could catch the scent.

No interest. So you did your best to wing the snacks at him.

A yelp! Sweet mother of mercy—his jaws cut loose for a second. You rotated, braced for further assaults.

Scarface was pawing at the right side of his face, whining. One of the stale old snacks must have clipped him dead in the eye.

For one tiny moment you felt bad for him. Then his head dropped below his shoulders. He was about to pounce again. You kicked out in desperation, eyes closed….

Both of your feet made contact.

Scarface thumped to the bottom of the staircase, laid out.

Shit! You felt terrible—instantly cursed. Steal a man's coke and his girl and he might move on with his life. But kill his dog? He'd probably hunt you to the ends of the Earth.

Without thinking you were limping back down the stairs, towards the dog, to see if you'd actually killed it. Then you heard a low growl.

Scarface popped up in full bristle, teeth bared, bloody.

Your blood. It took a second to recognize that.

You leapt up the stairs, four at a time. You had to lean more weight on your right. The tightness there turned to razor-wire. Then you were in the upper hallway and bounding, trying to remember what she'd said.

Third door on the left. Guest bathroom.

You collapsed into the third room, no longer caring if it was the bathroom, just wanting to kick the door closed. Shut out the beast.

You heard the door click shut and pressed your right foot against the wood, bracing it.

You could tell he was out there, hear him gnawing at the door with the side of his mouth. You reached up, locked the door. Gnashing turned to barking, guttural eruptions.

You worried about the neighbors being alerted but remembered what Ava told you—the whole joint was soundproofed since they used to get complaints about the studio bumping beats at all hours.

You flipped the light switch and caught yourself in the mirror. Bloody. Shaking. In track gear. The image ran ugly.

But at least you'd landed in the bathroom.

You were glad the mirror had to come down—seeing yourself in that moment brought in a rush of feelings and questions that were better not contemplated. You grabbed each side of the frame, lifted up, and pulled it back off its mounting screws.

The hole in the drywall was there, as she'd described. You reached in and found the plastic loop, pulled it off the nail in the stud. The loop was attached to a vinyl cord. Your shoulders strained to reel in the compressed duffel bag at its far end.

Seeing the loot gave you new confidence. You'd found your grail—your princess was waiting for your return. You re-mounted the mirror, used a towel to clean your blood off the floor and then wrapped it around your leg to staunch further bleeding.

Scarface's paws thumped against the door, nails scraping, not calming down. You scanned the bathroom for a weapon and found nothing that would allow you to confront the hound with confidence.

That left one point of exit—a small sliding window above the shower.

You slid the window open, popped the screen. You tied off the duffel bag to your CamelBak and used the vinyl cord to lower them to the ground.

The drop from the second floor was unfriendly no matter how you went about it. You managed to hang and exit feet first. Both legs felt equally savaged so you couldn't pick one to bear the brunt of the fall. Instead you tried to let your legs collapse and shift your weight to the back so you could somersault out of it.

This did not work.

Your left leg hit first. Before you could shift your weight your knee was driven into your jaw. A world-class uppercut delivered by yourself. For a moment everything was fireworks, copper, dust. Then your brain cleared out.

You'd made it.

Your contraband was to your left, Scarface was a distant threat, and you were only a quarter mile from an angel-in-waiting.

What you didn't expect was... well... any of it.

Ava was at the meeting spot, a dusty trailhead near the Wildwood hiking areas. That part matched up with what you'd pictured.

She'd stepped out of the car, closed the door. She'd left the headlights off. You couldn't see her well. You'd taken longer than expected to reach her, moving along with a limping trot. You began to apologize.

"I know I'm running a little behind but you won't believe..."

And then she hit you with the Tazer.

You were already on the gravel before you recognized the crackling sound, felt the darts piercing your belly.

For a moment you thought that you'd been shot. That Stump Lo had found the pair of you and you were dead for sure.

But it was Ava holding the Tazer, and she wasn't letting up on the volts.

Your right leg was folded underneath your body. With the next blast of juice you felt your calf pull too tight. Your fragile iliotibial band finally gave with an audible snap. You would have screamed if your jaw wasn't clenched shut.

Ava let up on the trigger. She said, "Bag!"

You gestured towards your pack and the duffel bag, thrown three feet to your side.

"Ava, what..."

She turned the juice back on. Grabbed the duffel, clearly not interested in conversation. She stepped closer.

"I'm going to release the trigger, but if you start to talk I'll Taze you until your hair starts on fire. Got me?"

You made your best effort at a nod.

She crouched closer. "You're not coming with me, but you should still run. You probably didn't even think of this, but Stump's place has a shit-ton of cameras. They make him feel gangster. He's no killer, but the people who supply him will not be pleased."

She'd been rehearsing this, leaving no room for emotion. Maybe she really loved you. Maybe this was some kind of test...

She continued. "You've probably killed me. This is what people will think. They will find a letter at Union Jack's, talking about how you'd been planning to rob Stump. You threatened to kill me if I didn't go along with it. You'd even joked about burying me out here in Forest Park and keeping the drugs for yourself. The girls I worked with last night think I'm scared of you. I really sold it. There are plenty of people who've seen you staring at me for hours. It will read as stalker behavior after the letter gets out."

"But, Ava..."

ZZZZRNT! You seized up. She was not trigger-shy on the Tazer.

"Don't try to find me."

Another long jolt with the Tazer. Then she was kneeling by your side, properly pegging you as too jellied for combat. Even in the dark, you could sense she was smiling. She was back at your ear.

"I did love the ring, by the way, but I had to sell it today. Easier to send off the single mother vibe without it."

Then she was over you. Her breath smelled like black licorice. She leaned in to kiss you on the lips.

And you, you sorry sonofabitch, you still wanted it. When her lips met yours you closed your eyes, hoped time would slow.

But it ended, and she was up and the Tazer was left in the dirt.

"You're smart enough to know I'm right. Get the fuck out of Portland."

"Ava..."

"Good luck."

Her car door slammed. Headlights slapped you blind and she was gone.

You hobble-dragged yourself three miles before realizing you couldn't go further. Dawn would come and you were far too savaged for your runner's ruse to help you.

You made it to a house which looked unoccupied. You memorized the street address, crawled to the backyard to keep from being spotted street-side.

You drained the water from your CamelBak, still felt Death Valley thirsty.

There *was* one stroke of luck in all of this. Ava left you with your cell phone.

Call it an oversight.

Your first phone call was to Uncle Joshua. He slurred a groggy "Hello?" but was alert after hearing your voice. You gave him the address. Said to come to the backyard of the house. Don't ask why.

He didn't. You'd run with him as best you could this last Thursday, knowing it might be your last time together. He'd started to ask you questions about late nights, your hitchy right leg. You'd cut him off.

"Things are just kind of crazy right now. I met this girl..."

Uncle Joshua had laughed and let out a slow, knowing "Oh." You'd worked hard to ignore your leg, picked up the pace. He got the message.

You hoped he'd pick up his pace now. You'd lost a lot of blood. How long did you have before Stump figured out he'd been jacked? How long before Ava's friends would have the cops scanning Forest Park for a body they'd never find?

A light turned on over the patio at the rear of the house. Could be on a timer—you weren't taking any chances. You crawled across the grass, spotting a large and thankfully empty dog house.

You crept in, found it surprisingly plush. Call it delirium, but you swore the west wall had an on-switch for a tiny A/C unit. Even the *dogs* up in the hills were living easy.

You leaned against the rear wall, set your CamelBak on your belly. Unzipped the pack. Pulled out your accidental insurance policy.

You'd broken in to Ava's place on Thursday night, knowing she was working at Devil's Point, to bring her underwear back. Ever since you'd stolen them you'd felt weird about it. They turned you on, but you wanted to move past connecting to people through their things. You had a chance to be with the flesh-and-blood girl. Starting out psychotic felt wrong.

But once you were in her place you couldn't help exploring. You rifled the bag she'd packed, wanting to see what kind of swimsuits she'd be wearing to the beach.

You'd been living with compulsion so long you didn't even question it when you pocketed the thing. She was going to need it with her. This way you'd be certain she wouldn't forget it.

But you could have left it in the bag. It was already packed. She wasn't going to forget it. Maybe, deep down in the recesses of your memory, you were thinking of Mary Ashford and Sarah Miller, and that twinge of pain kept her passport in your pocket.

Your second call was to Information. They automatically connected you through to a Customs agent at PDX.

You noticed silver sparkles in your vision that couldn't mean anything good. Zoning on the passport photo helped you focus.

God, she *was* easy on the eyes. Too bad she was murder on the rest of you.

You told the man on the phone what she looked like, what kind of uniquely marketable baby she was carrying. You told him that the woman's birth name was Jean Christenson, but that she preferred to be called Ava, which was short for Avarice.

He noted that the name seemed appropriate.

"More than you'll ever know, pal." You closed the cell, thinking of her last words to you.

Good luck.

Your chest began to shake.

You were still laughing when your Uncle Joshua arrived and spotted your running shoes sticking out of the tiny house in the stranger's yard.

He crouched down, looked you over.

"Jesus! Are you okay?"

In between gusts of mad laughter you managed to say, "Nope. I'm in a bad place. I'm going to have to run."

"Okay, we'll get to that. First let's get you out of that fucking dog house."

He managed to get you upright, with your arm around his shoulder and as much weight as you could bear on your dog-mauled leg.

Once he started the car he looked over at you, seemingly relieved that you'd stopped laughing. The pain of moving had killed the chuckles.

Your Uncle had a hundred questions on his face. He asked one.

"The girl?"

You nodded in the affirmative then, over and over, guessing he would understand: Yes I was a sucker I thought it was love and yes I'm still remembering her kiss and the worst part is that if you ask me if I am still in love with Ava gorgeous terrible amazing vicious Ava I might say yes despite it all Yes.

You began to shake, nodding, mumbling, "OhGodohGodohGod. . . ."

"Okay, okay. Take it easy. Trust me, you've just hit the wall. You know that's as bad as it gets. I'm with you. You're gonna get fixed up. You've got to tell me enough to keep you safe, but that's it. We'll go where we need to. And soon as you can foot it, soon as you get past this wall, the morning runs are back. And this time there's no dropping it. No goddamn way. Whatever's got itself inside of you, kiddo, we're going to hit the streets and clear it the fuck out."

He twisted his grip on the steering wheel, gunned his car down slender curving roads on the way to the hospital. Dawn was approaching. It was likely to be another beautiful grey-green morning in Portland. Could your Uncle really be willing to leave his home behind just to protect your mangled carcass?

You wondered at your luck, knowing this man.

He approached a red light, started to hesitate, took one look at you, and then pushed right through.

And you, you love-sick bastard, you finally let shock take hold.

The Witness at Dawn

Dale believed in both Christ and karma. But no matter how many prayers fell desperate from his lips, or how often he reminded himself of the reparations he'd made, he couldn't shake the guilt. It seethed through him, the heat-wired electricity of niacin flush. It wracked his stomach, left him with cramps that ran the length of his twisting guts.

Whoever killed Mark, Pete, and Steve, they're coming for me next.

The pistol was new to Dale, heavy and alien to his touch. Never had much affinity for guns. Tried to run his life quiet, calm. Tried to be a peaceful person.

That's why New Orleans never should have happened.

But it did, and now his friend's houses were sectioned off by yellow police tape, and he was cowering around his cold apartment clutching an oily gun.

Cops had asked Dale questions he couldn't answer.

"Do you know if your friends were involved in any sort of cult?"

"Maybe something to do with rituals?"

"Can you think of anyone who would want them dead?"

This last question was accompanied by long, sunlamp stares.

They think I did this. Want me to crack. But I *didn't do anything.*

And Dale couldn't help feeling that his friends got their just desserts. Not an easy thought, but it felt true.

He'd hid the news clipping in a cupboard three days ago, after getting the call about Pete's death. But Dale knew the picture was there. Meghan Farrington, her face newsprint gray, smiling from the obituary page. Twenty-eight years old.

She was twenty-seven when we met her in New Orleans. Told us charming stories about her father, Earl, a "Nawlins gris-gris man" who supposedly sold fake mojo to tourists and real hoodoo to locals.

She wasn't looking when Mark slipped the roofie in her bourbon. He promised we wouldn't hurt her; said she wouldn't even remember. But how could she not remember them? Pushing her down. Taking their turns. Steve, rotten on tequila, calling her by his ex's name, punching her kidneys. How could she not remember, with those bruises?

But I didn't do anything. I just held the camera and filmed them and pretended to laugh while they played with their rag-doll. I'm not like them. Never touched her.

And afterwards, when that evening's ugliness had cancer-crawled its way through the men's friendship and set them adrift from each other, Dale had tried to set things right.

He'd seen Meghan's driver's license that night and knew her name. Took him less than a day to find her on the internet.

Dale forged a friendship with her, posing online as a woman named Susan Jessup. He learned how fragile Meghan had become. That night at Mardi Gras now kept the girl isolated, house-bound.

Trust had become impossible, but somehow she'd opened up to "Susan Jessup," who claimed to have been a victim of similar abuse.

Dale felt crooked as hell, but couldn't let himself abandon Meghan after he'd helped to bring her to this state. He could fix things…

And when she revealed that she was pregnant, Dale mailed her cash. He skimped on his own groceries, settling for ramen every night so he could mail Meghan money for the child his old friends had raped into her.

Even these things didn't assuage Dale's guilt.

He burned the New Orleans tape; took it to the landfill and blazed it to lighter-fluid vapors. Green-black smoke in the moonlight. Dale prayed to Christ that what had been done might be undone, might be smashed to ashes like the burning tape.

But now Meghan was dead. Her un-named child had passed with her. Dale had been scanning the Announcements page, expecting news of Meghan's baby, when he saw her picture looking out from the opposing section.

"Complications during delivery." God, obituaries were always so sanitary. She and the child had been dead four days, their murderers hidden nine months back behind a rohypnol haze.

And those murderers were dead now, too. The karmic ocean had pulled them down to darker currents.

But I *tried to make things right. Whoever killed my friends has to know that.*

Dale dead-bolted the front door and slid the chain-latch into place. Whoever was coming would have to get past that first. He'd have them at gunpoint.

He settled into his bed, pistol on the night-stand with the safety switched off, sheets soaking up sweat.

3:14AM. No one knocking on his door. Maybe he had set things right. Maybe whoever was seeking revenge for Meghan knew that Dale wasn't like the others. Maybe...

"Dale..."

A woman's whisper.

A shape at the foot of the bed.

It was her. Hospital robe wet against her skin, stained dark. Arms cradling a child, tiny, still trailing its umbilical.

She moved quickly, skittering on slightly bowed legs to the right edge of his bed, where Dale lay paralyzed, his gun an abstraction of metal he'd never understood.

"Hold your child, Dale."

She laid the newborn on his chest. Its head lifted, wide new eyes staring into Dale's. The New Orleans video footage was playing on a frantic loop in its all-black pupils. And the child began to cry, the wail of something lost knowing it won't find home.

Dale looked to Meghan's eyes, pleading.

"But, please, Meghan... I didn't do anything!"

"*No. You didn't.*"

The infant's hands reached up, covering Dale's sight. They smelled heavily of gun oil. Tiny fingers curled in like talons and began to pull with the strength of a grown man's hands.

And as Dale felt his eyes being torn loose he knew that something terrible had been done and was, at last, being undone.

Consumerism

Ron, can you reach your mother from here? Yes… okay… and is she?

She is? Are you certain? And you've checked the jugular and carotid? Can you reach a mirror to check for breath signs? No.

Oh, dear…

No, son, I don't think I can move from this position right now. This shard of the bumper appears to have me pinned to the bench seat like a common Lepidoptera. You know, as a Byronic hero with a smattering of Randian objectivity flitting away in my mind, I can't help but feel disdain for this entire scenario. This is low.

Did I just call myself a Byronic hero aloud? Well then, it's out in the open. Your suspicions are quelled, correct? I'd never defined myself for you before because I felt you should find your own path and… Ugghh! That is disgusting. What is that smell? Dear lord. I thought the burning gasoline was bad, but that odor… her bowels have let loose, haven't they? Death moves like quicksilver.

Ron?

Stop touching her face, Ron. Recognize death's permanency and move forward. *We* are still alive—maintaining this status should be your only focus. Let go of her hair. You and your crippling sentiment; don't give that body a value beyond what it is now.

No, it's not your mom anymore. It's water mostly, some minerals. Gases. Proteins.

Check yourself for injuries so we can assess, repair, and mobilize.

No, we should be protected if the tank explodes. You may want to breathe through your t-shirt, though. Some of that smoke *is* entering through the crack in the dashboard.

Quell that braying, Ron. Your generation… I don't understand the value you've placed in vulnerability. Were this ancient Rome you'd be of age to marry and launch an empire. Have all the pugilists retired?

What is that ticking sound? It's coming from the engine block?

Well, I paid fifty-grand for this behemoth, and I believe it will hold. Those hippies in their little tin-can cars, they used to deride me on the roadway, middle fingers held up proudly. Fools protesting survival. Proto-agrarian communists denying progress. Denying man his greatness. Imagine *their* little car flipping four times and remaining as intact as our rig. God bless military design. Sturdy as a rolling mountain. I'd have bought the version with Gatling gun intact had that been an option. Had we been that well equipped I could have gunned that possum into the troposphere…

…

Ron, I don't think I can move my head in either direction. I'll need you to get loose of your buckles and crawl back here. Ronald?

Yes, I seem to be pinned. Good God, the back of my head is a-throb… your churlish weeping isn't helping a bit, either. Silence yourself, child.

Yes, I said "child." Never believe that age alone makes a man. And don't shift about too quickly. We're still on an incline and I believe too much weight on the right side of the rig will tip us back into a roll.

…

We should never have let you drive. A possum for Pete's sake… those animals are God's litter. Furry detritus. Just an animal. Nothing. Have you ever seen *me* swerve on the roadway before?

Yes, but have you ever seen me swerve to *avoid* an animal? That's my point.

What do you think the lifespan of a possum is, anyway? How many more years of mindless foraging do you think you've assured that ball of fur by dooming us to die here in the woods?

Well, we could die. Accept that. Any given moment. Remember your cousin Dane? He was vibrant up until the second he collapsed face-first into that birthday cake. Remember how you cried that whole night. "I saw his dead eyes! I saw his dead eyes!" That was your complaint. Strange how that didn't make you wiser. Just weaker.

I really cannot feel a single one of my limbs.

I've been in and out of consciousness, haven't I? Why can't I see the trees? How long have we been here?

We've lost the final vestiges of daylight, Ron, and yet you remain there, holding her. It's so absurd. She'll begin expelling gases soon. Maybe that will loose your sad Oedipal grip and we can try to get out of here.

The burning engine was providing much of our heat, wasn't it? Funny how quickly the warmth slips away once the sun drops. I still can't command an appendage, Ron. You'll have to get moving; make a run for that tiny gas station we passed about thirty miles back. You will be Pheidippides, and I, your Athenian tribe for the saving.

Ron?

Ron?

Speak, son! I'm hoping you can reach the Mag-lite in the flip-down console. I need some light back here, and your help. I've got to assess my condition and try to stop my bleeding—there's a static fuzz to my vision so I know I'm not getting adequate circulation here, Ron...

Hello? I can see you breathing, Ron, and I doubt you're asleep. I NEED THE MAG-LITE!

Jesus, son! No need to lash out like that. Okay, so it's embedded in her chest. How was I to know that, from this vantage point? Your anger is ridiculous.

Any chance you could get a solid grip on the light and free it for our use? I bet one solid tug would do the job.

Ron?

Ron?

It was my hubris, I suppose, to think us so invincible in this vehicle. Should I have packed flares? Yes, that's obvious. Water? Yes, even more obvious.

Perhaps, Ron, there's an errant package of Fritos on the floor near me. A Snak-Pak, maybe?

But this machine did keep us alive. I had to have it at first sight, this shining example of man's command over nature; our bodies reshaping steel, our minds designing perfect geometric infrastructures, our wills dredging liquid fire from the Earth's belly and converting it into unprecedented levels of speed, striking down drudgery and demanding progress.

And don't start, Ron, with your sniping. How you ever developed your line of leftist drivel while being home-schooled, I'll never know. The fact is that it is best to consume everything we can, while we can. Sustainability is a fantasy for those believing that humans were meant to exist forever as they are now—LIES!

I have never known such a level of thirst… Ron? I swear there was an extra Snak-Pak up near the driver's seat. Maybe some aspirin? This headache's gone thermonuclear.

We have to use up all the oil, Ron. It's what our bodies do. We consume. And when we are done consuming one thing, our bodies will learn to ingest another and our lights shall burn forever on. So said Darwin. So said Emerson—the conflict defines us. Ether and stardust swirling, colliding, sparking off into new shapes. If you had your way, we'd be stagnating on some insect-riddled farm right now, fondling possums and plucking fiddles while our teeth rot.

Oh… my head…

Well… dead ship captains on mosquito ponds, Ron! We'll not return to the stew. That doesn't match up on a theological or biological level. That's not why we're here…

Parched does not begin to define how I'm feeling here, Ron.

Your dad always wanted to be a poet, kiddo. I aspired, but aspiration was all that was within my reach. Playground injury, Ron. Age eight. Flew off the swings inverted, caught my head on the plywood marking the park's border.

The doctors never defined this clearly, Ron, but I believe that that *exact* moment was when I lost my grip on meter.

Pieces of you, Ron, they can die at a whim.

Especially, Ron, especially if you can't get your fucking whimpering little cur bitch of a son to bring you a GODDAMNED MOTHERFUCKING FRITO SNAK-PAK!

Your punishment, son… yes, your *punishment*, for even in this situation you must understand that all of life is a lesson, and you're lucky to have your elder to guide you… your punishment now shall be to understand survival. Basic animal survival… the way to soothe the reptilian bits at the back of your medulla so that you may live past this moment and continue to ascend to your higher human calling.

So wake up. Yes, that's it. Look me in the eyes, like a man.

The sun is rising. Your dark night of the soul is over, Ron, and you have to move forward.

Crawl back here. Carefully. Slowly. Keep the vehicle in balance. Your right leg looks dreadful, but it doesn't appear the femoral artery's been cut. That's good. That's good. You can do this, Ron. You can take your punishment and grow up strong.

Smell my breath, Ron. That tint to it, the thing worse than morning breath, that fresh cat-shit smell… that's me dying. And I can tell by the look in your eyes that my assessment is correct. I'm missing crucial human elements, aren't I?

Well, I could tell by the buzzing of flies at dawn, by the soft prickle of their landings in wide perimeter, that the rear of my skull is perhaps missing. I sense a gulf of tissue.

That bad, is it? The idea of me seeing another sunset with that much of my brain exposed to the elements is absurd. So it is that you, my only seed, must carry on as I instruct.

You can survive this, Ron. You are, at this moment, only an organism. And you must consume. Fluids, proteins. And if the Iroquois were right, perhaps a bit of my strength.

I proffer this now, the flesh of the father. Let my mind give you life. It is my last wish. It is your duty.

Tilt my head forward more? Perhaps that bit of glass by my feet will help you serrate….

Yes, you can do it. You must. Move swiftly, that this throbbing may abate and I may catch up with your mother at the soft, light gates of her heaven.

And gently at first, please… yes, that's it… please stop crying... no more sentiment… you are an animal now, and must remain so until you return to the world of man…oh, to be part of this Greek tragedy, it feels right, a poet's end… I am your Leonidas, eat well for you may not survive the day… yes, dig in… I'll not ask you to describe the taste… to paraphrase Joplin I suggest you take another little piece… Gorp! I can't… oh, God, a bit of blood in my eyes, I can't see much… your hands are stronger than I'd imagined them to be… how I love and despise you,

Ron… yes, burrow in, son, let your throat be gorged with my wisdom, swallow ages of evolution… oops, you've got a bit on your chin there, tut-tut, no waste in nature… they were right—there's no pain, no self-aware nerves in the gray matter itself… aaaaooooaahh… that last scoop touched off an old memory—the smell of the Atlantic in mid-winter New England, a hint of your mother's perfume… but what is this light… Oh, holy fire! Yes, Ron. I will live on through you… in you… carry on, consume, survive… swallow me down, Ron… take me deep, child, and become a man….

Trigger Variation

Does he know about the Mercabol? Damn it. Did I hide the gear last night?

Jackson pretended to stretch his neck as he scoped out his Spartan charm-free rental unit.

Thin mattress/weight bench/jugs of protein powder and amino fuel in the closest corner. Jump rope on the floor. Boombox with a stack of CD's placed neatly to one side, sitting next to a digital alarm clock.

No needles. No tiny glass bottles. Thank God.

But what if the shit's still out in the bathroom? Keep him busy right here. Keep talking.

Kane had just arrived, an hour earlier than expected, and was pacing Jackson's apartment, clenching and un-clenching his considerable fists.

Okay, what was I talking about?

Jackson started up again.

"I mean, didn't you ever think, for just a second, that maybe this lifestyle…"

"Maybe this lifestyle *what*, man?"

Jackson paused.

Okay, wrong tack. Focus, man. Don't act so shaken up.

He let his arms drop to his sides and hissed out a deep shaking breath. Felt the blood flow to his hands, veins bulging.

I'm heavy. Getting heavier. Finally. I don't think they know…

Jackson eyeballed Kane. Big, hair-trigger Kane. His superior by about 60 pounds and a few months of training. Thick, razor-shaved symmetrical skull and over-prominent brow. Gorilla physique. A guy prone to misunderstanding nuance. A guy deeply loyal to the EndLiners ideals. A guy who might just put a fist through Jackson's throat that very second for questioning said ideals.

Jackson cancelled his query/feigned mental drift.

Kane was watching him—studying him with his head turned slightly to one side, waiting for a response.

"Shit. I don't know. Having a fuzzy-brained moment. I haven't slept much the last few days."

Jackson noticed the oily rings around Kane's eyes and figured he was equally exhausted. They'd been training so hard…

"Yeah, man, I know what you're talking about. My brain's a little jacked at the moment, too. Last night I was curling and while I had the bar all the way up I started staring at the weight on the right side and seeing all the patterns in the gray metal, and then I looked up at myself in the mirror and I didn't know who I was for a second and I wanted to jump across the room and just fucking mash the dude."

"What?" Jackson asked the question with excitement in his voice, glad that Kane was going to let Jackson's earlier thought drop. Better for both of them.

Kane continued. "Seriously. I was so pumped that the sight of what I thought was another human being made me want to go kick some ass. It was like this force was behind me, pushing me towards him…"

"Towards *you*?"

"Well, yeah. And that's why nothing came of it. Because if I would have swung on the dude all I would have got for it was a broken mirror and a fucked-up hand. But I was *close*, man. Some borderline shit…"

They both smiled at that. Things had been sketchy for weeks, chaos sliding into their lives a little more as each day rushed by in anticipation of the big night. Jorge had gone to jail for trying to steal a crate of eggs (ostensibly, they all guessed, to be used for protein binging). Nate got pinched for rape, his own girlfriend the accuser, her broken right wrist making it an easy case for the cops to close. Kyle was arrested for brawling downtown, and was still wearing his "Your Mom is A Rotten Cunt" t-shirt when he was bailed out. Mitchell broke his ankle trying to clear a fence after getting caught in the middle of prowling an upscale residence (for reasons none of them could readily ascertain). And Frank had… well, Frank had crossed a line but *hadn't* been caught.

Their fearless leader, the man behind the EndLiner ideals, had gone out one balmy Thursday to spend the night sniping zoo animals with a rifle.

Frank saw it as further proof of human dominion, of the absolute power accorded our species, but Jackson could tell a lot of the guys were holding back a flinch or two while watching the footage.

Ex-straight edge kids, he guessed. Wanted the extra hardcore aspect they could get as EndLiners but still harbored their old pro-animal affection (or *affectation* as Frank would call it). Jackson got the feeling from Frank that his empathy ran as deep as a creek in Death Valley, and that all EndLiners were expected to exhibit that same coldness. And many of them did run frosty, these ex-edge kids who'd realized how much easier it was to deride and destroy. They discovered how *fun* it could be if you didn't mind abiding by their leader's occasional extremes.

As shaky as Frank's digicam footage was, it had been rough watching him drop the tiger. And the monkeys. A few of those twitched as they bled out. Other monkeys came right to the freshly-plugged bait, tearing out their fur in tufts, screaming at nothing until Frank scoped them down too.

And always, in the background, Frank's laughter. Like a sponge full of joy being squeezed out by his throat, his love for the midnight mercenary mission on full display.

Jackson had been paying close attention to the tape. He'd heard Frank whisper, "We win," after the last monkey dropped. Jackson had rubbed the goosebumps off his skin quick and mustered up the best laugh he could. It sounded as false as it was.

Kane had looked at Jackson then, too. Watched him closely.

He can tell something's off. Does he know about the 'roids? What is he telling Frank? We've been friends for so many years, man. Jesus, I shouldn't even be thinking about Kane like this.

But Jackson had been out on his own midnight missions with Kane and knew the kid that helped him limp home after his first bike wreck wasn't around anymore. Kane had developed a strong taste for the rough stuff, and there'd been a shift. They were EndLiners and now everything—everybody—fell into two categories.

The weak and the strong.

And God fucking help you if were even a momentary member of the first party.

The pillow fights were, of course, Frank's idea. Loosely, anonymously organized, being wholly un-associated with anything EndLiner. General net shenanigans got it done. Emails, IM's with an address and a single message: *Bring a pillow and be ready for battle*. Frank paid a guy to pay a guy to set the ball in motion, and the results were great.

The first fight—at McGrady's public park—pulled a few hundred combatants and ended with a ration of bruises and grass covered thick with expelled feathers.

Arrests: zero.

Jackson had watched the officers from the periphery, studied their faces, guessed at their reactions. Some smirked—writing it off as the further infantilism of a worthless generation. A few cops kept their itching hands hovering over their pepper spray canisters. Some wished they'd brought their own pillows.

The second fight was in the town square and pulled double the numbers. This time the media was invited. Everything stayed anonymous but now people who'd never even heard of the term "web browser" knew about the events.

Those crazy kids, they commented, there's worse things they could be doing.

What Jackson couldn't tell Kane, or anyone else for that matter, was that he was starting to have doubts about the big night.

There was no name for the event. Frank wasn't big on marketing.

"No catchy slogans orsimple images to tag up on a wall," he'd said. "Being an EndLiner means respecting one thing: Human survival. If you need a ten step plan or a secret handshake or a goddamned secret Mason reach-around, then we don't need you."

Keeping the idea at the forefront—that humans were the one great species on Earth and that they must, at any costs, become ever-stronger—that's what Frank did. He tapped into primal urges and desires. Fighting/fucking/feasting. The things that came with power and strength.

But you had to work for it. You had to get big. Local stores ran short on protein powder/milk/eggs/chicken/steak. The guys involved with Frank stayed loosely connected, per his net instructions, but when they did meet in person their conversations invariably drifted to three topics—lifting programs, combat techniques, and music (predominately of hardcore variety).

The straight edge kids ate it up because Frank thought that their power should come without the taint of drugs. His ideology freed them from believing in the nobility of anyone other than themselves; saved them from the inevitable letdowns that the rest of humanity had to offer.

And they liked the fact that he allowed meat and promiscuity back into their lives. Many of them had grown skinny and anemic without their old diet of animal flesh. Surging sex-drives had made the ascetic lifestyle a bitch. Now they were bigger/more dangerous/sexually aggressive to the point where you could taste the hormones when a group of them entered a room. And they were going to the same punk/metal shows, throwing around considerable added weight, and getting blown in the parking lot while blast beats still rumbled against the roof of the venue.

It was ape heaven.

At least that's how Jackson was starting to see it.

He'd been enchanted at first. Like a lot of the EndLiners he came from a shitty household scenario. It was close to standard issue with their crew. Jackson's particular brand of bullshit was father-oriented.

His Pops was an unshakeable, almost admirably tenacious alky. Even the drunken traffic wreck that broke his dad's right leg and put Jackson's mother in the grave hadn't slowed down his bottle draining mission (his time "in the cups" as he called it; shooting for charming but coming off resigned).

After that particular mom-slaughtering indignity, Jackson had been taken away by the state and started the eighth grade as a technical orphan before his dad figured out who to payoff—with money from mom's life insurance policy—to get his kid back.

Back home. Two years of listening to the fucker sobbing over the sound of empty bottles clinking. And then it was legal emancipation/ dropping out/working groceries at the Shop N Save for rent money. Freedom, pretty much, aside from the occasional late night phone call filled with promise and apology.

I'm so sorry, Jackson. I hope you know it. I try so hard but I don't think you'll ever see that. Enough talk though, right? Show and prove time. I've been thinking about joining a gym, and maybe I can even go back to AA if they don't keep pumping God up my ass and... I don't know. I'll quit talking, Jacky, and I'll show you something.

Once in awhile the old fucker sold it sincere enough to tease out a sliver of hope.

It was that hope—and how his father used it—that led Jackson to hate the man. When Jackson was teased by those chances to see his father as a *father* and not just the drunk that spawned him—and when those chances were inevitably smashed like empty bourbon bottles—that was the worst of it.

That was what made him want to be *hard*. To be big, and better, and clean, and powerful.

To be an EndLiner.

But as Jackson stared at the injection kit in front of him—a slim needle and a small glass bottle with a label reading Mercabol, underscored by some Asian writing he couldn't translate—his doubts returned.

I'm just as hooked as Pops.

Jackson killed the bad thoughts, recognized they could only take him in one direction. He drew fluid into the syringe, wondering if it was really horse testosterone like the web ad had said, and then pushed the needle into the meat of his left thigh. He grimaced at the intramuscular burn, pulled the needle, and watched one drop of fluid emerge and slide loose down the side of his leg. His thoughts ran so morbid that he felt the expelled drug drip was his only way of crying now, and his face flushed red with embarrassment at the lameness of his own maudlin bullshit.

Can your fucking emo lament. Lift. Don't think. Get bigger.

He pressed Play on his mini-stereo and then hit Shuffle. As Death Shall Fall/Morbid Descent/Strength Over All on rotation. Great, raw shit by men bloodied on their own instruments, singers collapsing lungs to let you know that the world was a brutal place, that will was all you had. The first disc was from Denmark and Jackson didn't know what language it was in, but he could *feel* it regardless. Power had little to do with language.

The Mercabol kicked. Jackson hit the bench and pumped the barbell until he had to roll it off him and onto the floor. His blisters popped and oozed blood. He'd been hoping they'd callous more—he wanted 1800's whaling-ship hands. But the sight of the blood made him feel right.

I'm hard. I'm doing what others cannot. Will not. They're sleeping now, and I'm growing stronger.

Visions hit his brain.

Terror-type: murder/rape/destruction. He pictured his fists calloused over, cement-hard, smashing anything that got in his way.

Visions of fear: Frank finding out about his 'roid habit. Frank setting the other men upon him for training. Dog meat in the center pit.

Doubts: Needle worries—did he have guts like this without his secret injections? EndLiner worries—just what the hell was their big night really going to be like? Always worries—what made him think he'd ever be better than his father?

Shake it off. Don't overthink. Keep pushing. Get bigger.

He dropped to the floor for crunches and supermans and then did push-ups on his fists to keep the filthy carpet fibers out of the ruptured blister pools in his palms. He popped up and grabbed the jump-rope. He worked the rope triple-fast, setting time goals on the clock, not relenting until the right minute clicked over.

More push-ups. Deep-lung breath like spoiled meat popping back off the carpet.

He chugged water. He smeared the blood from his hands across his face and chest. He flexed just to flex, to feel his new size. He silent-screamed along to his music, face straining the way he'd seen in the videos.

He desired—anyone to contradict him right now/anyone to suck him off right now.

He wondered—how had he ever questioned that this was the right path?

He flexed again, shaking in the dark, whispering "Fuck you" because it felt right.

* * *

Home from work, Jackson always checked his answering machine before doing anything else. He was one of the five people left on Earth that didn't have a cell-phone so he spent most of his work shifts at the Shop N Save wondering who was calling him and what he was missing. EndLiners moved in small groups for their "training"—to tint their activities as the sort of random violence people brushed off when they caught it on the nightly news—but Jackson was connected to four of these small groups and didn't ever want to miss out. He'd learned a lot during their short forays—how quickly he could run with a stolen crate of Rapid-Bulk powder in his arms (pretty goddamned fast), how hard it was to break a man's arm (not very), how to make a noisy bar turn quiet (return to the place where you broke the guy's arm, accompanied by five guys who look just like you).

He noticed his finger was shaking as he reached out to press the Play button next to the blinking red light on his answering machine.

Look at that, champ! The shakes, just like Pops... way to go! What're you hooked on?

Jackson ignored the nagging thoughts. They crept up now and then, although he'd acknowledged his new reality—he was addicted to the life of an EndLiner. So were his friends. They were getting off on violence, but at least it was violence with a purpose. They were fast-forwarding human evolution, bringing...

Jesus P. Christ, man! You believe that? You buying what some crazy monkey-sniping fuck sold you through your MySpace account?

Jackson pressed the button, anxious to hear something other than the voice inside his head.

"Message One," said the digital woman.

"Hello? ... Anybody there? ... You there, Jacky? Okay, well, I wish you were home. I've got some great news and... well, I'd rather tell you in person... Okay, so you're really not there. I'll just tell you. I've met a great lady. Her name is Rhonda and she's been *so* good to me, and helped me see some things straight. The part I need to tell you about is that, um, she found a way to get some financial assistance through the city and she's going to pay for me to go rehab out at Pinebrook and I've agreed to go and that's pretty much that... Shit, bud, I really wish you were home... The thing is I've got to go in today, like three hours from now, and then I'm cut off from everybody for the whole first month as part of the deal. I was really hoping you'd come see me at her place. She's at 6705 Kent on the northwest side and I'll be there with my luggage in the next hour and I was hoping...Well, I don't know what I was hoping. It would be good to see you, Jacky. It would be really good. I know you don't have any reason—"

A sharp beep cut the message off.

"Message Two," said the digital woman. Jackson expected to hear his father's voice continuing. Instead it was Frank's, slow and determined.

"Bring a pillow and be ready for battle."

That was all Jackson needed to hear.

The big night was going down in about three hours.

Jackson pressed Delete on his answering machine, clearing out the false hope and the call to arms.

He ran to the cache in his bathroom, where two glass containers marked "Mercabol" were waiting.

He placed the gear reverently by his front door. He'd inject at the last minute to make sure he was cresting high tonight.

Then he was back in his bedroom, hunched over his pillow with a pair of scissors in hand.

His music was on blast. Fuck the neighbors.

Jackson smiled, thinking one word.

Tonight.

Car engines rumbled around them, dust stirred by boots floating ethereal before headlights. There were maybe one hundred men, perhaps a few less than that. Jackson estimated their combined weight at about ten tons.

Ten tons of muscles and gritting teeth, and each man holding a pillow.

Each pillow a tiny Trojan horse containing: brass knucks/billy-clubs/wrenches/hammers/fist packs/etc. No guns—Frank had been explicit about that. Any idiot could wield a gun—tonight's message would be delivered by the flesh of these men. With the help of a few handy tools.

It would be a show of human strength. Of what the species could be, of what it had to be if it wanted to stay on top of this rock.

Frank addressed them, his voice clear and booming and without the slightest tremor:

"I'll keep this short. You don't need any propaganda to put a fire into you, because *your* fires are already burning. They always have been. That's why you've heard the call. *That's why you're here tonight*. You see the world for what it is. A giant rock, floating in space, over-run by beasts. And you see the world for *how* it is—teeming with life, which means it's also teeming with death. Destruction. Entropy. *We* haven't been convinced otherwise by our strip malls and safe, tightly packaged industrial lives. Nature is *not* sentimental, nor does she respect intellect. The apex predators of this planet are still here because they understand the way the world works."

Frank's volume increased. The words came faster. Jackson found himself swaying from left to right, stirring up more dust. He noticed Kane was doing the same. Knuckles cracked around him. Heads rolled/neck vertebrae popped from the strain of over-pumped muscles.

"The strongest beasts *crush* the weak. They consume *without sentiment. They conquer*! The laziest of beasts are slaughtered *and those that struggle most survive*! This is the truth of our world and any opposition is founded on whimsy.

"The people of our country have gone soft without true opposition. They compete with each other in bullshit corporate games to earn fancy SUV's, desperate to protect their soft, weak bodies with a steel shell, so *afraid* of the world around them. They tell themselves that they are enlightened, that they've escaped their animal roots and have taken humanity on a higher course. These are easy to believe when your food arrives shrink-wrapped and drinking water comes with the twist of a faucet. *But take those things away and see what happens. See how fast the laws of survival take hold.*

"Each of you has a mission tonight. Some of you already know what that is, and you *will* succeed! The rest of you will follow me as we begin our path to glory.

"Tonight you will show the world what the human race was meant to be.

"Tonight the fire that I see in your eyes will sweep through this city and bring it back to life!"

Jackson watched Frank watching them, staring down each of them and none of them, playing up his messiah moment for all it was worth.

"This is your time to define who you are and what you are! This is your time to take your rightful place in the world! So I ask you…"

Frank put his fists up in the air.

"ARE YOU WITH ME?"

The roar that filled the air left no doubt about the response.

With that the tribe of born-again savages began their march into the night.

Jackson knew he was bleeding from a deep gash over his right eyebrow, but the wound seemed to be gumming shut, and he'd washed the blood out of his eye at a public water fountain.

I think I shattered that guy's jaw.

The man was about two blocks east of Jackson now, likely still lying in the pool of blood that had been spreading wide under his splayed face.

He had it coming. Try to cut me with a fucking broken bottle...he's lucky I didn't kill him.

"You should have killed that guy, Jackson."

Kane had found him.

"I think he'll die, but you could have made sure."

Kane had dived all the way into the big night. His wife-beater was Pollacked with blood spatter in varying degrees of dryness. Jackson thought he could see a glint of white bone where Kane's knuckles had split open, but it may have just been the weird arc-sodium light from above. The black S (for Strength, he'd said) on Kane's forehead was now smeared with sweat from exertion.

"You take care of that gash, Jackson?"

Jackson nodded in the affirmative.

"Good. We have to keep moving. Frank said that if we stick to our small groups and stay in motion it'll take them way longer to pin down what's going on."

"I know what he fucking said, Kane."

"I know. Just making sure that bummy bar fucker didn't cut loose your brain with that busted bottle. Being all stoked on steroids doesn't make you Superman."

Shit, he knows.

How does he know? Does he really know? Don't let this escalate.

"Yeah, right, man. I'm all juiced up. Whatever."

"Jackson, I've sparred with you. I've been in the group shower with you at the gym. And I'm not as fucking stupid as you think. Your arms are big like mine, but they feel puffy. You've got a nasty patch of back zits going. You put on 20 pounds in two months."

"Hey, I've been working my ass off, just like..."

"Shut the fuck up. You're going to lie to me? To *me*?"

Kane had him pegged. This was a no-graceful-way-out scenario. Best he could do was damage control and be ready if Kane charged.

I'm big now. Maybe I can take him.

"Okay. Yeah, I've been cycling. I wanted to be ready. I was so stressed out about tonight and I needed to be sure I could hold my own. I know it's not *pure* like Frank wants it to be, but..."

"Excuses. You know who you sound like right now? Kill it, man."

"Does Frank know?"

"No, but he will if you don't end it right now. Things are only going to get rougher after tonight, and you need to be stronger than that. Not in your body, in your mind."

Jackson guessed he might have felt relief at hearing this, were his system not so awash in the chemical stress-bath this night had become.

"Alright, man. I swear. I fucking swear on everything—no more of that shit."

This is another chance. I'll show Kane I mean it. I'll prove I'm an EndLiner. The next asshole that gets in my way is going to find out what kind of a man I am.

"Okay, then," Kane said, "let's keep moving."

Jackson agreed. Staying in motion kept your blood pumping. It would keep the thoughts about Jackson's lies on low/conflict on high.

The beast who struggles most survives, and all that.

Besides, if we slow down we'll have time to think about what's going on. About the fact that we're running around town assaulting people at random. Because Frank said to.

And because it feels good. No, great. It feels great.

Some part of Jackson's mind felt guilt at this last thought, but he started to walk with Kane and let the feeling fade in the face of motion. The air across his skin felt warm, almost a caress over his throbbing forehead slash. He'd ditched his pillowcase back at the first rumble, as had Kane, and he felt streamlined by their forward inertia. Jackson's weapon of choice, a five pound barbell he'd planned to hold in his fist, had proven unwieldy. Kane still had a small, steel-rod enforced bat with the word "Grendel" written on the side.

They'd grown up in this town, and now Jackson felt they were wandering its streets like a Death Squad. The idea gave every second a bizarre power.

"Kane, we're changing everything tonight."

"I know, man! It's fucking awesome! I'm so glad we're on this squad and didn't get stuck with the grocery store run. Maybe those guys will catch up later tonight."

On the short walk from the clearing to downtown Jackson and Kane had managed to listen in on a few mission details. Rumors or not, neither had any idea. Supposedly there was a crew headed up to the reservoir. Frank had instructed everyone to stock up bottled water the week prior, so Jackson guessed this detail might be true. Another crew was likely headed to the warehouse-sized grocery store on Berger to inject the butcher shop's meat with some homegrown bacterial culture. A third crew was headed to the *real* pillow fight at the Sternwheeler Mall parking lot that Frank had set-up as a decoy. They would watch the cops there and walkie-talkie out to Frank when the lawmen were made aware of the more serious rumbles that were being launched elsewhere.

Jackson pictured the cops there at Sternwheeler, laughing, watching the feathers fly, thinking, "Man, kids these days…" while downtown had gone slaughterhouse.

He actually hoped they'd catch on sooner than later. Part of him wanted an excuse for their crew to slip back into the shadows, and part of him just really wanted to beat up a fucking cop.

The faster he walked with Kane, the more the latter felt like the truth. They walked like giants. They were lions/Kodiak bears/sharks that never slept. And this town was theirs until someone else could prove otherwise.

The Black Rabbit was a dive bar on the southernmost tip of downtown.

It was here that Frank had begun his series of public executions.

The public, of course, had no idea that this was to be the case. Nor did Jackson until he and Kane approached and saw Frank bring the mallet down.

The man in the brown corduroy jacket let out a scream that squelched on impact. Metal met skull and kept moving, bone went smashed-pumpkin wide and slid curbside on brain. The man's body spasmed until Frank brought the mallet crushing down again, this time at the neck. A woman in a red denim skirt and cowgirl top screamed out, "Harold!" and two EndLiners held her back, one seizing the opportunity to score a fist full of tit.

Frank lifted his head from his work, smiled, and shouted out, "NEXT?" He used one thick leg to roll what used to be Harold to one side, clearing a space in his impromptu killing floor for whoever else was to be randomly doomed.

Two EndLiners Jackson knew by their nicknames, Chud and Scam, walked forward with another man from the belly of The Black Rabbit. Jackson guessed that there was a whole crew in there, that EndLiners had taken the place over. They'd likely have secured whatever firearm the owners had behind the counter.

And Harold, poor brain-panned Harold, must have tried to oppose them.

This new guy, he was *definitely* an obstacle to Frank's game-plan. Morbidly obese, three chins deep, barely contained by a too-small Schlitz t-shirt and a faded pair of blue jeans wrapped around surprisingly skinny legs.

"Kneel down," Frank commanded. Jackson edged closer, as if his proximity would reveal to him whether or not this was real.

This can't be happening, right? This is happening. I think it is...

The fat man hocked a snot-ball at Frank that hit his left forearm. Frank slopped it off with his right hand and stepped closer to his captive.

"I like that spirit, man. Where the fuck was that when you sold your soul to the Yumm Corporation for ten cent tacos? It's too late for you."

The man tried to throw his girth around but Chud and Scam weighed as much in pure muscle. The big guy quickly recognized that and slumped.

"That's what I thought," Frank said. Then he brought down the fist-sized steel end of the mallet. It didn't kill the man but was enough to make him lose his legs. Chud and Scam dropped the body and let Frank finish his work.

Jackson's heart beat faster. His breath had doubled and he couldn't tell if he was smiling or grimacing.

Am I enjoying this? Is it just the Mercabol?

Frank took two more decisive swings at the fat man's head, and then—almost as if he hadn't been involved in the murder that was bleeding out below him—he was holding his walkie talkie up to his head and listening intently.

He leaned over to Chud and whispered something. Cops must be on their way.

Frank had said he had a plan for dealing with law enforcement, but not one that allowed for direct combat. At least not yet.

"Okay, folks, only time for one more." Most of the "folks" watching Frank were EndLiners, although a few were bar rats who'd edged towards the front but couldn't muster up the guts to take any action.

Chud and Scam were back quickly.

The man they held was small, and curled in on himself. He wore a blue dress shirt tucked in to a pair of khakis. Jackson noticed one side of the collar was buttoned down while the other was loose.

Why would I notice that at a time like this?

The man already looked as if he was resigned to death. He could barely keep his feet under him. Had he been crying?

Again, a woman rushed out after him, but she was quickly restrained by a few of the gathered EndLiners. She had a short, permed haircut and a pair of round wire rim glasses on. And she looked furious.

Her face was bright red. The veins at her neck bulged in a way Jackson found admirable. She screamed, "Don't you hurt him! What the fuck do you think..."

Scam backhanded her and she would have dropped to the ground unconscious had Frank's men not been holding her.

The captured man lifted his head. "No, Rhonda!"

Help help me, Rhonda...

Jackson almost had time to laugh at his own joke.

Wait, Rhonda?

Jackson looked at the man.

Dad?

The man looked at Jackson.

"Dad? *DAD?*"

Frank was lifting his mallet as if he hadn't noticed the development.

"Frank!"

"What?" His voice rolled out in a low monotone. No inflection. Nothing human about it. And Jackson guessed that gave Frank great pleasure.

"That's my dad."

"So what? We found him here, drunk off his ass. He's just another one of them. The weak. The failed. The wasted. Should he live because you're sweet on him?"

They were all watching him. His brothers-in-arms were around him now, their mania disturbed, eager to continue their takeover, waiting for the next kick, the next snuff. Even Kane was twitching to his left, "Grendel" in hand, his face twisted and un-readable.

Shit. I'm alone here.

Jackson eyed his father, the man who had seen fit to bring him into the world despite the fact that he'd always love his boozy oblivion more. He felt the grunting breath of the animal tribe he was running with, could smell them around him.

There was no opposing them. He could give them a hell of a fight, but turning on them now probably meant death for his dad *and* himself.

Why is the old bastard here anyway? What happened to Pinebrook?

Is this man worth dying for? Dying with?

Who the fuck is he?

Jackson looked his father in the eyes and said a single word.

"Rehab?"

The old man shook his head from left to right as his eyes drifted to the ground. His voice came out small from between his hunched shoulders.

"I just wanted you to pick up the phone. I just wanted to talk to you, bud. I'm sorry. I..."

Jackson cut the old man short by stepping forward and planting a kiss on his forehead.

Then he stepped back and things felt still. None of them knew how to react. The scenario didn't fit into the new code they'd chosen.

His father was shaking, his face hot-red and streaked in new tears.

Frank raised the mallet again, although Jackson didn't know whether the next blow was intended for him or his father. Jackson sensed Kane at his side, saw his fist tight around "Grendel", ready to swing.

None of these things mattered. Jackson had said his goodbye to this man.

All that was left now was survival.

Jackson threw all his weight, from the legs up, into his right arm. His fist connected with the top of his dad's low-slung head causing Jackson and his father to topple in unison and from that moment there were no more EndLiners and no more lies and Jackson couldn't blame the Mercabol for this because the fury he fell into ran deeper and truer than any chemical reaction. His fists clenched like they had at his mother's funeral where his father had asked for a chair at graveside because he was too drunk to stand any longer and now Jackson clasped his hands together and swung them down on his father's head.

If there was a face that resembled Jackson's under all that blood, it was disappearing.

Jackson's arms grew tired. His rage began to subside. A soft gurgle pushed its way from his father's throat.

He was never me.

Never me.

But maybe he loved me. Maybe...

It doesn't matter.

Don't think. Finish it.

Jackson could tell that the men he'd been with were running away because Rhonda was trying to pull him off and saying something about the cops and it became obvious to him that he was the only one who could see he was saving the man they called his father from a slow and terrible death to be suffered at the foot of sadness—this immense sadness that the man had fallen in love with and then cultivated and tended to like a rare and exotic flower.

And so Jackson's fists fell again, sure and steady, the echoes of his final mercy sounding long into the night, saving them both from the burden of being human.

The Gravity of Benham Falls

He's taking me to the place where we lost Michael.

This thought, more than the speed of the car and the sight of barely illuminated trees blurring past, cemented Laura's unease. She hadn't been up this way since the day her little brother disappeared, and never planned on returning. Now this "date" with Tony was dragging her back.

Laura silently cursed herself for not coming up with a better way to make money. Her current plan wasn't getting any smarter, or easier. Could she even call it a plan? How many small town drug dealers could she seduce and steal from, before one of them caught on and decided to hurt her, or worse? Word would travel; she'd be in danger. Tony, the guy driving, seemed like the type that would own a gun.

When the headlights of the car cut through the wispy road fog ahead of them and illuminated the sign reading "Benham Falls-Fourteen Miles" she realized that this was *not* where she wanted to be. Anywhere else would be better. Then she forced herself to remember her dad, lying in bed at home, under thin sheets, lungs barely pulling oxygen while he dozed in and out of a Vicodin stupor.

He probably still wishes he had a cigarette right now. Well, we can't afford any, damn it. I can barely afford the doctor's appointments, so we're just going to have to disappoint the Marlboro man.

The thought of her freshly divorced dad—mom bailed when the diagnosis dropped—and of his mounting bills at St. Peter's Hospital, re-focused her on the task at hand. The guy in the seat next to her had to fall in love, or at least lust. The faster, the better. The last chump, he was stupid with love after just two days. Love earned trust, and trust earned secrets, like where the guy kept his cash, and that Rolex he wore only on special occasions.

A shoebox. These guys, they all want to think they're Scarface, and they all end up keeping rolls of cash in a little cardboard shoebox.

Laura tried not to enjoy her cleverness, but failed. A smile was spreading across her face, helping to ease the piano-wire anxiety that was sinking into her chest.

She shifted in the tan leather bucket seat of the '68 Camaro, giving

Tony an eyeful of leg as her short skirt hiked up her left thigh. Tony glanced over quickly, caught the flash of skin, and turned his eyes back to the road. He grinned.

"Almost there, babe."

It was the first thing he'd said since he picked her up earlier that evening. Laura was fine with that. She didn't want words. She might start talking and mention the wrong thing. Draw suspicion. Or she might start talking about the time her family visited this same forest and came back missing one person. She might mention how they never even found Michael's body.

No, she was content to play with the electricity in the air between them. Better to turn this into a fantasy. Reality could be so unpleasant.

Laura pretended to yawn, pushing her chest forward with her arms raised above her head, moving her legs slightly so that her pleated camouflage skirt hiked up even further.

It was her turn to grin as she saw Tony shifting in his seat. They were both swimming in tension, nerves on full alert as the stereo blasted and the air that rushed in through the windows grew cooler.

The road became thin and curvy as they approached the entrance to the Tolaquin County Forest, but Tony didn't slow the car for a moment. He slammed through the corners. The rear right tire spit out gravel as it caught the soft shoulder. Laura wanted to tell him to cool it on the alpha-male stunt driver shit, but she didn't want to disturb the chemistry of their little game.

This was a game she had to win. Till now, it had been easy. Asking around town, finding out who the local dealer was. Getting his name. Tracking him down.

In another life I'd make a great cop.

Earlier that day she'd met Tony at the Chevron. Marco at the pool hall had said that Tony kept the Chevron job for appearances, and it was an easy place for people to drive through and buy whatever Tony was selling.

Laura saw Tony squeegeeing the window of a mini-van, checked out his broad shoulders, his jet black hair, his olive skin, the way he filled out his oil-smeared jumpsuit, and shouted, "Hey, nice ass!" She loved playing the aggressor.

Tony walked over and scoped her out in return. He let a slow, straight-tooth smile bloom across his face, and said, "Thanks."

Laura licked her lips, slow, and said, "What's your name?"

"Tony."

"Well, hi, Tony. You got a pen?"

He pulled a pen from his shirt pocket and handed it to her. She wrote her name and cell-phone number on a twenty dollar bill, folded it, and slipped it in one of his front pants pockets.

Two hours later her cell phone rang. "Hey, Laura, you wanna do something special?"

It now appeared to her that by "do something special" he meant "drive out to Benham Falls and get naked." At least that was the subtext to the tension that hung heavy in the speeding car. Laura was just happy her plan was working. Her dad and home were over a hundred miles away. She'd need a place to sleep tonight. Hopefully Tony had a nice, big bed with a down comforter and some thick pillows. Hopefully Tony had a heavy, hidden shoebox, and slept like the dead.

Hopefully we can head back to town soon, and get the hell out of this place.

The Camaro rolled to a stop as they approached the gate between the paved road and the dirt passage that led to Benham Falls. He hopped out, swung the gate open, and slid back into the car.

He turned to Laura. "They don't want people up here in the spring. It's still pretty cold at night, and the area around the waterfall can get icy."

"So?" she said, trying to maintain her attitude even as she cringed at the idea of stepping into the freezing cold in a short skirt and thin, black tank top.

"So," he said, "people have died up here."

She pictured her own little brother, five years old, smiling in front of the waterfall on a sunny afternoon.

Is that my last memory of him? Has to be. This is the last place I ever saw him.

Laura tried to stop remembering, but the echo of her parent's panicked voices screaming her brother's name still entered her mind. Instant gooseflesh, shivers.

"Don't worry, though, I'll make sure we stay warm."

Tony slid a calloused hand over her knee, then drew it toward the inside of her thigh. As his hand shifted a feminine-looking bracelet, with blue and black beads, slid down his forearm to his wrist, jangling on its way down. The beads formed the outline of a horse's head, raised and proud. Laura wondered if it was a trophy from another conquest, or if he just felt comfortable wearing pretty jewelry. Either way, this guy was different enough to be interesting, and the warmth of his fingers made her cheeks rosy. Laura didn't expect these feelings. Romance, so far, hadn't been par for her twisted course.

She smiled at him and said, "Just make sure I'm taken care of." Laura laughed, trying to come off sly, to ignore her urge to hop in the driver's seat once he got out and drive as far from here as fast as she could.

They drove for four more minutes and then he slowed, killing the lights and the engine. Laura could hear the roaring waterfall through the glass windows of the Camaro. She immediately hated the surging volume of it. It was the soundtrack to the worst day of her life. Laura pushed those feelings down. Right now had to be about Tony, and nothing else. She had to earn his trust or soon she'd lose another family member.

He could be dead right now. While you're away robbing lowlifes for medical money, he could have wheezed out his final breath. Alone.

Laura ignored the voice. Listening to her conscience was not an option.

She stepped out of the car and slammed the door, instantly feeling the cold bite of the higher altitude and the dampness of the waterfall's backspray. Tony walked over to Laura and grabbed her delicate left hand, enveloping it with his.

"Follow me. I'll show you something."

She followed him through the woods in the dark of the moonlit night, towards the sound of the waterfall. He walked with a sure-footedness and Laura briefly pictured herself as a notch on his bedpost.

"You bring all your girls up here, Tony?"

"No," he said, through laughter, "just the special ones. My family and I used to live in a house bordering the park so I'm pretty familiar with the area. Used to play here as a kid."

Laura was surprised by how much she liked Tony's voice. The first guy she'd stolen from, her old boyfriend Mark, and the second guy she robbed, Adam, they both had something nasty in their voices. A greasy sort of power. Tony sounded different. Still, she was cold. Her feet hurt. She wore platform shoes with crisscrossing straps on top, picturing this as more of a booze/cigarettes/dancing type date. She didn't plan on this nature hike with Ranger Tony. Still, the firmness and warmth of Tony's hand made her feel safer.

Tony guided her past a patch of trees into a clearing. Laura hadn't seen Benham Falls since she was small, and she was still stunned by its sheer grandness. The nearly full moon reflected off the water, giving the whole area a shimmering, light blue glow. The hundred foot wide river was raging over the lip of the waterfall, about three hundred feet above them. The water roiled furiously at the point of impact, sending out a spray that within seconds coated her like cold sweat.

The memories—the sounds of her parents' voices crumbling and growing hoarse as they yelled for Michael, the look of instant despair on the face of the park ranger who couldn't help them—all of it wanted in to her head. Laura knew she had to stay in motion to keep from thinking. Maybe Tony could distract her.

She leaned in, ran her tongue lightly up the salty skin of Tony's neck and then whispered in his ear. "It's beautiful." Somehow it wasn't a lie. The falls couldn't be denied their majesty.

His hands found the curve of her lower back and he kissed her. She could feel the beads of his funny bracelet pressing against her skin, strangely warm even through the fabric of her tank-top. Then they were kissing, intensely for a moment, then slowly pulling away. Laura found herself thrilled at the newness and willingness of Tony's kiss. The kiss was good enough to make her think maybe this night could be okay; that maybe she was meant to come here and create good new memories to erase the old. The start of a new life. Tony pulled away.

"You've gotta see the cavern."

He grabbed her hand and they continued down the trail towards the base of the falls.

"This used to be called Sotsone Falls, after this Indian lady. She was a princess, like an Indian princess, with the Tolaquin tribe, and back when they were relocating her tribe, she came up here and jumped off the falls in protest. Some way to go, huh? Well, supposedly, she's *in* the falls, haunting them, cursing them, whatever. You're supposed to be able to see her face in the falling water during a full moon. Anyway, people kept dying up here, falling and drowning and stuff, so they renamed the place Benham Falls in the thirties. Weird, huh?"

"Yeah." Laura said. "Pretty weird."

Inside she was trembling. She fought to keep it from showing; Tony was just starting to open up to her. She wanted to tell him that changing the name of the falls didn't stop anybody from dying up here.

Then she looked up to the top of the falls and for a second she saw the Indian woman up there, staring back at her, pointing at her with one long finger.

She shook her head and turned away. A trick of the moonlight off the mist.

They reached the bottom of the falls and Tony led her across a series of lichen and moss-covered rocks that played hell with her slender ankles. Soon they were behind the waterfall, standing close to each other beneath the low ceiling of a cavern carved out by the falls. The smell of minerals was sharp, and the sound of the falls was deafening. The cavern was barely illuminated with the thin, gray light cast by the moon's reflection off the falls. A cold drop of water fell from the black cavern ceiling and splattered on Laura's scalp dead center. She was about to complain about the cold and her shoes and the hike, to say, "Hey, this cavern's just lovely but we should go *now*," when Tony grabbed her and pulled her in for a deep kiss.

Tony's kisses were so sweet, so genuine in their urgency and attraction, that for a moment Laura was capable of forgetting again. He bit her lip playfully; he kissed her ears. He chewed at her neck and kissed the corners of her lips.

She sighed with pleasure; the shaking exhalation turned to thin vapor. She watched her breath float upwards, away from the shimmering light coming through the waterfall.

Tony kissed the hollow at the base of her throat. His lips felt so good on her skin, like a release from the ugly thoughts this place had forced on her, from the sickness that had permeated her new life with her father.

She tilted her head back, exalted, smiling.

That was when she saw the dead boy on the ceiling of the cavern.

Michael.

Her brother had black sockets where his eyes should have been, two holes in a pale, angry face. Thin trickles of blood ran from his open mouth. His little corduroy pants and yellow t-shirt were tattered and soaked dark crimson. He was floating down from the ceiling towards her, his arms and legs spread wide, and she was frozen with fear, oblivious to Tony's urgent kisses.

The little boy floated closer to her and one tiny hand reached out toward her face. She could not move as she felt four cold fingers press against her forehead.

A black veil fell over her eyes and she couldn't tell where she was, or who she was, or where Tony was. All she could do was *see*.

A small boy, at the top of the falls, picking up an old, beaded bracelet. The child, attracted to the bracelet and its horsehead pattern, slid it on to his wrist. Little Tony was a lucky boy that day. All smiles.

She saw that same boy pushing her brother into the river just north of the falls.

NO! Where were my parents? Where was I?

The vision provided no answers. It could only show her what her brother knew from that point on. The intimacy of his pain.

Michael, in his yellow t-shirt and corduroy pants, went over the falls and hit the water so hard his eyes were forced from his head.

Michael had yelled Laura's name on the way down. She'd always been there to help him before. Helped him tie his shoes. Helped him reach the cookie jar. But at that moment, everyone had looked away. That moment was all it took. Nobody could have heard his voice over the sound of the raging falls.

The vision shifted, became blurry and liquid.

Somewhere much further away she could feel hands around her throat.

After putting on the bracelet, Tony had been a busy boy.

She saw Tony throwing his new puppy dog over the falls. It yelped before the splash.

She saw him return to the falls as a teen. This time he threw a woman over.

Then another woman, and another. First he choked them, then he threw them from the top of the falls.

It was ritual; Sotsone's final protest repeating without end.

The fall and the maelstrom beneath it tore them all to pieces, collapsed their lungs and filled them up until they sank, swirling in the current with all the others. With Michael. She could hear them all howling under the water, torn, and restless.

She could hear Michael whispering to her.

Wake up.

Laura awoke from her vision to see Tony on top of her. While she'd watched the memories of her dead brother, Tony had pushed her body to the stony ground. The veins in his face bulged and he had his right hand clamped tight around her throat. The beads on his bracelet rattled as he choked her. She gasped for air and found none.

Laura regained consciousness as her hand touched the icy waters of the river flowing beside her. Tony's voice barely broke through the sound of her own blood rushing back into her head.

"You know, Laura, you could stand to lose some weight. Do you know how hard it was to carry you up here?"

Whatever it was she'd liked in his voice, it was gone, replaced by the same greasy confidence of the guys she'd hustled in the weeks before. That all seemed so distant and petty next to her need to pull in a full breath though her crushed windpipe. She couldn't help thinking, "This is how dad feels when he breathes."

Dad. No... I can't die now.

"I asked you a question."

She moaned, unable to respond with her maimed vocal cords. Tony continued.

"You tasted sweet, when I kissed you. But then you started shaking, and your eyes rolled back in your head. I couldn't keep kissing you like that. The look in your eyes was… wrong. I decided to take care of business."

Unable to speak, Laura raised a middle finger.

"I'm not going to pretend I don't enjoy this. I mean, *she* tells me to do it, she has ever since I found this bracelet, but I love it more every time. I kind of regretted pushing in that first kid, but it was just too easy. It's like fate put him there. All alone. And she was whispering to me. *Push him in. Watch him fall. Do it for me.*"

Laura hated Tony, the way he spoke of her brother. She wanted to say, "That wasn't just some kid. That was my brother, Michael." She wanted to kill Tony and knew that if she could find the strength she'd have no problem performing the act. She might even like it.

She tried harder to breathe, to think a clear thought, to find a way out of Tony's sight. He kept talking, enjoying the sound of his own voice. Something buzzed beneath his words. Something old. Something that had savored so much death it couldn't understand anything else.

"I like watching the women fall. That's the best part. Just for a second, right when they go over the edge, they kind of hang there, like *she's* holding them up, and then they drop so fast you wouldn't believe it. Sometimes they look like they're flying. Especially when they don't scream on the way down. I don't think we'll have to worry about that with you, will we?"

His hands dug into her arms, lifting her toward the edge of Benham Falls.

"You know, none of the bodies have ever surfaced. I guess the falls holds them down there. Keeps them hidden for me."

Laura felt his grip tighten as they approached the edge. The cascade here was raging as the river shot out and plummeted to the stormy water below.

Vertigo reeled through her body as the swift winds above the falls whipped around her.

She wanted to cry, to run, to scream at the madness and cruelty that brought her here. She hated her stupid plans, her father's cancer. She wanted to escape; to get back home and save her father the misery of losing another child's life before his own. Laura could not resign herself to this last, cold swan dive.

Then she heard Michael speaking inside of her head.

His voice a soft whisper, felt underneath her skin.

"Let go now."

She trusted the voice. What else was there to trust?

Laura let go. She let her body go limp and felt her ankles roll out from beneath her. She pitched forward, dead weight over the yawning precipice. Tony, who was still holding her arms vice-grip tight, had no chance to escape the fall.

Gravity took them both. They fell faster than the river had in its thousands of years.

On the way down, Laura saw the women.

Their white faces were just beneath the surface of the water. Over a dozen of them, empty white faces with hair and skin floating loose around them. None of them had eyes. All of them had gaping mouths, teeth bared, locked in a scream.

Tony and Laura's bodies rotated in the fall, and Tony struck the water first, with Laura on top of him. His body crunched beneath her, and then they were underwater, with the women. Cold, loose skin pressed against her as the thundering waterfall pushed them all under. Hands, all bone and sinew, tore Tony away from her. Teeth scraped her skin as they chewed away his hands, releasing her.

Her freedom from Tony's hands did not matter. She was trapped in the plunge pool, struggling to reach air and being pulled further and further down.

She heard a terrible tearing and popping sound, and the water around her grew warm. Laura could see that the dead, empty-faced women had chewed open Tony's belly and torn his limbs from his body. His gutted torso was still in their frenzy, his mouth wide in shock.

Laura struggled, trying not to inhale, but her lungs demanded it, and she pulled in a deep, liquid breath. Her lungs filled with water as the dead women swarmed.

No... I brought him to you... I'm not dead yet... I have to get home... my dad... Michael... please...

She could taste death in the water, and sank deeper until she felt a tiny, cold hand on hers, pulling with all its strength. The women's hands clamped down like talons, but could not hold her. She closed her eyes and felt the water parting before her, then falling away.

Moments later she found herself on the mossy shore near the base of the cascade, vomiting gouts of water and pulling thin breaths into her crushed chest. She was shattered and bone cold. Her skin wore the deep lacerations of the pale women's rage. In spite of all this, she was alive. With each breath, pain sunk its teeth through her splintered ribs and reminded her she was still in danger. The cold of night was sinking in. She imagined that if she died here the women would crawl from the water and drag her back in, back down to where they were hidden.

She stood and wavered, fawn-like, and stumbled towards Tony's car, away from Benham Falls. Halfway back to the car she stooped and picked up a fist-sized stone. "Please let one of the car windows break easily. Let me remember how to hot-wire the ignition without getting shocked." Laura felt like if there was ever a night someone was answering her prayers, this was it.

As she reached the clearing, and Tony's car, Laura heard a noise, thin and high pitched. She was bleeding from her left ear and turned her right towards the sound. The laughter of a small boy, a sweet echo from her childhood, drifted through the trees.

Somehow, Laura found the strength to laugh along.

"Goodnight, Michael."

Moments later she was in Tony's car, listening to the engine rumble, wondering how far away any hospital was, and how much money she could get for a vintage Camaro with a busted window and a scrapped ignition. Most importantly she thought of home, of holding her father.

She wheeled the car around and slammed the gas pedal. The entrance to Benham Falls became dust, then darkness.

Cathedral Mother

One little piggy dies and the whole crew goes soft.

Amelia saw things for the way they were. No bullshit. You had to see straight or The Machine would grind you down, leave you blind, fat, and confused. *Stare at the hypnotic box. Have another slice of pizza. There's cheese in the crust now!*

She brushed aside a chest-high sword fern, feeling the cool beads of a just-passed rain soaking into her fingerless climbing gloves. The redwood forest was thicker here, and the gray dusk light barely penetrated the canopy. Amelia tried to force herself calm, taking in a deep breath through her nose, picking up the lemony tang of the forest floor, a hint of salt air from the Pacific, and the rich undercurrent of moist rot that fed the grand trees and untold species. She imagined herself in the time of the Yurok tribes, when man had a fearful respect for this land, before he formed the false God of the dollar and built McMansions of ravenous worship.

She found no calm. All thoughts trailed into spite. All long inhales exited as huffed sighs of disgust.

Goddamn fucking humans. The worst.

When she joined The Assemblage she had felt like they understood. They *got it*. They could see The Machine for what it was—a vast system established solely to allow the human virus to replicate and consume at any cost. And The Assemblage had formed to restore balance.

She'd only met one other member of The Assemblage, as a precursor to her redwoods mission. Their group thrived in the anonymity of a subnet supposedly facilitated by a sixteen-year-old kid who'd been vying for membership in a hacker group with a classy name—World Wide Stab. So instead of having a batch of finks and fuck-ups gather in somebody's musty patchouli patch living room with an inevitable COINTELPRO-variant mole, The Assemblage existed only as a loosely organized forum of people who understood The Machine and challenged each other to disassemble it in as many ways as possible.

Minks were liberated from a farm in northern Oregon, their pricey cages devastated after the exodus. Two Humvee dealerships in Washington got hit, one with well-placed Molotovs, the other with thousands of highly adhesive bumper stickers reading "NAMBLA Member and Proud of It!" Chimps were saved from HIV testing at a bio-tech development firm outside of San Diego, and subnet photos showed them being returned home to a preserve in Africa (where, Amelia guessed, their lack of survival skills probably got them torched as "bush meat" shortly thereafter). Every Wal-Mart in New Jersey arrived to glue-filled locks on the exact same morning.

Not everything The Assemblage pulled was to Amelia's liking, but overall they seemed to be one of the only groups out there worth a damn.

That was until the Oregon tree spiking incident shook them up.

She'd been shocked too, initially, when she opened the forum thread. The title read, "97% of Oregon Old Growth Gone—Don't Fuck With Our Last 3%." Two quick clicks on the title and she was staring at a grainy, zoomed-in digital photo: a logger's face turned meatloaf, head nearly bisected, left eye loose of its orbit. Text beneath that: No more warning signs for spikes! Let's *really* put Earth first! Feed the worms another tree killer!

The Assemblage, for all its rhetoric and snarky misanthropy, was not prepared for murder. Buddhist members cried bad karma. Pacifists quoted Gandhi. Anarchist kids sweated clean through their black bandanas, wondering if eco-terrorist association charges would make Mom and Dad kill the college funds. Membership dwindled in anticipation of Fed heat.

Amelia, however, was applauding. The Oregon spikers got it right. Now The Machine was short a cog, and she knew any logger working that territory had a new thought in their head: *Is this worth dying for?*

She was inspired. She knew that acres of redwoods south of her home in Eureka were about to be offered up as a smorgasbord to a conglomerate of corporate interests, one of the final parting gifts from King George's administration.

She had hiked those territories since her childhood, and even now she trekked there with her son Henry. The trees there were giants, vast even among redwoods, some topping thirty five stories tall, with trunks over twenty feet around. To her they were great and ancient things, representatives from better times.

To grow for thousands of years only to be destroyed for the "cubic feet" needed to house more goddamned MOB's (Morbidly Obese Breeders, Assemblage code for the common-folk)… Amelia couldn't stomach the idea.

She planned. There were only a few months until the virgin forest was to be royally fucked by bulldozers and cat-tracks and chainsaws and cranes.

Despite being consumed with finding a way to stop The Machine from gaining penetration, she tried to stay balanced.

Nights were for plotting—surveying and copping gear and staying tuned to those few voices on The Assemblage that still raged and let her know she wasn't alone.

Days were for Henry—homeschooling and hiking and lessons in doing no harm. Late summer heat let them swim in a pond near their property, sometimes until dusk brought out flurries of gnats and insect-chasing bats. These were the sorts of things she pointed out to Henry, to remind him that he needn't be jealous of the TV shows his friends talked about.

Not that she let Henry see those friends too often. Their life was very contained, and she couldn't risk outside influence turning her son into another one of… them.

She never intended to become a Breeder, and had a hard time accepting the extra pressure she was creating for the taxed environment. But she reminded herself that she had not had Henry for selfish reasons. She'd been young, and confused, and had made the mistake of being seduced by a gangly hippie boy named Grant, who was drifting through town with a few hundred other friends on their way to a Rainbow Family gathering.

She was pulled away from the boredom of her grocery store stock clerk gig in Eureka, and spent over a year wandering the US with the Family, dropping acid and shitting in woodland troughs, shoplifting steaks and air duster (for cooking and huffing, respectively). Free love gave her a nice case of genital warts and a disappearing period.

Grant, lover that he was, offered to sell off his Phish bootlegs to pay for an abortion, but by the time she'd really put the pieces together she was already in second trimester, and the kicks in her belly had her feeling like this kid was closer to alive than not. She killed the LSD and nitrous habits and smoked a lot of weed and ate buckets of trail mix and waited for the Rainbow Family train to circumnavigate back toward Eureka.

The train didn't quite chug fast enough and she ended up having Henry on the outskirts of a field in eastern Oregon, near the Blue Mountains. A girl named Hester, who claimed to be a midwife, shouted at Amelia to breathe. Then, once she confirmed Amelia was indeed breathing, she shared what she must have thought was comforting wisdom.

"The Armillaria mushroom that grows near here is the biggest living thing on Earth. It's underground. It's like three miles wide."

Then she wandered off into the distance, perhaps to find this giant mushroom, leaving Amelia alone to have the most primal experience of her life.

She felt abandoned for a moment, cursing Grant for his carelessness, herself for being seduced by the irresponsibility dressed as freedom that brought her to this Third World state. But loneliness was swiftly crushed by a series of contractions and a sense of animal purpose. Then everything was waves of pain, and a sudden release, and the sound of tiny lungs taking first air. Amelia collapsed with her boy, loneliness long forgotten.

She was cradling Henry in her arms when a dirt-bag named Armando wandered by and offered to help. He also, she later realized, wouldn't stop looking at her crotch. Still, he had a Leatherman, and in cutting her umbilical, was the closest thing Henry had to an obstetrician.

With her infant son in her arms she'd found it easy to beg enough change to get a Greyhound Bus ride back to glorious Eureka.

Since then she'd done her best to raise Henry outside of an ever-sickening American culture. If she had to be a Breeder, she'd make damn sure that her contribution to the next generation gave back to the Earth in some way. Since she couldn't trust Henry to the goddamned Rockefeller Worker Training Camp they called Public School she'd had to reconnect with her parents and beg enough of a stipend to support her and the kid.

It meant her parents got to visit Henry on occasion, but she was sure to let him know that these were Bad People. Industrialists. Plastic makers. Part of the Problem. They were piggies.

Still, they kept her and Henry in the food and clothes business, and Amelia took a secret joy in spending their money on the various laptops and servers that maintained her connection to the subnet and The Assemblage.

And lately she'd been spending their cash on climbing gear. It had taken her a precious couple of weeks to come up with her plan, but if she pulled it off she'd be able to protect the forest *and* keep it from being tied to her or her new associate.

She'd drafted "Cristoff" from another subnet board called Green Defense, where he'd developed a reputation for being too extreme. His avatar was a picture of Charles Whitman with the word HERO embossed at the bottom.

They vetted each other via subnet friends. "Cristoff" agreed to drive up from San Francisco so they could get to work. Real names, they agreed, would never be exchanged.

Posing as husband and wife—Mr. and Mrs. Heartwood, har har har—they hooked up with a local arborist named Denny who gave lessons in recreational tree climbing down by the Humboldt Redwoods State Park.

Henry was allowed to spend a week with his friend Toby (whose family she found the least disgusting).

She and Cristoff were quick learners. They picked up "crack-jamming" on day one, which allowed them to free climb a redwood's thick, gnarled bark by pinning hands and feet into the crevices. Day two taught them how to use mechanical Jumar ascenders, rope, and a tree climbing saddle to get much higher. This was called "jugging," a term which Cristoff found amusing.

"I'll tell my buddies I spent all week crack-jamming and jugging with a new lady friend."

Who was this guy? *And* he had friends? That was concerning.

Still, he could climb, and was willing to help her with the delicate work they needed to do up in the unprotected redwoods.

At night she wore a head-lamp in her tent and read up on great trees: Forest canopies held half of the living species in nature. The top of the tree was the crown, which could be its own ecosystem, several feet across, filled with canopy soil up to a meter deep, hosting hundreds of ferns, barbed salmonberry canes, even fruit bearing huckleberry bushes. These crowns were miracles of fractal reiteration, with some sprouting hundreds of exacting smaller versions of the main tree, all of them reaching for the sun. The redwoods were one of the last homes for legions of un-named prehistoric lichen and some canopies even inexplicably harbored worms and soil-mites previously thought to be extinct.

She was particularly happy to read that both HIV and Ebola were postulated to have come from human interaction with canopy dwelling primates and bats. These trees were already fighting back. It gave her mission a sense of camaraderie. She would work with these noble giants as an advance warning system. *Don't fuck with our last 3%.*

Amelia and Cristoff spent the last part of their lessons learning a technique for which they'd paid extra. Skywalking was a way of manipulating multiple ropes and knots in the upper canopy, allowing you to float from branch to branch without applying too much weight. Properly done you could even move from crown to crown.

They *had to* be able to do this, as the crowns they'd be leaving would be far too treacherous to allow return. They were going to create a logger's nightmare up there.

That was the plan—To spend a week camped among the canopies, working to saw dozens of branches just short of the snapping point. The loggers and climbers call these hanging branches "widow-makers" and with good reason. Falling from stories above they could reach terminal velocity and they typically tore loose an armada of forest shrapnel on their way down. One turn-of-the-century account of a widow-maker dispatch simply read, "Wilson was ruined. Pieces were found five feet high in surrounding trees. The rest of him was already buried beneath the branch. Most could not be retrieved for proper interment."

How many loggers would be splattered by her old growth nukes before they asked the crucial question?

Is this worth dying for?

That *was* the plan, at least until Cristoff decided to get in a fight with gravity.

There are different types of branches on a redwood. The higher branches can be thick as most regular trees and are rooted deeply into the trunk. The lower branches are far narrower. Between handfuls of strawberry granola Denny had told them these lesser branches were called epicormics, or "dog's hair" for slang. They were easily shed and not to be trusted.

Cristoff was getting comfortable in the trees, pleased with his progress. Denny told them not to be surprised if this felt strangely natural, since all other primates were at least partially arboreal.

Cristoff's inner monkey had him gassed up and proud after a few strong ascents. Cristoff's inner monkey started feeling an imaginary kinship with the tree. The kind of false trust that let him think a batch of epicormics would hold as well as a single trunk-rooted branch.

He was sixty feet up, ten feet past the climber's "redline" cutoff for survivable falls. He ignored Denny's request that he rope a higher branch. The last thing he said through the walkie talkie was, "I've got this."

The redwood, clearly disagreeing, decided to shed some weight.

The sounds were as follows: a sharp crack as the branches separated, a shocked yell accompanied by a terrible whooshing sound as gravity got serious, and at last a chimerical whoomp-crunch as Cristoff created the first and only Cristoff Crater at Humboldt Redwoods State Park.

Technically, per Denny's lessons, he was supposed to yell "Headache" if any object was falling, even himself. His neglect would be forgiven the moment Denny and Amelia approached his body.

Cristoff was breathing, but the crimson gurgles at each exhale screamed hemorrhage, and compound fractures at the femur and clavicle had happened so fast that the bone still jutted white and proud with little blood to emphasize how shattered the man was.

Still in shock, Denny informed Cristoff that he shouldn't move.

As far as Amelia could see, this was a non-issue. Whoever this Cristoff was, she had a hard time imagining he'd ever move again.

Denny held out hope, lucking into a cell phone signal and getting Air

Life dispatched.

Amelia tried to get Cristoff's eyes to focus on hers, but his were glazed and the left had gone bright red. She could hear a helicopter in the distance.

She prayed for telepathy. She stared at the broken man and thought, "Don't you say a motherfucking word."

With that, she turned and walked to her rental Chrysler. Denny's eyes stayed fixed on the injured man as "Mrs. Heartwood" gunned the car out of the park, leaving an odd impression, some cheap camping gear, and the crushed shell of a man she hoped would die, and fast.

Weak men were shaping Amelia's world. First Grant left her with an STD and a kid. Then the spiked logger's greed and split skull became the catalyst that weakened the resolve of The Assemblage. Now the man she knew as "Cristoff" turned snitch.

It wasn't intentional, but the bastard (real name: Richard Eggleston) had managed to make it to the hospital, and the opiate mix they pumped into him for pain management left him delirious. His night nurse picked up enough chatter about "tree bombs" to feel comfortable playing Dutiful Citizen and calling the Feds.

The Feds got to his computer gear. The subnet that hosted The Assemblage was fluid enough that they were able to block Fed access and re-route themselves, but speculation about what might have been on Eggleston's hard drive had a variety of already-freaked underground groups on full black helicopter alarm.

Worse still, The Assemblage had gone even more limp-dicked. Even staunch hard-liners she'd once trusted were calling the glimmers of her plan that had gone public "monstrous and irresponsible."

She put her stress in the wrong places, snapping at Henry for minor transgressions like leaving his crayons out. She was forgetting to eat.

Then a new voice joined The Assemblage—Mycoblastus Sanguinarius. *Black bloody heart.* She looked it up and discovered the namesake was a tiny lichen that revealed a single dot of blood-like fluid when ruptured.

He signed his posts as Myco. She assumed the member was a "he" since the writing had a masculine terseness, but there was no way to be sure.

Myco posted an open letter to anyone who might have been involved in the aborted "redwoods plan." He begged them to contact him privately, saying that he might have a way to help them reach their goal without shedding any blood.

He had to be a mole, right?

She ignored Myco and tried to come up with her own new plan. Random spiking? Fire-bombing bulldozers?

The stress amped her self-loathing. *You say you hate humans. Well, what do you think you are, bitch? What do you think Henry is? Chain yourself to a tree and starve out. Pull the media into this. How much explosive could you strap to your body? To Henry?*

These were not safe thoughts. She pushed them away. She tried to stay focused on a real option. The loggers would gain access soon.

She sent a non-committal message to Myco. *What's your plan?*

Two days later Myco sent a response, and it felt legit. He *was* government, and he was upfront about it. He held a position of some influence, and if he had the right information he could get it in front of someone who might have the power to halt the government's release of the property.

The problem was that the property was in a weird transitory status, off limits for government-permitted climbs even for the research sector. He needed someone who knew the area to engage in a "ninja climb" and acquire a number of biological samples. Depending on what was found, the rarity of the species and its "viability for government use," he might be able to prevent the destruction of those groves.

But who was this guy? This was a classic COINTELPRO move. He wrote like a professor, which could place him with DARPA or one of its extensions. Could just be an FBI grunt telling her what she wanted to hear. And would it be any better if the property was retained "for government use?"

Or was this some old hippie college teacher trying to regain his idealism after trading it for a BMW in the 80's? Maybe his son was in the California legislature? Maybe his nephew was the goddamned President?

Who knew? But she trusted this subnet, and if he promised they'd never have to meet then she felt there was enough safety in the agreement. There's no way he'd be able to guess which trees she'd climb. The groves were too dense, the old timber too wide.

He assured her that all he needed were the samples, and she could leave them in a place of her choosing, as long as it was temperate and hidden. Then she just had to forward the location via GPS coordinates.

It would be a shame to waste her climbing lessons. And she'd been dreaming of these trees, somehow still standing proud for another thousand years, after all the little piggies had destroyed each other. In her dreams the skyscrapers fell and the redwoods swayed in the moonlight, returned to their post atop the world.

She responded to Myco—Please check Assemblage regularly. Location of samples to follow.

After sending was confirmed she crawled into bed with Henry and spooned him, despite a few sleepy grumbles. She pulled the blankets tight around the two of them and kissed the back of his head.

I'll protect us, Henry, from these humans.

All of her gear was black, from boots to ropes to pack. Even her Treeboat, which would allow her to sleep in the tree hammock-style if needed, was damn near invisible at night.

Dusk had passed now, and her anger was shifting to nerves as she tried to recall climbing techniques. She moved quietly. The yielding forest floor, rich with decomposed needles and ferns, absorbed much of her noise. Where moonlight broke through the thickening canopy it revealed large clusters of redwood sorrel, the heart-shaped leaves still glowing emerald green in the slight illumination. It was beautiful.

I will save this place.

She picked a full moon night, thinking it would give her better natural light once she cleared the canopy and reached the crown. Until that point she'd have to stay to the shadows.

Myco told her that the older the tree was, the more likely it was to be biologically diverse. She searched for the base of a redwood that looked about three cars across, and briefly shone her headlamp to check the coloration of the bark. The "newer" trees, only a few hundred years old, would have reddish brown bark while the eldest would have shifted to a stony gray.

Her tree finally presented itself, after forty minutes of hiking deeper into the grove. Light had simply ceased to find a home. To her right she saw the outline of the blockage, a tree thick as a blue whale reaching up to heights she couldn't perceive.

She ran her hands across the bark, imagining herself at the foot of some planet-traversing colossus who was standing still to allow her up for a visit.

She used a pair of night vision-equipped Zeiss binoculars to scan the base for a solid climbing branch on which to start. The best option was about one hundred and forty feet up, though several epicormics presented below that. She thought of "Cristoff's" ruptured eye and wrong-angled bone shards and immediately canceled any thought of risking the lower points.

The best solution was to shoot a weighted fishing line over the good branch, then use that line to pull a rope back up and over. It was a patience game, and she set herself to it, unpacking a crossbow with a pre-threaded dull-tipped arrow.

Four tries and she found purchase. After that it seemed easy to rig up the rope and lock in her climbing saddle and Jumar ascenders.

She began her climb beyond the world of the humans, praying that the tree's nightlife would yield something Myco needed. She stopped at each major branch and briefly flipped on her headlamp, extracting a plastic container with a micro-fiber lid as instructed by her mysterious correspondent. The lids allowed oxygen in, but nothing, even water, would find its way out.

At mid-height she managed to pry loose a tent spider entrenched in a bark pocket. Its eyes gleamed purple in her headlamp.

She scored fragments of lichens, some shaped like leaves of lettuce, others like tiny clothespins, and still others that looked like green beard hairs.

Just before breaking into the crown she spotted an inverted blackened chamber about three feet wide, the damage from some fire that likely burned before the birth of Christ. Tucked just inside the fire cave she found a blind salamander, its damp wet skin speckled with orange dots. She grabbed a chunk of moist canopy soil to include in its container so that it might survive the voyage.

The salamander wiggled in her fingers. She stared at it, wondering how the hell it got up here.

Speaking of which, how did I get up here?

Strung between two branches, hundreds of feet above the Earth, staring at some tree lizard. Way out of cell phone range and one mistake away from instant death. So far from home, from Henry.

Aside from the thought of her son, she was filled with exhilaration rather than fear. This was a world so few had ever seen. And she was going to save it from her terrible species.

Emboldened, she pushed upward to the crown. The moon was there to greet her, blindingly bright and so close she could touch it.

Amelia was confused during her descent. Happy, ecstatic really, but confused. She felt as if her time in the crown was a dream. Beautiful to be sure, but… those things couldn't have happened, right?

She'd been gathering more samples—a variety of berries, more lichen than she could count, even a bright white worm she spotted nosing out of the canopy soil. But then she'd… what?

Shimmers of light. *She'd found the trunk pool.* Dead center in the crown, the main trunk had collapsed inward and hollowed out, allowing water to collect there.

She'd reached in with a plastic sample container and immediately felt a sting in her exposed fingers. Was it the cold? But seconds later her hand filled with warmth. It spread up her arms and unfurled in her chest. She'd closed the sample container and tucked it into her pack.

Then she remembered feeling an overwhelming sense of joy, and safety. Thoughts of rotten Grant or all the pigs snorting around down on Earth turned to sand and were blown away. A dumb grin slid across her face and the moon blurred through her tears—a white puddle surrounded by oil.

But did she really unhitch her tree saddle and carabiners? Did she really let her body drop into the trunk pool, and float there, picturing herself as a tiny red hummingbird sitting in the palm of a kind and loving God.

It seemed insane. But when she reached up to feel her hair, it was still sopping wet.

"I had a moment of rapture," she thought. And she didn't care if it was real or not.

She descended carefully, methodically, and placed her cargo in a safe place before the sun cracked the horizon.

After cleaning up and communicating her drop spot to Myco, she drove to Toby's parents' house to pick up Henry. She still hadn't slept, but she couldn't wait to see her son. There was something so lovely about him. She smiled at the thought of him and her chest ached in his absence. She sped across Eureka, keeping an eye out for the erratic driving of the tweakers that inhabited early morning commutes like this. Not that she hated the tweakers. Everyone had their problems.

Jesus, what?

Amelia had been clean of the poison of drugs for a long time now, but she could swear she was being washed over by waves of euphoria. She wrote it off as sleep deprivation and adrenaline.

But when she got to Toby's she found that instead of honking and waiting for Henry to come running out, she practically jumped out of her car and ran to the front door.

Shit. I'll have to talk to the parents.

I love the parents.

Oh, God.

Thankfully only Henry emerged from the front door. Amelia saw him recoil as she crouched down to sweep him up. What a boy…

"Momma, you smell funny."

"Well, kiddo, you smell, too. You smell *great*. God, I just love you SO MUCH!"

She kissed him full on the lips, a big wet smacker that she was sure would have embarrassed him if Toby were watching. Oh well, she'd slap one on adorable little Toby too.

She set Henry down. He looked up at her, his brow furrowed. "You okay, momma?"

"Yes, honey, I'm better than ever. You want to go get some pancakes?"

With that he nodded "Yes" and took off running for the car. He *never* got pancakes. High fructose corn syrup was a poison, one of the favorites of The Machine.

But it felt so right to make him happy. She wanted to hold him close and kiss him all over his little face.

He was already buckled when she got in the car. He was rubbing his sleeve back and forth on his lips.

"It tingles, momma."

"Bad tingles, like burning?"

"No, like peppermint. It's kind of nice, I guess."

"Are you sure?"

"Yup. It's really nice, actually. Really nice."

She and Henry were barely eating anymore. They felt constantly tired, though they found they were happy just cuddling and drinking water. Lots of water, to the point where Henry would laugh at the sloshing sounds when either of them moved around.

Their temperatures ran hot, but never to the point where she started thinking Emergency Room.

Amelia did worry when the sores appeared on Henry's chest and arms. They reminded her of the splotches on the tweakers that tried to shoplift at the grocery store she'd worked for. Her boss had told her that was caused by battery acid in the meth.

She applied A & D Ointment to Henry's sores and got a cool washcloth for his forehead. That seemed to give him more energy. He asked her to tell the story again, about climbing the great tree and meeting the strange creatures and swimming in the sky pool and saving the woods.

He loved the story. He loved her and told her so, over and over again.

* * *

He was dead when she woke.

She could tell right away. She was so hot—sweating under the blankets—that his body was like ice against her chest.

And something was very wrong. Because his chest was not expanding, but his belly was. His abdomen was thrumming like it was filled with boiling water. Worse, while her animal instinct got her away from his body, she found herself back in front of the sink, refilling her favorite glass with tap water. Good God she was thirsty.

And happy.

Happy? Fucking Christ—Henry is dead. Something is moving in his belly.

They'd both been crying for days now, but they were tears of overwhelming joy, at their luck that they might be alive and filled with so much love.

Amelia wanted true tears. Part of her brain was screaming, begging to collapse to the floor, to crawl back to Henry and wail.

What was happening?

For days now, their lives were only bed/water /love. They'd heard helicopters roaring overhead last night, and it was a wonderful sound. That man should fly was so amazing.

No. Henry is dead. Nothing is amazing. Figure out what's going on.

Drink some water.

No.

Go to bed.

No.

She hadn't turned on her computer since sending her last email to Myco. *What a beautiful name. What a great man!* Amelia wanted to scrape all this love out of her skull, but it came at her in insistent waves.

Myco had responded: Your woods are saved. Your collection efforts provided us with not just one, but *two* viable interests. Rest assured that this grove will be protected for some time to come, though public access will be greatly reduced. However, the trees will be saved, and I would like to let you know, in the confidence afforded to Assemblage members of course, that one of the lichen you provided us may hold the key to boosting white blood cell counts in patients with severe immune deficiencies. The other sample of interest was a microscopic parasite found in the water sample you provided. We expected protozoa but actually discovered a never-before-seen type of copepod, a tiny shrimp-like creature. We can't tell whether it has been self-sustaining in the tree for thousands of years, or if it was just recently dropped there by a wet-winged osprey, but we do know that it possesses an ovipositor for egg delivery and that the eggs have this miraculous viral coating that likely induces confusion in the host. It's similar to how a parasitic wasp breeds, but it is *so streamlined.* You've done our group a great service and we believe that this little management tool may help us to control invasive fish species off Florida and elsewhere. Congratulations!

She deleted the message.

Henry's body was twitching under the blankets.

Drink more water.

Get in bed. Love your son.

Protect him.

She refused the voice. It was a virus. Myco's precious streamlined management tool had killed her son, and it would kill her too. And for the first time in her life, she could embrace her death.

But not Henry's. Poor Henry.

Before she died she was going to send a message to some of the piggies. Somehow they'd led her to this terrible place. *All these humans...*

Amelia cleaned herself, ignoring the shifting in her own belly and the "love" that whipsawed around her brain.

She dried and put on her only perfume and spotted a few sores blooming on her skin. Nothing some foundation couldn't cover up.

She slid on a short skirt and an old black t-shirt. It fit perfectly—the last few days' fast had done right by her looks.

No underwear. None needed.

She would walk to the outskirts of the grove, where she guessed gun-sure soldiers and salivating business men were already setting up perimeter in anticipation of harvesting what she'd found.

There was an old redwood stump there which had refused to die. It was fifteen feet across and rimmed on all sides by new redwood trunks growing from its edges. The locals called these "fairy circles" and a few romantic visiting botanists had termed them "cathedrals."

She would claim this cathedral as her own and would invite every last man to join her.

She licked her lips in anticipation. She was already wet. Her upper thighs tingled. Like peppermint. It *was* really nice.

Humanity needed a management tool. And she would give it to them.

With love.

The Brilliant Idea

You had the brilliant idea this morning, at dawn.

You rose to a noise from outside, a trashcan overturned by wind, spilling fetid food for early-rising dogs. In this moment—sleep a mucous haze over your dilated eyes, mouth tasting soured bacteria, hearing the clang of metal against concrete—the idea landed.

It was genius, the answer to every question you'd ever given up answering, the unifying concept that could surely explain God to the world in a way that we could all agree on.

This idea was too big. Maybe it's the sheer processing speed required. Synaptic overload. That Ambien you took. Your brain couldn't hold it. The further your eyes opened, the more this idea slipped away like the organs of a suddenly skinned man.

Then you were Awake—not in some grand spiritual sense, but the corporeal—and the brilliant idea was gone.

All that remains is this phantom feeling that you *knew*... something.

Tears come. They are extra-salty; you drank too much wine last night.

Skipping your morning habits, you shelve your shower and your half-conscious masturbation and instead sit at the kitchen table with a pad of paper, scrawling words like "stardust" and "sub-cellular." But they're never more than words.

You head outside; start knocking over trashcans. Perhaps there's an auditory trigger? Each can produces a clang before fast-food bags tumble free and grease their way into the gutter.

Nothing.

The world needs this idea.

You drink, smoke, meditate.

You create Goldbergian devices—alarm clock/sewing machines that drive needles into the soft pads of your feet, causing you to wake suddenly.

Months pass. You can't focus. Your job's terminated.

Despondent, walking home, you barely notice the semi-truck running a red as you shuffle through the crosswalk.

The horn sounds. Headlights fill your vision.

The brilliant idea is there, glowing, closer, closer, almost within your grasp.

Then it hits you.

Simple Equations

Minna knew that her fits were a blessing. She'd never stated this fact to anyone. Not her husband Jakob, nor her son Garin. Not even to her mother, who Minna knew viewed the writhing black-outs as a curse which might one day steal away her precious child.

At the funeral Minna had wondered if her mother might still be alive, had she understood the nature of the attacks. Perhaps the heart-crushing stress of caring for a tormented child would have been alleviated if Minna could have explained the glorious *glow* that she felt during the fits.

Her mother could only have seen the child, and later the young woman, in a state of extreme duress. Eyes rolled white. Teeth gnashing. Back arched in a contorted "U" that threatened to snap the spine and spread open her stretched-thin belly. She could never have known the sights, the glow, that Minna had experienced as her body bore its own assault.

Inside that state Minna had seen new worlds. Alien languages formed by numbers and angles and whorls, and images of a galaxy in which forces shifted gloriously. Minna had seen these images from so great a distance that all the chaos and movement had been reduced to simple truths, which she later learned to speak about and document to great effect at the Technical University in Darmstadt.

As a child she called these things she'd witnessed The Beauties. As a woman she relented and referred to them under the name which her male counter-parts at University used: Physics.

But in her heart, still: The Beauties.

And the things she witnessed during her fits served her well, or as well as they could. Her brilliance with the language of movement allowed her occasion to matriculate and complete a doctorate at Technical. Although she was forbidden from filling an academic post, the sheer value of her knowledge permitted her to work—always unofficially—alongside minds like Hemholtz and Muller. She aided Wuerzberg with his radar research at Telefunken.

She was afforded little to no wage for these efforts, but found the opportunity to test the ideas of Prandtl, or dissect the effects of flow velocity, too alluring.

It was her chance, in each of these studies, to speak the language of The Beauties outside of the blinding moments in which she'd envisioned them. It felt heretical to do anything else.

And now her talent with "physics" had brought her to Nordhausen in the Harz Mountains, as the primary member of an airborne weapons development group.

It was here that she'd had her most recent and terrible fit. Terrible because during her last attack the glow had abandoned her.

She'd seen nothing, knew nothing of the fit until it was over. And instead of coming to with an even more keen sense of how the world was, indeed, in exact order, she woke to the realization that something inside of her had broken.

She'd pleaded for her husband Jakob then, called out for him to lift her from the floor of her small house. Such was her agitation upon recovery—she had forgotten Jakob had perished three years before in France, when the war had not yet seemed real to her. She'd called out for her son Garin, too, who had been away working as a guard at the Maidanek camp for as long as Jakob had been dead and buried.

Minna was finally found there on the floor, soaked through from exertion, by a Nordhausen guard on night duty.

She'd asked to be shipped out of the mountains, to see a doctor better than Kuntzler, who she knew was fiercely held in the grip of alcohol at most hours, but due to "security reasons" she was never allowed to leave the factory grounds.

She knew too much about the weapons program to risk transporting. Kuntzler assigned her to two days of bed rest and left it at that.

Since the day of that empty, thieving fit she had been unable to move her left arm, and the left side of her face was nearly dead to the touch, its eyelid drooping so heavily it obscured and twisted her depth perception.

Worse, her thoughts and memories seemed to have been scattered to the periphery of her mind, and recalling the way to mouth a certain phrase or spell common words became a chore.

The men around her—the guards and fellow researchers and craftsmen of the Nordhausen munitions factory—now looked at her differently. She heard whispers and caught smirking glances.

As a woman she'd felt that her power at Nordhausen had always been in question; this new and damnable disability was sapping what little influence she'd once wielded.

The factory labor—hollow-faced Jews shipped over by Koch from Buchenwald—still regarded her with fear, and she cursed herself for finding comfort in that. After all, their fear was misplaced. She'd never harmed one of them. In fact, she'd quietly protested the banning of the Jews from the University back in'38, at risk to her own life. The unearthing of this fact had almost prevented her from receiving her development position at Nordhausen, but in the end the intellectual prowess and value of Minna Konig's mind had proven too valuable to the Führer's project.

Now Minna wondered how much more time she'd be allowed to complete her work. She'd been sequestered to the harsh terrain of the Harz Mountains for years now, toiling at Nordhausen to develop an unmanned flight craft that could accurately deliver bombs to the territory of their enemies.

The factory itself, aside from its attendant development offices, was a rough place. Parts of the weapon production and storage area were being built into the mountains themselves, and the laborers that toiled at this task were dying at a rate Minna found surreal. These dead men were carried out on carts, and were quickly replaced by new skeleton-thin workers.

About two months back a laborer had attempted to sabotage the massive steel press, one of the few machines too large to fit into the mountain-side tunnels. The normal punishment for this, for anything outside Nordhausen's rule of law, would be to hang the man in the gallows beside the factory. These hangings took place daily, sometimes for what seemed like hours. But the soldier in charge of the man must have grown bored with the noose.

Minna heard the story later, how the saboteur had been forced at gunpoint to wedge the upper half of his body into the press. How after the machine had done its work the other men who attended to it were forced to scrape the remains away and return to work, sliding steel plates into the maw of the blood-slicked machine.

Minna avoided these parts of the factory as often as she could. Instead she stayed in the research office, toiling away for hours with her pad and pen. It was hard work for Minna but initially she'd reveled in the language of it. Angle of attack, curvature, mass, all of it rolling like honey on her tongue as she formulated trajectories and wingspans and frame designs. Even when Jakob had passed, she refused to acknowledge the reality of what she was creating.

The ends are not important, she told herself. *The universe will work in exact order, as it always has.*

She knew she was being seduced by a chance to speak The Beauties, and to do so with greater authority than she had been able to at University. But this was knowledge that she held in utmost restraint and it only crept into her mind on long nights when she could not find sleep. It was then, as the cold winds of the Harz Mountains howled against the small frame of her house, that she allowed her mind to be over-run with thoughts of Jakob, and the terrible way the men at Nordhausen treated their labor, and the effect that her love affair with her visions might one day have on the flesh of the unsuspecting.

She could only clear these terrible thoughts by whispering the name of her son.

Garin.

Garin, please come home.

They said that a miracle had saved Garin during the American's attack on Maidanek. A bullet had glanced from his high cheekbone and proceeded to tear off a substantial portion of the left side of his skull. Somehow a field doctor had managed to escape with Garin's unconscious body and had sealed shut the wound, suturing the flap of skin and hair that had been torn loose by the gunfire.

The piece of skull lost in the injury had never been recovered, but Garin still survived the trauma. He fought a fever that peaked at one hundred and five degrees, and his body staved off an infection that threatened to creep right up to the vulnerable soft concavity where Garin's skull used to be.

Once he regained consciousness he managed to speak his mother's name. Minna was well known among the higher ranking officers, who wanted to respect Garin's apparent request.

Looking at him now, slumped forward in his wheelchair with a thin string of drool running from the right corner of his mouth to his shoulder, Minna guessed that they just wanted to be rid of him. And deep down she loathed herself for feeling the same way.

He's finally here, but he's never coming home.

It wasn't supposed to be like this. You were supposed to be here to help me.

She looked at her dead arm, saw how loose and separate it was from what she felt was her body.

I need you now. You can't need me.

She hated herself for thinking it.

Minna wondered if he was in there somewhere, thinking and struggling to speak just as she had done ever since her last fit. She hoped his mind might be healing, growing stronger.

Her eyelid was drooping less than it used to. Perhaps he was on the same slow road to recovery. In her brighter moments she believed that this was the truth and it allowed her to find her own words more easily. She'd discuss her job with him, she'd reminisce about Jakob. She even, for the first time in her life, tried to explain her vision of The Beauties to him, but gave up when her tongue couldn't find a way around the ideas.

She settled for gently washing Garin's wounds and combing his hair on the side opposite the injury. She'd tried to bathe him the week before but with one arm it had been too difficult to shift his body. On top of that, she'd noticed he'd become aroused when she'd tried to wash his groin. While Minna hadn't been disturbed by it, Garin had emitted a low moan and started to cry. As best he could, he'd tried to shake his head from left to right.

No, Mom. No.

She respected his wishes but worried that her inability to completely clean him would let infection creep back in.

Her work at Nordhausen had slowed to a near standstill. She felt a strange relief at the fact— *This weapon won't help anyone. It won't help Garin.*—but knew how dangerous it was to be of no use to the men of Nordhausen and the Reich.

How long will it be until they bring in someone like Reinholtz to continue my work?

And the jokes at her expense were beginning to feel more like threats. She heard comments about the "worthlessness of the feeble-minded," the curse of the "useless eaters" and "life unworthy of life."

Minna tried to return to her work full force, although she could get none of the men at Nordhausen, not even Kuntzler, to help attend to Garin. He was a reminder that none of them could tolerate. But Minna knew that her weapons work was the only way to return to the status quo.

If I can get this craft to fly, if we can get a few dry runs to clear the right distance, then they'll know I should remain here. Perhaps they'll even increase my wage and I can bring in an outside doctor to help Garin heal.

She worked for two days straight, coming home only to feed Garin soup—chicken noodle was his favorite but she had to make do with a thin tomato puree—and to make sure he knew he wasn't alone.

Minna prayed for another fit, something to strike her down so she could rise again and know exactly how to make the Nordhausen project a success. She focused on finding the right words and calculations until sweat dripped from her wrinkled forehead.

Her renewed efforts were working.

She designed a new wing flap that would allow the craft to stabilize even over sharp mountain winds. She perfected her fuel equation to maximize distance. She recalled bits of her work with Wuerzberg and proposed ways to equip the weapon with radar guidance.

The effort exhausted her. She requested a soldier to shuttle her home from the factory.

Her driver didn't make eye contact. He didn't speak a word.

This is wrong.

She'd had the thought so many times before—when she'd stolen from her mother to buy hard candy, when she'd tossed a book which Goebbels had banned into the pyre at University, when she'd buried Jakob, when she'd thought about all of the destruction her project might create.

But none of those moments had felt as wholly wrong as when she'd read the letter that had been delivered to her residence.

Minna had hoped that the letter might tell her that a doctor had finally been assigned to come help Garin, as she'd been requesting. Instead she'd received notice that both she and Garin were going to receive "the finest care" at the Reich Work Group of Sanatoriums and Nursing Homes.

As a scientist she was supposed to be insulated from the daily goings on of the war. But she'd heard of the Reich Work Group, and understood the nature of their "healing." Even if she could convince someone that she and Garin were becoming healthier, she was sure her University protest from '38 would resurface. She'd be shunned—they might even declare her insane for once having favored Jews.

The Reich had clearly decided, with the utter finality the Work Group represented, that Minna and Garin no longer represented the best interests of the great race.

We must escape.

As soon as she had the ridiculous thought and her mind tried to put together all the permutations of the idea, there was a knock at her door.

Kuntzler entered and in a few acidic, boozy breaths, explained that the requisition had already been filed, that they were patients in his care, and that he would personally supervise their transfer to Work Group tomorrow.

He did not hesitate to add that an armed guard would be standing outside the door to her house all evening. To protect her security in this time of transition, of course.

The guard was kind enough to listen to her. Her words, her promise, and the banded bundle of cash she placed into his hands assured that he let her and Garin pass.

Minna had difficulty moving Garin's wheelchair in a straight line. With only one arm to steer she had to lean the weight of her hips against his back and felt the heat of his body through the chair.

During the long, slow slog to Nordhausen she stopped occasionally to look up at the stars, or to kiss the tops of Garin's hands. She'd been doing so since he was an infant. He had delicate, beautiful hands, and she forced herself not to imagine the work they may have done at Maidanek. Rather she let herself feel his pulse and heat through the thin skin of her lips.

They can't have us, Garin.

All the chaos was reduced to this simple truth—the huge steel press machine in which she cradled her son was made to exert monumental amounts of pressure at an incredible speed.

This pressure had already proven its potency on flesh and bone.

That Jew died trying to destroy this thing.

Feeling the immense power of the apparatus that held her and Garin, she realized what a fool's errand it was to try and break it. Some things were too large, too immutable. There were forces around them which would not slow against resistance.

She'd toured the main floor at Nordhausen many times; she knew from watching the star-marked laborers that it took about a minute for the machine to build up to the explosive release of the vast black panel above.

Minna used that time to speak her husband's name with love.

Jakob, please forgive me. We had to escape.

She whispered kind words to her only child and ran her fingers through the still thick hair on the right side of Garin's head.

The building sound of the great machine began to fill the empty factory.

Minna was ready. She placed her lips to Garin's, closed her eyes, and waited for The Beauties to complete one last equation.

Cortical Reorganization

Mandy Vasquez let the sun soak in, hoping to retain the day's heat when cold, wet night rolled in and left her shaking. She'd begged up enough cash to score tonight, so at least there was one guaranteed warm evening ahead of her.

"Listen, lady, do you want some money or not?"

"Oh, sorry…" Mandy hobbled over to the blue sedan, maintaining a delicate balance on mismatched prosthetic feet (the left—a curved spring meant for disabled athletes, the right—a regular foot with fake skin that swelled on rainy nights). She snatched the cash from the woman's hand, caught the smell of a new perm.

Gotta stop zoning. I'd be out three bucks if that light would have turned green.

Mandy stepped back to the curb thinking this new intersection was working out fine. She'd only been in Portland for a few days, but they seemed pretty free with the cash. She made sure her sign—DISABLED, WAITING ON SSI, PLEASE HELP GOD BLESS!—was upright, then flinched as a streak of pain ran through the sole of her non-existent right foot.

That was the worst, the terrible pain in feet she didn't even have. Like being forced to give birth to a kid you weren't allowed to keep. Hurting for nothing at all.

That's why she got high—it killed the ugly feeling that ripped through her missing heels, like hooks driven through meat, tugging ever upwards. The dope let that agony sluice into the gutters and trickle to nothing.

Another shock of pain hit the space where she didn't exist. She held back tears and lifted her sign higher.

Martin Vasquez hated the drive home. Early summer weather had him cooking. Run the A/C—kill the ozone. Open the windows—fill your lungs with exhaust. No conscionable way to avoid roasting.

Today was worse. March 14th. Mandy's birthday.

She's thirty-one today, if she's still alive.

March 14th meant pounding booze and pretending the wreck never happened. Pretending that he'd stayed awake, that he'd buckled Mandy in. Wishing he and Estrella hadn't been so young and poor when Mandy needed them to be rich and mature and strong. Wishing that he had it all to do again, to never abandon his crippled four-year-old in the fruit section of a Shop-Rite.

Mandy had such beautiful brown eyes, with flecks of gold in them. He still saw them, some nights. Stupid dreams.

He rounded 13th and his fresh-bought bottle of SoCo rustled in its paper sack.

You talkin' to me, buddy? Let's get started.

Martin twisted the cap loose, let it click to the plastic floor-mat beneath his feet. Quick cop-scan, then he knocked back two stern slugs, let the burn spread.

He pictured the calendar in his kitchen, today's date reading "Mandy 31." Easier to swallow another shot, let his focus go soft.

Martin pulled up to a four way intersection and spotted movement to his right.

Mandy wished the man would let go of her hand. The light would go green soon, people would start honking. This guy was interrupting the flow of her grind.

"I've seen your eyes in my dreams," he said.

"That's dreams for you. Now let go of my hand and get the hell out of here."

You had to be stern with the freaks.

The man flinched at her words, shook his head.

"Yeah…sorry…" He dropped his gaze to the bottle in his lap. Mandy pulled away quickly, happy she still held the twenty he'd waved at her.

The light turned green and after a moment's pause, the man drove on.

Mandy hardly noticed. She was thinking of tonight's score and the liquid pleasure that would roll through her limbs and calm the screaming phantoms haunting the places where she'd died.

A Flood of Harriers

We're on the reservation now, so the blasting bass from the stereo goes into silent mode and the car drops to exactly whatever speed it says on the road signs. You come through here calm and quiet, especially if you look like me. The Kah-Tah-Nee rez is mostly Paiute and there isn't an Indian alive that's going to give the look of love to a ginger-haired white dude with a mohawk. Not on a sweat-river-down-your-back heat-blast of a day like this. Not in this place, where the meth and the booze have jacked-up and sludge-brained the populace.

The Kah-Tah-Nee rez is a charmer. Greatest frequency of drunk driving accidents—affirmative. Highest child mortality rates in the state—every year. Corrupt cops—big old check. Some punk kid like me caught a bullet to the face last year during a traffic stop. Spooked witnesses said the kid wouldn't kick up any bribe cash. Got uppity. Got his brains plastered to the tempered glass behind him. Cop caught a temporary suspension, then got pinned by the Feds for meth traffic while on *that* little vacation.

You drive the exact speed limit through here, hold your breath and pray to the Gods of Invisibility. *Dear Gods, Please let me and my lovely girlfriend Sage pass this gauntlet until we are among a group of people that our ancestors didn't attempt genocide against. Let no tire pop. Let my speed remain a smooth constant. Let my presence go unknown. Amen.* The impulse is to speed until you clear the rez, to rush towards the comforting sight of the next concrete Wal-Mart behemoth. But don't. It's not worth it. Picture bits of your own skull stuck in the upholstery, that nice tan bucket seat turned dark red.

Slow down. Enjoy the drive. Sage looks beautiful in the seat next to me. Five years together and she's still a stunner. She's reading a *Glamour* magazine so she can get angry at it. She's one of the new breed of feminists that likes to constantly decry the effects of the skinny, blonde, big-breasted, All-American Beauty Myth, while, of course, trying as hard as she can to look exactly like the girls in the magazines. Awareness, even awareness coupled with anger, isn't always power. Not that I'm complaining; I get nervous when her armpits start to show stubble. I tell her otherwise of course, because I admire her attempts at personal growth, but when it comes down to it I prefer the shaved-and-primped porn star look. I don't really want to stick my dick in some idealistic, earthy Sasquatch.

"Look at this shit, Darren. They've got this girl posed, passed out in the gutter with her panties around her ankles. You want to tell me what this has to do with selling pumps? Seriously."

I could say something in response, about rape fantasy as a commodity and the saturation of shoe-fetishism in American porn, but it's boring preaching to the choir. She and I both read the same AdBusters, go to the same town hall meetings, use the same compost pile, get the same e-mails from lefty groups pretending they aren't socialists. So I say nothing, just shake my head from left to right and purse my lips and huff a breath out through my nose to let her know that I'm with her in her parade of constant disgust.

I can't let her know, ever, that I jerked off to the ad before we packed the car up this morning. Sleaze presses my monkey-brain buttons. The cerebellum doesn't always offer a counter-move. Let her think I'm enlightened.

Sage slurps up the last of her 32 oz. iced cappuccino through a red plastic straw and turns to me with unexpected urgency.

"I have to use the bathroom."

"What? We just stopped back at the top of the pass, and you'd already drank most of your coffee by then."

"I'm not arguing with you about the size of my bladder. I just need to go. Bad. Whatever the next stop is."

"Shit, Sage, that's in about forty miles, outside of South Barker."

"What about one of the stores up ahead?"

"No. Remember, we don't stop here. Ever."

"We're going to have to, Darren. My bladder infection isn't all the way gone yet and I seriously need to go. Don't be a control freak."

"I don't stop at the rez."

"Why? Are you a racist? You afraid you're going to get scalped? Whatever your hang-up is, you need to can it and find me a bathroom."

I don't tell her my reasons. Never have before. Never needed to. She might peg me for the scared little white guy I am. Besides, not even counting today we've got about nine hours of driving tomorrow before we make it out to the Burning Man festival, and I want to keep this car clean of tension.

"Okay, I'll stop at the next restroom."

That earns me a series of soft kisses on the spot next to my right ear and a hand sliding up and down my thigh.

"Thank you, baby," she says. "Find it quick."

State park facilities. Sunny day. Lots of traffic passing by. Ramp for fisherman to slip their boats into the Sheenetz River. Two outhouses, one for men, the other, women. Looks clean enough. Why not?

My compact blue Ford sedan stirs up dust as I pull a quick right turn in to the rest-stop. My bladder's starting to feel a bit full, too, and this stop will let me make the rest of today's drive in one haul.

Hop out and stretch. Let the slight, warm wind blow across my lower back and dry some of the sweat puddled there. When the lower half of my shirt touches my back again it feels cool and wet. Goosebumps, and the hairs on my arms are up.

Sage is putting make-up back into her purse, and then bringing it with her as she steps out of the car. She also stretches, giving me a good look at her long legs, barely encumbered by a short black skirt. The wind must have caught her, too, because now I can see her nipples through the thin white fabric of her tank top. I'm starting to wish that this little rest-stop had more trees so we could hide away for a moment and have a nice travel-fuck. She smiles at me like she's thinking the same thing, then ducks her head like she's shy. Too cute. The girl can press my buttons.

She starts to walk towards the bathroom and I finish my stretching with a wide, open-mouth yawn and look down at the river. The sun is bright off the water, white-silver, and the area downstream from the dock is dotted with dried brush. The opposite side of the river is walled in by a sheer, tan stretch of rock, high enough that a jump from it would guarantee shattered legs. At the far right border of the park I see an old, leafless tree with a trunk wide enough to cast a few feet of shade.

There's motion from inside that shade, then a voice, loud and deep across the park.

"Hey, girl! I want your ass! Now!" Then laughter. More shapes moving. Five shapes, all visibly in motion now, as if they'd been invisible in their stillness before, sitting beneath that tree. Waiting.

We should get back in the car. Now. Right fucking now.

I hear the women's bathroom door close behind Sage. Too late; the girl's on a mission. Not going to let a catcall bother her.

Focus on the dark space by the tree. There are five of them. All men. All seated or resting on the ground. Still laughing, watching me. Two are shirtless and wearing old blue jeans. One guy, lying on the ground towards the back of the shade, is morbidly obese. When he laughs his girth barely moves. His lungs and diaphragm must be so small under all that fat.

One of the shirtless guys stands up. He's looking right at me. This can't be sustained. This will lead to something. Act casual. Move your feet. Soon the men's bathroom door is behind me and I've latched it and there are enough flies buzzing around in here to block out the noise of the men laughing outside. I try to stay in motion. I piss quick through a fear-shrunken dick and then squirt a couple drips of anti-bacterial cleanser onto my hands and rub them together. Even in this heat, my fingertips have gone cold. My head feels like there's a wool hat of electricity over my skull and I can sense my heart is kicking double-time. You couldn't find a drop of spit in my mouth with a microscope.

There are men outside this small bathroom yelling that they want my gorgeous girlfriend's ass. The best odds say that they are Indians, and I'm a skinny white kid with a red mohawk. This is like being a Nazi and wearing a yarmulke into the heart of Israel.

The world has just gone real. The pleasant harmonic fuzz of daily life has been stomped to the concrete with atomic bomb speed. I'm fucked.

I hear Sage stand up in her bathroom and buckle her belt. Shit.

We're fucked.

I unlock the bathroom door and grab the handle. For a split second I can't seem to push it open and at that moment I know that one of them, one of the men from the shade, is going to keep my door held tight and not let me out and the others are going to step into my girlfriend's stall when she opens her door and then they'll have her and they can lock themselves in with her and rape her and beat her down and cum on her and piss on her and I'll have to listen from inside this shitty bathroom, surrounded by a legion of flies, and I'll hear everything, every last moment, separated from her by a thin wall, and when they're done…

But then the door does open, as if the wind across its surface had given it a moment's extra weight, and I'm thanking God until I see that the man that was looking at me earlier is now headed my direction.

I stand in front of Sage's bathroom door. Five of them. *Goddamnit.* How can I stop five of them? Only one is headed towards me. I'm shaking but trying not to let it show. Things are moving so fast that it seems my brain is a second behind, disconnected, not altogether worth having. Hard to think. Fight or flight? Never fought a day in my life and I can't run and leave sweet, delicate Sage here. What other options?

He's ten feet away now. The other four men in the shade are standing, expectant. Can I take this one guy if he starts swinging? Would the other four leave me be if I beat this guy? Right. The guy's definitely an Indian, dark skin marked in all directions by inch thick scars. Oily black hair smattered with dust. Lip scar from a cleft restructure. Moon-surface pock marks from cystic acne. The booze on his breath hits me at five feet away. This guy's a wreck, and he's not wearing shoes. The sight of his bare feet pulls the breath from my chest. Something about seeing his feet caked in dust.

At three feet away he speaks up. "Hey, man, I need to talk to you." He's talking loud enough for his friends to hear. I'm their entertainment.

"Okay, yeah." *Say as little as possible. Don't puff your chest out. Don't let this escalate. Be ready if he swings.*

"Sorry, man, but you can't have that here." His right hand points up at my head. His left hand hovers near a slim shape in his pocket. "People 'round here are crazy. They see you with that hair, you could get hurt." He's smiling a three-tooth smile, happy as hell to watch me twitch. "Not everybody's like me, man. People 'round here get crazy. You know that's a tribal haircut, right?"

"Right." I don't think telling him that I'm trying to go for a Mad Max/Travis Bickle look is going to mean shit to this guy. I'm a target, regardless of hairstyle. I could have stopped in here with a fully shaved head and he would have asked me if I was a Nazi. He's looking at me with one eye, his other floating slightly to the left, un-focused.

"You Scottish? You sound Scottish."

I must sound Scottish when I'm about to piss my pants, or maybe it's the red hair. For just a second I'm thinking that this is my way out, that I'll tell him I'm Scottish and we'll kick back with some beers and joke about how the English fucked both of us over and that'll be that. Brothers-in-arms. But what if I can't sustain an accent?

"No. I'm not Scottish." This response leads him to step closer towards me. His left hand slides into his pocket, towards the thin rectangular shape. His breath is heavy and thick in my nose now, like dumpster breeze on the wind. Old eggs, gallons of cheap, pissy lager. His focused eye is locked on mine.

"I'm not scared of you, man. I just left Reno, with the Paiutes there. Proud people. We made sacred shirts so I wasn't never afraid. We did the Ghost Dance. Got into some trouble, though, knowhatImean?" He gestures to the inch thick scars on his body, what appear to be stab wounds interspersed among faded prison tats. A crucifix with the word "Wokova" across its horizontal arm. Another on his left shoulder reads "FBI" and beneath it "Full Blooded Indian." Doesn't he know Full Blooded Native American would be more PC?

He's covered in these marks, black ink and flesh wounds. He knows what it's like to fight. If something starts, I'm decimated.

The door clicks open behind me. Sage steps out, her make-up refreshed. Her innocence makes my heart ache. She's been dolling up for what could be our last day on Earth. The look she gives me says she's been listening to our conversation, though, and now she's ready to get the hell out of here. I slip her the car keys and am waiting for the guys to come rushing towards us.

The men in the shade whistle at her. Mr. FBI in front of me doesn't even look at her. All his attention's on me. He smiles again. "Pretty girl. What's she doing with a guy like you?"

I hear the passenger door close behind me and knowing that Sage is in the car gives me a moment's relief. She isn't locking the doors though. Doesn't she know she's in danger? Or is she being brave and leaving it open for me? Shouldn't someone else be pulling into this rest stop soon?

"Cat got your tongue? Rude, man. Rude. Listen, don't stop here again. My friends are about to go crazy on you. But I told them I wanted to talk to you first. I got this watch I need to sell."

Should I reach for my wallet? Could be my quickest shot at getting out of here. I tell him I could use a new watch, and he tells me that he'll have to give it to me later but I can buy it right now. I don't ask him the price. I know what it is.

I hand him all the cash in my wallet, three hundred in twenties.

As he takes the money with his right hand his left slides from his pocket. Before I can retract my arm he's grabbed my hand and he's slashing across the top of my forearm with a dull silver box opener. The pain is sharp and immediate and the sensation of the blade touching bone turns my stomach.

He's still got my hand and he pulls me in close and spits on my face. His saliva is hot and it's in my right eye and trickling to the corner of my mouth. He's whispering to me in my left ear and in my right I can hear the men in the shade laughing and shouting.

His breath feels damp on my face. "*You NEVER come back through here. Ever. This is our land, stupid white bitch. This is our place.*"

Blood is running in a steady stream from my arm to the dust below. Muddy spatter is hitting the front of my sneakers. Sage, thank God, is still in the car. I can hear her screams through the glass.

Mr. FBI's hands are on my chest now, pushing me back and down and I'm turning even as I hit the dirt, to scramble back to the car and get in and lock it and bail out of this place we never should have been.

Sage has already got the key in the ignition, and she hits the auto-lock just as my door closes. I start the engine and begin to pull out of the lot in reverse. Going forward would steer me by the shade tree and that's not a chance I can take.

Mr. FBI is standing behind my car now, box opener in one hand and my cash wadded in the other. Sage sees the gash in my arm and her screams gain volume. I can't take her freaking out right now. I yell back, "Quiet! I've got to get out of here!" Mr. FBI is smiling at me, laughing. I start to back up and he kicks my bumper. I feel the kick through the seat of my car.

I start to back up again and now he's dancing.

We did the Ghost Dance.

He's chanting something and inscribing small circles in the dirt with his feet. As quickly as the dance began, he's done and steps to the side. He's letting me go.

The exit to the place is on a slight incline and my right tire catches the soft shoulder, almost spinning my car into a drop that would pull us end over end to the river below. Back to where they are.

Sage is crying now. *OhmyGod, ohmyGod, ohmyGod...*

My arm is still dripping, and I can see dust in the wound. The dust of that place.

This is the beginning of our vacation.

When you lose your friends here, at the Burning Man festival, you lose them for days. The desert shifts time around you. The dust storms, the wind, the drugs, the sense of having drifted into a separate reality, all of these things break down the way your brain used to function. By the end of your first night you've seen an all-male gangbang, watched two dwarves get married at the foot of a giant temple, snorted enough Charlie to make Scarface jealous, fondled a theremin dressed as an alien, and fallen asleep at the foot of a door to nowhere. This all before you see your first sunrise.

No surprise that the place is tough on relationships.

Sage was pretty shaken up in the first place, and no matter how much I tried to get her to relax, the Kah-Tah-Nee rez scenario keeps her freaked out. Paranoid. I'm the one with seventeen stitches. I'm the one who can still feel the spit on my face (*Looks like he's got Phantom Saliva Syndrome, Doc*). I'm the one who had to ask his parents to wire extra travel cash. But Sage is the one making this into her deal. Her trauma.

And we did not come here for trauma. We came to party. But she could barely party anyway, with her "friend of Bill W." bullshit and her twelve steps and her insistence that we stop and meditate every hour and absorb the peace of the desert. I'm not here to get centered. I'm here to escape into the chaos.

So that's what I bought. One big fistful of chaos.

I've never seen mushrooms like this. The guy that sold them to me said his name was Scheme. I told him that was a tragically dodgy name for a drug dealer. He told me $30 bucks could buy me a ticket to outer space. Said the 'shrooms came from the Moapa reservation and were used mainly for religious ceremonies. The idea of my drug money eventually trickling back to the Indian population pissed me off, but I've seriously never seen mushrooms like this, so small with such a bright purple tint. Besides, they burn The Man down tonight, and there's no way I'm going to be within shouting distance of sober for that social call.

It's about three hours till the big wooden Man gets blazed and I want to be peaking when he topples over into his own funeral pyre. I've got no girlfriend obligations, no friends to slow me down, a CamelBak full of filtered water, a dust mask, and warm clothes on.

Sage put clean bandages on my arm tonight, moments before she decided to take off with her new yoga friends, Dale and Kristin. She was getting ready to leave our tent and I leaned in to kiss her. She pulled away.

"What?" She's been hyper-hesitant towards me since our bad time at the rest stop. I can't figure her out.

She speaks, carefully, like she's been thinking about this for our whole vacation. "Well… I'm having a strange feeling about you now, like something changed since you got hurt. You looked so scared. You just didn't look like the guy I thought I knew. And I feel like luck or God or whatever is all that got us out of that place. I don't think you could have protected me." She breathed out heavily like she was about to tell me I had terminal cancer. "I just don't feel safe with you anymore."

Sage kissed me on the forehead like I was some lost puppy about to get the gas chamber treatment, and then she stepped out of the tent and zipped it up behind her. If she would have stayed I'd have told her that I don't feel safe anymore either.

I'll try and find her at the center of The Burn tonight. We can straighten things out.

But first, I've got some mushrooms just dying to be ingested. I dig into the Ziploc bag and pull them all out, all the little bright purple stems and caps. Best to eat them quickly, the whole batch at once. They tend to taste like the shit they're grown on.

I'm chewing, and they've definitely got an earthy taste, but it's one I can't quite place, or at least I don't want to, because the flavor most reminds me of the dust I huffed down when Mr. FBI cut me and pushed me to the ground.

Stranger still, the wound in my arm begins to throb as I swallow the last bite of fungus. But the throb isn't my heartbeat. The rhythm is not my own.

The drums can eat your blood. The drums can eat your blood. They move in circles. Sing words I can't understand. Try to melt into the dirt. Try to crawl inside. We are swallowing everything. This whole desert runs on gasoline. We are not separate. All plunder. All rape. We are reptiles. We will eat your children. Keep your drums. Keep them away. Have a blanket, let it soak into you, join the stitches and I'll skin you alive. Unravel. Consume. Swallow.

Try to breathe. This dust storm can't last. I'm surrounded. Can you hear them? Where's Sage? She's shrinking away. Gone. I'm cold. I'm naked. Why am I naked? Thirsty. The Man is burning somewhere; I can see the flash of the blaze through the dust, light gone soft in the storm filter. They're around me. Every direction. I can't keep them away. I can't make them BE QUIET!

This dust is ancient. A wall one thousand feet high, pointing at the moon. He appears like a cloud. The dead are alive again. We were one but you ate us to nothing. Wokova, your dance will bring the flood. Your armor will make us safe. We are all around you. Pull you back through yellow-black. We'll keep you alive till sunrise and eat your tongue to steal your lies.

Dancing in circles all around me. The sky is opening up and the spears are raining down. They will eat my heart. The drums are finding their way home. I can't stop throwing up. I bit my way through my stitches to try and set the drums free. My blood is still pulsing on the ground. Tiny eyes in the soil. Watching. Waiting. Shit. Help me. Sage? If I'm still naked when the sun rises I will be burned black. Burnt to dust. Floating. Breathe me out.

The land will return. The water will be made of flesh. Wokova is coming. The Earth will breathe again. Wokova is risen. Balance will return. The drums can eat your blood. The drums can eat your blood. The drums...

You can try to imagine it. You can picture what it must feel like to walk naked back to your camp covered in the dust of the playa, with a bloody arm and your own vomit dried on your chest. You would know how hard it would be to get the well-meaning hippies to leave you alone, to not drag you back to a med tent. Or you could imagine the fear that you see on the faces of people who came here for bliss, the people whose trips you are utterly devastating with your wrecked appearance. You can grasp all that.

You might even be able to understand what it's like to hear drums that can't be real coursing through your bloodstream. You might be able to picture the phantom blurs of bodies dancing in circles around you as you shamble home. Could be a trick of the light, right?

But is there any way to truly understand what it's like to unzip the flap to your tent and find the girl you love lying there dead? To understand that she's gorgeous and naked there, with her legs spread, so much so that you're instantly aroused despite the fact that her eyes are wide open and staring at nothing and there's old vomit pooled in her mouth and caked in her flowing hair? When you smell the booze on her breath, the stink of the alcohol that she'd sworn off by oath and will so many years ago, would you know that she'd found something to make her feel safe again? And would you be surprised to find you can only think one word?

Would you ever understand what it's like to be there at the foot of the dead, bathed in new sun, whispering the word "Wokova" like a holy prayer?

.45's come cheap. I'm just glad that Scott's brother still lived in Aston. His place was an easy stop on the way back towards Kah-Tah-Nee. Even when I was little, Scott's brother Dean always had crooked guns. No numbers. Said he bought them at truck stops from cranked-out drivers doing a little extra traffic on their long hauls. Didn't say much more than that.

Even now, when I show up at his place still covered in dust and withering away inside of a gray velour track suit, he isn't the talkative type. He notices that my sleeve is crusted to my arm with blood and say he knows a doctor who can fix things without reporting them. I shrug it off. What can I tell him?

I'd see your doc, Dean, but this open wound is the only thing keeping me from hearing the drums. In fact, it was healing up and I cracked the scab open this morning, just outside of Modesto on I-5. Didn't want to see the shapes dancing around my car anymore so I took my house key and raked the wound until the blood started flowing again.

Nope. I just keep quiet and buy the gun and feel its oil soaking into my skin.

I'm confused by Dean's question as I leave.

"Hey, Darren, don't you need to buy any bullets for that?"

I keep quiet.

The sign tells me I'm now entering the Kah-Tah-Nee reservation and I start to cry. Last time I saw a similar sign Sage was sitting there next to me, sipping on her coffee, planting sweet kisses in the soft spot by my ear. Now she's gone, cooking away in a little tent in the desert until the wind spreads the smell of her and other campers come calling.

And I'm back here, smelling gun oil in my nervous sweat and hearing the drums inside my blood. The wound has scabbed over again and the drumming is so loud I'm having a hard time staying focused on the road. I can try and think in the space between the drums, but I keep losing the plot and these words keep repeating in the place of logical thought.

Wokova.

Balance.

Revenge.

Fifteen miles. Seven. Almost there. These drums are smashing around in my head. I feel heat on my lips and chin and realize I'm bleeding from both nostrils. Bloodshot eyes stare back at me through a vertigo haze that makes me feel like the world is on permanent tilt.

My body is in the grasp of tremors, shaking to this rhythm that was never mine. The sun drifts behind a mountainous ridge and dusk floats down, spreading gray light across the Sheenetz River. I can see the rest stop. My pulse is the sound of long dead tribesmen calling down the flood.

They are still here. The men in the shade. But now they aren't laughing. Can they hear the drums too? Apparently Mr. FBI is their permanent mouthpiece for tribal affairs, because he's stepping forward with his box cutter in hand and saying, "Man, you get in an accident or something? You deaf? I told you not to come back to our place."

The drums are so loud now. Can they see me shaking? With the sun gone there is no more shade, just dim light and dark shapes. I feel a drop of blood slide off my chin. The four-hundred-pounder shouts out from beside the tree.

"You lose your pussy somewhere, little man?"

I raise the gun up with my ravaged arm. They register it quickly and appear more angry than scared. I level off at Mr. FBI and he doesn't flinch. I'm not the first sick white man to aim a gun at him. He's resigned to it. He looks straight at me with his one focused eye.

"Pull the trigger, man. Because when you do, my friends will fucking kill you, and I'll be free."

The dancers are around me now. They're surrounding Mr. FBI and I, and they seem real. The drums get louder, too loud, and I grind my teeth together and I can feel the enamel cracking, my teeth splitting down the middle and now there's this pain that accompanies each beat of the drum, this soaring red fire that courses up my gut every time another invisible hand falls to a skin pulled tight, and there's only one way to make this stop before it tears me to shreds.

Wokova. Balance. Revenge.

They watch me as I lift the hand that isn't holding the gun and plunge the fingers into the wound on my forearm. I'm scraping. I'm digging. Get the sound OUT.

The wound opens and instead of dripping to the ground the blood sprays out fast, too fast, and too much of it, forming this thin mist that spreads quickly through the air.

We are all in it now. The dancers. The Indians. Whoever I've become. We are all standing in this red mist, breathing in the drums. We are breathing my blood, our lungs pulling a lost pulse from the sky.

Wokova. Balance. Revenge.

REVENGE.

I aim at Mr. FBI's head and pull the trigger on the .45. His good eye goes wide as the hammer falls on nothing.

Click.

I pull the trigger five more times, letting each empty click echo through the sound of the drums.

Revenge is here. And it is theirs.

They are upon me in seconds, all of them. The sound of the drums, the mist we are breathing in, the sight of the gun, all of it has brought forth an old rage. Not anger and booze and cheap, easy hate.

Rage.

Box cutters become talons. Fists become great stones. Their ancestors dance around us while they consume me. My teeth crack against smooth river rock. They float away, broken bits of white bone flowing over red clay. A fist grabs the front of my dusty mohawk. Claws enter my scalp at the top of my forehead and then I feel fingers sliding under my skin and pulling up, pulling back. I can feel them sawing it free and my head drops down to the river stones as the men raise my scalp in the sky. They drink the blood that drips from the shank of skin and hair. They are chanting a name. Wokova. Bringing a flood to cleanse the Earth.

Mr. FBI is chewing at the back of my neck, tearing at the skin with his few remaining teeth.

They are becoming as hungry as we are.

And I can see by the light of the new moon that the waters of the old river are rising fast.

The Encore

Thirty deep black strands of hair from the bedroom carpet.

I am collecting what remains of my beautiful Zhao-shi, just days ago murdered by her defective heart.

Before her passing, Zhao-shi was capable of flight. Toured the world as part of the Dynasty Circus—The Suspended Woman. 747's her daily commute. Paris, Tokyo, London. Seldom earthbound, whether borne by flying metal behemoths or her own luxuriant hair.

Acrobats, contortionists, fire eaters—none matched her radiance.

Fifty hairs entangled in her brushes (I'd combed her hair for an hour before calling the paramedics; held my face to it, swallowed its cherry scent).

She was the girl with feather bones, floating before red backdrops, her arm-length purple-black hair tied tight to a silken blue rope, arms and legs fanned, swimming against gravity, winning. I would watch for the drift of butterfly dust crossing the stage-lights' beams.

Could I sleep, I would pray this image into my dreams.

Twenty-seven hairs from the shower drain, gently washed until they squeak.

I've been offered dope and therapy. Her friend Bai, equally confused by Zhao-shi's early death, even offered me sex as sympathy.

All are empty solace.

Seventy-two hairs on her clothes.

Zhao-shi's been dead three hundred fourteen hours as of… now.

Time will slide past like nothing, then constrict; every second is suddenly stark, cold. And *lonely* like I'd never imagined.

It's all quicksand. Just a matter of how long I can drift.

Ninety-four strands are hiding, entwined with silvery party tinsel, coiled around the motorized carpet-scrubber in our vacuum.

The tensile strength of a single hair fiber is equal to copper wire.

There's not enough left of her for a hangman's knot, but any knot will do.

The chair topples beneath me. I hover for a moment before gravity asserts itself.

Although I can't breathe, I taste the scent of cherries.

Zhao-shi holds me again.

We float home.

Laws of Virulence

INTERNAL MEMO: 08/07/2010

CASE: F-DPD0758 (CDC NORS-Water Report ID VEC147, Received 08/03/2010 via State Report OMB No. 0920-0004, Submitted by: Dr. Lorena Santos of Pacific Grace Clinic)

ETIOLOGY: Unknown (comparative specimen analysis in progress, genus/species/serotype may require new designations)

CONTAMINATION FACTOR: C-N/A, Unknown

SURVIVAL FACTOR: S-N/A, Deaths can be attributed to case though comparable pathogens have displayed symbiotic behavior

DOCUMENT INSERT: Verbatim transcript of post-containment etiology determination interview with Subject 5 (Matthew Hall). Due to active vector status (transmission mode remains classified as Indeterminate/Other/Unknown although enteric Phase 1 possible) subject interviewed in iso via 2-way audio. DPDx program active/engaged. Elimination & Control team at ready.

Recorded at Director's Request/Classified Confidential 1-A. Speaking: DPD Director Cliff Selzer, Matthew Hall

CS: Hello, Mr. Hall.

MH: [No response]

CS: I'm going to be frank with you, Mr. Hall... Can I call you Matthew?

MH: You can call me whatever you want.

CS: Very well, Matthew. I need you to understand the situation we're in right now. How important you are. How much you can help us.

MH: I'm not important. I'm the least important person you've ever met. And I don't give a shit about helping you. And if you don't get me something stiffer than this glass of fucking tap water then I'm not saying a word.

CS: Matthew, I'm afraid that water is all we can provide you right now. But if you cooperate there could be adjustments to your Stay Profile.

MH: You get me a bottle of Maker's and a shotgun. You promise that. Then I'll tell you everything.

CS: You know I can't do that.

MH: I don't know what you can or can't do. I don't even know who the hell you are. You strip me naked. You spray me down with some kind of goddamn fire extinguisher and make me sit in the dark in three smaller and smaller rooms. I thought you were cooking me alive in the last one.

CS: Matthew, that was all for standard decontamination protocol. We're trying to protect you and others.

MH: So am I safe now?

CS: "Safe?"

MH: Decontaminated?

CS: [Long pause] We're not sure, Matthew. That's why it's so important you tell us what you know.

MH: [Garbled] fucking shitbirds. Just let me die. Please.

CS: That's very selfish, Matthew. There are millions of people in this country who don't want to die, and you're putting them at risk. If you won't speak with me will you at least consider filling out the form we've placed in front of you?

MH: [Sound of pen being thrown across room, striking floor. Sound of Subject 5 expectorating on form CS115.]

BREAK IN RECORDING

MH: Now that's more like it, chief. Aaah, that's more like it.

CS: I suggest you slow down, Matthew. We don't know how alcohol will affect the specimen or its interaction with your body.

MH: [Sound of gulping.] Shit on your specimen, chief. [Sound of belch.] Oh, Jesus, that fucking burns.

CS: It's 100 proof, Matthew.

MH: No, not the booze. That stuff is silky. It's the fucking crawler. Sonofabitch never stops working on me. I knew it. Your precious little detox rooms were a waste. [Sound of fabric rubbing on skin.] See, my mouth is already bleeding. Then I'll get the fucking seaweed eyes. Then you guys will wish you already would've given me that shotgun.

CS: "Seaweed eyes?"

MH: Yeah. It's like lace under the eyes, or like… like they're bloodshot but the blood is dark green.

CS: And your wife displayed this condition?

MH: Claire had it first, and then…

CS: Then your daughter?

MH: [Long pause. Sound of gulping.] Yeah… Myra.

CS: We've performed a full sweep of your apartment, Matthew. We're aware of your loss and I promise you we understand how difficult this must be.

MH: Did you burn them?

CS: No. Our procedure dictates a course other than destruction…

MH: Quit fucking around and burn them. Please. Give them that. Claire always wanted to be cremated and… I was going to do it myself, before you guys booted in my goddamn door… please. It's the last good thing I can do for them.

CS: The sooner we know what you know, the sooner we can honor your request.

MH: Promise?

CS: We will do our best to keep funeral processing in motion.

MH: Well, cheers to that. [Sound of gulping.]

CS: So, at what point did you notice the discoloration in your wife's eyes? And were there any notable signs or symptoms prior to that? Vomiting? Fever? Abdominal cramps?

MH: There are probably some symptoms I didn't even notice. To be honest, we weren't talking that much. I mean, this all happened last week and it happened so fast. But she was always bitching and crunching on Tums and popping Tylenol, so… I mean, running a daycare center is hard work. She used to joke that children could only grow by stealing your energy and happiness. But she liked it, she really did. Hell, she was pretty much raising Myra without me.

CS: Our records indicate you lived together.

MH: [Brief laughter.] Depends on how you define living, chief. We split rent on an apartment and had the same last name, you know... Sometimes I'd take Myra to the park. She was too little to go on the swings or anything, but she liked to smell the flowers and watch the other kids play… But Claire would have been the second person, after me of course, to tell you that I'm a piece of shit. A real charity case. So the truth is that I didn't notice how wrong things were until they'd gone way past wrong.

CS: What did you observe first?

MH: Well, I woke up after Claire every day, and I'd make the bed to pretend I was useful in some way, and I noticed some little spots of blood on her pillow. Nothing too serious looking. But then she got home that night and had a hefty cough. Plus, her breath had become pretty toxic.

She'd block it with her hand but the smell would float across the whole room. And this smell, chief, it was like a dead hooker's pussy stuffed with old shrimp. But worse. It crawled into your nose like it was living. She started burning nag champa incense, so she must have smelled it too.

CS: Is that when she decided to go to the hospital?

MH: No. Claire is… Claire was a tough one. I was starting to feel a little sick, too, and Claire figured we had some food poisoning. It was her birthday a few days before, and I'd been out "job hunting" at the Pussycat Palace. You know the place?

CS: I'm aware of it.

MH: So you've seen Cherry Headrush dance before?

CS: No, Matthew. But I'm aware of many venues and chains because of their prominence on our regional disease vector maps.

MH: Oh. Shit. [Sound of gulping.] Well, I'd flipped for this girl, Cherry. And they'd just extended my unemployment for another three months so I was feeling flush. Spent almost my whole check in one afternoon, hogging up the lap dances. Milking a cheap beer buzz for hours. And then my cell started vibrating and a Reminder message pops up: CLAIRE B-DAY DINNER TONIGHT. Only the "tonight" is spelled like 2-N-I-T-E which means Claire programmed this into my phone so I'd remember. [Long pause.]

CS: Please continue. The food poisoning?

MH: So I'm running late, very buzzed and most of my cash is already in the Pussycat's sterilizer. But I have to try and pull myself out of this so I hit Chinatown and looked for something fancy to cook up. Chan's Market has a beautiful red snapper on discount, so I cop that, pick up some lemon and capers, and get two fancy chocolate Cupcakes at Dreampuff's.

SEE SEPARATE DOCUMENT INSERT FOR RELATED DIRECTOR ORDER: DPDx multi-venue deploy/search/surveil. Full containment authorized. Andolini appointed Team Leader.

CS: Sorry about that break, Matthew. You've been very helpful.

MH: Do I have any choice? Really? I appreciate the second bottle, but you might want to give me a bucket if I'm going to keep going. Although I'd have no problem shellacking your little desk here.

CS: Consider us well-advised. Please continue.

MH: Shit, man… it seems obvious, doesn't it? I barely had any time to bake the fish before Claire got home with Myra. I brushed up and changed my clothes and put on some Alicia Keys even though I can't stand that shit. Lit a couple of tea lights I found under the sink. But I still fucked it up. I still fucked it up. [Pause] The fish looked good by candle-light. Looked delicious.

CS: You think the red snapper was the original source of the sickness?

MH: Thing is, I was pulling off the sober act, but I had to burp. And that just ruined it. One hundred percent. Like a strip club came out of my mouth. Claire pegged it, and laid into me, even though Myra was sitting in the room in her little bouncy chair and we'd sworn not to fight in front of her. And I mentioned that and we tried to enjoy the dinner and pretend that something was okay and nice and we didn't even notice how raw the snapper was until we'd taken out half of the fish.

CS: So Claire was guessing that the raw fish had given each of you food poisoning?

MH: Yeah. She was toughing it out until Myra got sick, too. Because that didn't make any sense. Myra was still breastfeeding, so she never had any of that nasty snapper. But she was coughing and having the blood speckles just the same.

CS: That's when she visited Pacific Grace, toward the beginning of August?

MH: I think so. I was sort of on my own thing while this was happening. Sleeping on the couch at night. Hiding at Pussycat's during the day. I told myself I was in exile, giving Claire some space to forgive me. But I was really just doing the same old shit. Living in a worn down strip club booth, paying Cherry to hip-hump me. Hoping that Claire and Myra would start feeling better. That maybe Claire would start feeling so good she'd build up the mojo to finally drop me.

CS: When did you find out she wasn't feeling better?

MH: Well, Pussycat's kind of extradited me back to my family. I was already putting off that rotten jellyfish smell and... let's just say there aren't enough dollars to make a stripper let you cough blood in her face. I didn't even see it coming. Just sitting there half-chubbed and dead drunk and BOOM! No tickle in the throat. No warning.

CS: Do you happen to know Cherry Headrush's real name?

MH: You're kidding, right? [Sound of bottle opening/sound of gulping.] All I know is that I was home and starting to feel pretty rotten myself, and I can't imagine how Claire was managing to run the daycare like that. All those little people screaming. "I want. I need. Watch me. Love me." Jesus.

CS: This was the Morning Sun Daycare on Stanton?

MH: Yup. So, Claire stumbles into the house and she and Myra are both coughing and they have those triple-dark circles under their eyes, and seeing them like that makes me feel like I managed to sneak into Hell without dying. Just worthless. No, worse than that—fucking evil. [Long pause] Claire said the lady at the hospital gave them both two I.V. bags to rehydrate them, and that they needed to go back tomorrow for more diagnostics. But she thought it might be a parasite, like one of those squiggly little gut worms you get from eating sushi in Ohio.

CS: Did she suggest you go with them?

MH: Of course. And I was thinking it was the right thing to do. I was starting to feel weak in my bones. But the next morning I wake up and they're already gone and there's a text on my phone saying that they're both "feeling much better." Which was weird, because they'd been coughing like crazy all night. Just brutal sounding. Wet. Like I'd guess TB used to sound.

CS: So... a productive cough followed by an apparent return to vigor?

MH: Sure, chief. However you want to call it. It spooked me because I was still under the weather. But I pegged that up in my mind as booze-related immune suppression. All those sauced little white blood cells getting bitch-slapped by the bugs in my system.

SEE SEPARATE DOCUMENT INSERT RE: Viability of ethanol [or variant] ingestion as chemical deterrent to life cycle of [un-named parasite/parasitoid CASE: F-DPD0758].

CS: So when did it become evident that Claire and Myra were still… unwell?

MH: [Prolonged sound of gulping.] You want to hear the rest, you get me a loaded shotgun. I promise I'll only fire it once.

CS: Not an option, Matthew.

MH: Okay. Fuck it. I better get the truth out before the goddamn crawler starts telling my story. [Pause/sound of shuddering exhalation.] I knew they were still unwell when I found their tongues. Claire's was in the bed, tucked under a pillow. Dried up already, like jerky. And Myra's…

CS: Please, Matthew.

MH: Myra's was in her crib, next to her favorite pacifier, the one with the orange dolphin on the back. And I've got to tell you, chief, between my half-sick, half-drunk stupor and lack of sleep, I felt like I was dreaming. So I did what seemed like the right thing. I threw the tongues in the garbage and kept on tidying the apartment. Like I could organize away what I was seeing. Like I could clean up reality.

SEE SEPARATE DOCUMENT INSERT FOR RELATED DIRECTOR ORDER: DPDx forensic detachment to attain SW Sanitation schedule/ potential combing of landfill [use of trailing dogs authorized]. Retention of tissue from Subjects 3 and 4 Top Priority, presence/absence of eggs to be communicated ASAP.

MH (continued): So I had the place pretty spruced, and I was waiting for them to come home. Claire wasn't answering her phone. And my nerves were on four alarm blaze, so I had some bourbon close by, just to keep things mellow until I could figure out what was going on. I'd call her phone. Five rings. Voice mail. Nothing. Take a swig. Five rings. Voice mail. Nothing. And they still weren't home by 9:00pm.

CS: Records show you called Claire's mother.

MH: Three or four times. But she never picked up. And I thought about calling the cops, but I knew my speech was slurring by that point. What would I tell them? There was no crime, and they'd probably guess it was just another wife bailing with the kid, leaving the stew-bum behind.

CS: But their tongues? That must have…

MH: Can't see that impressing the cops either. Just a way to induce them to pack a straitjacket. Besides, if I mentioned finding their tongues… I'd been on a steady drunk trying to bury that detail, hoping I was just losing my shit.

CS: So when did you next see Claire and Myra?

MH: Never again. I think the night they came home from the doctor's was the last time I really saw them.

CS: Matthew, the chronology we've established shows the three of you were in that apartment for almost two days before we…

MH: Before you decided to bust into my place and stop me from finishing my work? Listen, chief, this is hard enough to talk about. So let me lay it out for you without all of your interjections and then we can clear up your questions later.

CS: [Long pause.]

MH: That's more like it. So what I'm saying is that I saw Claire and Myra again, but they sure as shit weren't my Claire and Myra. At some point that night I'd finished my bottle and given up on my phone crusade. I remember thinking, "She finally left me." And I remember feeling so relieved. No one would expect anything from me after that, you know? I'd cop some menial job, enough to service a studio apartment and child support. I'd push for a few weekends a month with Myra, just enough to not feel guilty when I show some stripper a picture of my kid. I think I'd been waiting for a long time for a chance to fall apart.

CS: Matthew, I need to know more about your wife and child, and time is a factor. We have a staff psychologist you can speak with later if you need to get more familial issues off your chest.

MH: Courtesy is a short-lived thing around here, huh, chief? All right then, shitbird... So I passed out on the couch, if you can believe it. Noble. Noble guy. And when I woke up they were sitting at the foot of the couch, both of them, very quietly and... holy shit... and Claire was nursing Myra, and her head was tilted, and she was staring across the room at nothing, like she was back on Paxil, and they both had those goddamn seaweed eyes. And Claire had both of her breasts out and the one that wasn't in Myra's mouth was... it was kind of lumpy, like it had been stuffed with tapioca, and the nipple looked raw, just red meat raw, with these blisters around it, some popped, some filled up with the same dark green that was in her eyes, and...

CS: Hold on for a moment please, Matthew.

SEE SEPARATE DOCUMENT INSERT RE: Confirmation of multiple gender-specific intra-species transmission methods as seen in CASE: F-DPD0674. Student population under Sector 6 Quarantine should immediately be grouped same sex for confirmation/testing of all fluids for presence of concurrent microparasites.

CS: Okay, we're back, Matthew.

MH: [Garbled/indistinct vulgarity.] My tongue is starting to feel numb. [Sound of coughing/spitting]. Aw, Christ, chief.

CS: I'd suggest drinking some water. We need you to finish your account.

MH: Yeah, well... suggest in one hand and spit in the other and see which one fills up first. [Sound of laughter/sound of gulping/sound of empty bottle set down on table.] What you have to understand is that I thought I was dreaming, seeing Claire and Myra like that. Between the guilt and the hooch, that kind of nightmare fits right in. But then Claire put one of her bony bird hands on my ankle and she turned toward me and smiled. And I swear to God, these two wiry antennae uncurled from in between her teeth and started swaying in the air. So of course I lost my shit. I rolled onto my side and chucked out my guts on the shag carpet, and it's just bile and bourbon and I get that post-puke rush where things feel okay for a moment and I'm thinking I'm awake now and then I turn back towards Claire. [Long pause] She's still smiling at me and this voice comes out of her mouth and says, "Empty. Feed." And she's got her other breast cupped and I swear it's dribbling this shit like fucking wheat grass juice. [Pause] And Myra… Myra pulls off the other breast, or at least her lips move away, but there's something else pushing out of her mouth, something with those same feelers wiggling, and it's latched on to Claire, right on her tit, and it's got these two tiny claws pinched on and its body is pulsing and hunching, and these plates on its back are clicking together and I can see through this thing's belly, where the skin is clear and its guts are filling up green. And Myra's eyes look almost black, but I can still tell they're rolling back in her head…

CS: Claire could speak?

MH: They both could. But Myra… she didn't have any words yet, so she would smile and her lips would pull back, but all that came out… Have you ever seen that footage of dolphins being massacred in Japan? And Claire's voice was different. There was a lisp, like her mouth was too full, and there was a sort of hissing to it, like cricket legs or… [Pause] And the smell that came from them filled up the room. It was like being stuck in the dumpster behind a seafood wholesaler on a hundred degree day. Made me throw up again.

CS: So why didn't you call 911?

MH: Are you listening to me, chief? This strikes you as a rational response fucking situation? I had no bearings. I asked Claire a question, thinking that this time she'd give me a normal answer in her old, sweet voice and I'd be all the way awake, but it came out with no authority and just made me feel smaller and detached and more alone. But I told her I was worried and that I wondered where she was yesterday and she smiled again… I'm thinking that's the only way the thing could move around in there… and all she says is, "Work. Feeding." And I say, "You were at the daycare?" She nods and says, "Feeding. Growing. Most will be born." Then she looks down at Myra, and her nose curls up like she's disgusted, and she says, "This one is dying. This one is too small." [Long pause/sound of soft crying.]

CS: Matthew, I'm sorry. I'm so sorry. But the more detail…

MH: Details, chief? Go fuck yourself. I did what I did. I tried to save them. I tried to fix it. To fix them before anybody would have to know…

But it was too late. I could barely stand, but Claire was always pretty frail, and this fucking bug thing had wiped her out. So I tried to help her first and it wasn't too difficult to get her hands belted behind her, but that thing… that thing had teeth or mandibles or whatever and Claire started to shake and even with all the lamps in the room turned on my head kept making a shadow over her face and Myra was squealing and stomping her heels down where I left her on the carpet and I couldn't tell where the thing in Claire's mouth ended and the rest of her tongue began and when I cut in with the box knife it started bleeding so bad… But for just a moment Claire was looking straight at me, and even with the green lace it looked like her old eyes and then she spit right in my face. Right in my face, and she meant it. And her mouth was half-filled, and I noticed the blood from the thing and my wife wouldn't quite mix, so there's your details chief. Then her lips pulled back and the eyes were still Claire's eyes and she said, "You did this to us."

CS: Matthew, she…

MH: She was right. She was right. Even after I managed to finish cutting through, and I'd pulled the goddamn thing out of her face and smashed it under my foot… You want more details? The shell of the thing started changing colors and it hissed and sprayed a yellow mist out of its mouth after I set it on the floor. What the fuck does that? Even after I got the thing out of Claire she still had her eyes trained on me, just bullet-eyes, and she couldn't have hated me any more. And I couldn't fix her, because she was already weak and I don't think she could stop from choking on all that blood. But I thought that Myra… [Long pause.]

CS: You didn't try to remove the "crawler?"

MH: I didn't want her to bleed like Claire. So I thought if I could just kill the bug that maybe it would just detach and… and I was thinking of how they cook lobsters, and I tried to keep the water in a tin can and hold her over it, but the steam was making everything slick and I couldn't get her mouth open at the same time and… so I thought that the burns would heal, you know how they say that the inside of your mouth can heal so fast, and then at least she'd live, and I didn't put the sponge in there for more than twenty seconds, but the thing was hissing and it tried to curl in on itself, and Myra started shaking and making fists and then her eyes were open and they were looking right at me, right into me, and…

CS: Matthew?

MH: They were right. There's nothing… [Sound of empty glass bottle being shattered.]

CS: Matthew, please. There's no need to…

MH: I did this. I did this. I… [Sound of Subject 5 collapsing on floor. Sound of wet coughs/exhalations. Faint sound of specimen clicking/squealing from interior of Subject 5. Sound of door opening/boots shuffling/Subject 5 moved to stretcher.]

CS: Goddamn it, [REDACTED]. I said plastic bottles only. Triage?

DPDx: Subject 5 at ISS 75. Both major sources of blood flow to brain severed, trachea punctured. He was committed.

CS: The specimen?

DPDx: Significant damage. Suggest immediate retrieval attempt.

CS: Agreed. Prepare for transfer to Surgical Theater 8, movement protocol in place.

DPDx: Confirmed. [Brief pause.] Director?

CS: Yes?

DPDx: If I didn't know better, I'd think this dead fuck was grinning right at me.

CS: Could be a symptom of the parasite attempting to exit the damaged host. Stay far from his mouth until we've assessed specimen mobility. And let's keep it moving. Perhaps Matthew's got a second chance at fatherhood.

DPDx: [Muffled laughter] Yes, sir. Rolling out.

END TRANSCRIPT

States of Glass

The Caller ID reads "Unknown" but the man on my phone says he's with the Thurston County Coroner's Office in Washington. I know precisely zero people up north so I peg the call as a prank or a particularly grim dialing error.

Darry is travelling on business, but I spoke with him this morning. He was fine.

Mistakes like this happen every day, right?

I can smell my breath on the phone, stale hints of cinnamon toast and mimosas light on the orange juice. The voice on the other end continues to intrude into my lazy afternoon, verifying my name is Elloise Broderick, and the sunshine coming in through the kitchen window suddenly feels too hot on my skin. That heat and the tone of the voice create a flash-fever in my belly that spreads quickly to my fingertips. I can imagine flowers wilting next to that warmth, petals curling, dropping.

Delirium. The blood in my head whirlpools down, a tornado spinning out of existence, rendering me transparent. So when the voice on the phone says, "I'm sorry to inform you that your husband has been in a fatal traffic accident," it's easy to imagine that the "you" being addressed is someone else, maybe someone standing directly behind me, someone older, someone who has three kids and a half-paid mortgage.

Not that the statement regarding the death of that other husband will hurt that person less. But it would seem, at least, appropriate. More real. Because my husband's not dead. Can't be. I've only had him two years since last October. The expiration date for a guy like him is so far off that I can't even conceive of it.

"You" could, though. The "you" being addressed on the phone has had her share of life, with its troubles, even its deaths. She isn't the one with weekend bar-hopping plans and a yellow plastic cell phone in her hand that feels sweaty and toy-small. She isn't the one getting nauseous, eyeing the distance to the kitchen sink because her belly might evacuate its contents. "You" understands mortality, may even have found some strange peace accord.

Mistakes like this, I'm sure they happen all the time. That's why I ask the misguided voice on the phone if I can see the body.

Static, then a hesitant, "Yes… actually we are required to have someone, family or friend, identify the body, to satisfy coronial procedure. But you may not want to be the one who does this. The accident was high velocity, and the body… "

Then he's telling me about the condition of this body that's not Darry's; how useless the dental records will be in the absence of, you know, teeth. He details the projected speed of impact, the rain on the roadway, the delayed response from authorities that allowed physical evidence to be dispersed by passing traffic.

Even finger-printing is a lost option. The poor bastard that they think is Darry tried to shield his face on impact. His delicate, thick-veined hands are as much a part of the interstate landscape as his well-bleached enamel.

Crow's breakfast, all of it.

His teeth now tucked in SUV tire treads, chewing up pavement.

If he didn't have his mind on the road before, well…

I'd caught a bad case of gallows humor during my short-lived stint at the Windy Arbor elder care facility. An old man named Percy Heathrow caught me weeping in a storage closet, sorry little red-faced me unable to handle the sight of all these intentionally forgotten people slogging away their last years. He called me over. I came forward, chugging back snot and wiping the corners of my eyes with the inside of balled fists. He didn't say anything, but his knobby hands floated down to his waistline and lifted up his shirt. I thought I was about to get perved on. Instead I saw a fresh colostomy bag hanging from the side of his belly, "SHIT HAPPENS" written on the plastic in black felt-tip.

That got me through the week; that moment where Percy and I were in on the cosmic joke. Since then my humor's veered obsidian black. So somehow my face harbors a misplaced smile even as this coroner dumps details.

The kind of wreck Darry's been in is called a "rear under-ride." This is what happens when a car hits the back of a semi-trailer and keeps going. The Freehoff trailer Darry didn't brake in time for acted like a guillotine on tires. Darry's death would have been instantaneous.

Because it's not really Darry we're talking about, I laugh quietly at this part. The voice on the phone said "instantaneous" like auto-dealers say "zero down," like it's a blessing. Like this guy they think is Darry died so quick, he might just come back.

This information is conveyed in the programmed, caring polite-speak of someone who talks death all day. It's me applying the realities, putting sauce on the steak. I remember a semi-snuff video Darry had me watch with him, how at the moment this hapless Russian girl got hit by a train she turned from a moving, breathing person to a flying sack of tissue and bones and nothing else. I've seen that side of death. I'm de-sanitizing this whole affair. Easier work for the brain than coming to grips.

"There are a few tattoos, Mrs. Broderick, that we believe could assist in the identification process."

I pictured Darry, home from getting his second tattoo, showing off the still-bleeding black cursive lines between his shoulder blades. There it is, stuck under his skin, my name marking him forever, more than any ring—Elloise. I'd run my fingers through the soft, warm ointment coating it and felt the abraded ridges where his skin had been torn by needles. This feeling, I think of it later, months later, while I'm masturbating. It helps me finish.

I prefer those tattoos that look like Japanese tapestries—dragons and whirlpools, ornately-scaled fish. But I couldn't argue with the intensity of seeing my name trapped under his skin.

His first tattoo, some random black tribal band encircling his left arm, he had that before we met. The kind of mark that binds you to the Tribe of Other Dudes Who Think That Shit Looks Cool.

His phrase for it was, "Purely aesthetic."

My response—"But it *looks* stupid."

We never spoke on it again. Verboten, you could tell from the silence following my comment.

Yes, I know his tattoos.

I ask for the address of the morgue before the voice can say anything else about identifying ink. The address is in Olympia.

Darry's "Introduction to Data Marketing" conference was in Olympia too, downtown, just off the water. Maybe I'd visit him at his hotel *after* I told the people at the morgue that I'm sorry I couldn't be of assistance. Wish them the best of luck, offer telegrammed sympathies to "you."

They'll want to apologize for the worry they've caused me.

They're used to apologizing, I'm sure. Mistakes like this...

Sweat beads along my hair line. If it runs I'll get hairspray in my eyes, like some cosmetic company test rabbit. My stomach is not altogether in the right place now. It's plastic-wrap tight around a belly full of nothing, relocating acid to the back of my throat.

The phone call has had the necessary effects.

It's the *unnecessary* effects that have me so goddamn confused.

Moments after I hang up the phone I get this feeling—warm, sweet molasses spreading down the inside of me from underneath my belly-button. That's the start. Then fullness, a subtle pressure as I expand against the fabric of my underwear. Then my heartbeat heads south, steady, filling me up, exposing my nerve endings.

The phone call's natural response should be crying, right? Even with my textbook denial there should be tears at the rims of my eyes, waiting to run down my cheeks.

No tears. And I need to get off.

I try to rationalize. This sudden urge is a biological sidekick to mortality. It has nothing to do with Darry. I'm not a whore, not sick. We oppose death by fucking. It's our weapon.

But Darry can't *ever* know how the false news of his death has triggered this need…

He can't know how much his death makes me want to fuck. More precisely, how I have never before, not in the recorded history of Elloise, so desperately wanted *to be fucked*.

These responses, my denial, my instant want… I can see them for what they are, but I can't shake them. So I stay in motion. I start packing bags for the drive up to Oly.

The new focus—grabbing my toothbrush, deciding which gas station will have the best mocha for the road, not looking in the mirror, not getting my vibrator out of the closet, picking my favorite towel because I never like hotel towels, wondering how long my sandals can go without falling apart, remembering that Darry is still alive, remembering that mistakes like this are commonplace, getting the gummies out of the corners of my eyes, putting fresh saline solution in my contacts case, not calling Darry's gorgeous friend Peter, not even thinking about how big Peter's hands are, not even letting this stream of thought go any further…

STOP!

Deal with the problem.

I flop onto our bed and catch a quick whiff of Darry's sweaty sleeping-boy smell, soaked into our lumpy old goose-down comforter. I'm so used to Darry's smell that my nose won't pick up the scent for long. An accepted part of my life. No need to process.

I undo the top button on my pants. I can't separate the buckle of my belt quick enough. Reason has vacated this moment.

My fingers do their work, tracing the paths of familiar sense memory, making my back arch and my stomach tighten. I can't remember the last time I was this wet.

I can't remember the last time I felt this good.

Slow circles turn to pressure. I close my eyes and there's Darry's friend Peter, watching me, lying next to me, sliding one of his huge hands up and down my belly. I can feel the calluses on his hands, an accumulated roughness that Darry's data marketing job would never give him.

I'm close to coming and Peter turns into the checker at the grocery store, the one with the jet-black hair and blue eyes, the one that told me about the detergent coupon. His breath still smells like black licorice.

Behind my closed eyes, far from my desperate hand, parades of men are waiting for their turn with me.

Hips are lifted, calves are squeezing tight. So close. My body drops back into the comforter and stirs up another wave of boy-smell.

I smell *my* boy. My Darry.

I can't come.

The wave crashes that quickly.

Fucking Darry.

I try again, try to climb the peak, but now I'm numb. I'm only touching myself now, meat on meat, no sacred shock of nerves. Just a sudden guilt, virus-quick through my system, flushing me with heat. Staring at the ceiling with my right hand cupped against pulsing warmth. Thinking about the last thing I want to acknowledge.

Darry and I have been together so many times in this bed. Too many times, I guess. That's why I've needed more lately—my fantasies, the images that I've transposed onto Darry's body while he's inside of me.

I don't think he's caught on. Even with me always turning the lights off beforehand, and asking him not to make noise, and asking him to come in from behind. Even with all my delicate fantasy preparations—these little tricks that allow me to screw another man when I'm married and faithful to a fault—he hasn't seemed to notice.

The thing making it easy for me to ignore who he is while he's inside of me—his weakness—is that he loves me too much. I guess his love is *my* weakness, too, because the love itself—his fingers running through my hair at night, his hand soothing my sore belly after I developed my first ulcer—is wonderful. His type of true, warm affection is more suffocating and alluring than any hotel fling or office tryst.

The idea that this lust, even now creeping back through my skin, is suddenly upon me because Darry's dead and now I've got a chance to be with other men… it worries me because it feels true. And knowing that it's wrong hasn't given me power over it.

If he is dead, I'm sick. Sick and alone.

I'm thinking too much. I sigh a long, shaky sigh and can feel myself on the verge of tears now, but I don't know if I'd be crying for Darry or myself. I just know I hate the delicacy of trembling air leaving my chest.

In five more minutes I'm in my car, headed north on I-5.

Even as my right leg becomes fatigued to shaking from the two hundred mile drive, I take comfort in the inappropriateness of my situation; in the fact that I've received this misguided message. It'll make for a crazy story at the least. I wonder how Darry will respond when I tell him that the rear end of a semi-truck tore off his head.

He'll want details, of course. To flesh out the morbid fantasy of his own brutal, blood-and-diesel demise. I'll tell him about this drive—how I flinched at every bit of sulfur-smelling road-kill that littered the roadside, at every tuft of skunk hair shifting in the wind of traffic. How the bright red flashing brake-lights of each semi-truck I passed were fists squeezing my heart.

Tonight, as we're curled up in bed together, I'll lay out the whole absurd affair for him. And he'll laugh. That's the easy thing to do. I'll feel the familiar heat of his breath on my neck, rub my head against his chest, and we'll both acknowledge this strange truth:

For a moment, he was dead.

This is what the world, excepting us, had believed.

The coroner's name is Brad Fuller, and he has hands that could casually palm a basketball. Or a human skull, which must be a more common occurrence for him. He's tall and butterfly symmetrical. Strong forehead. Wide jaw. Alpha all the way. He smells like nothing because he works in a place that goes to great lengths to smell like nothing, provided you don't take a deep whiff. Brad's younger looking than I expected from his professional demeanor on the phone, and I wonder if he's even past his third decade.

I'm smiling at him and extending my hand, saying, "Nice to meet you, Brad." I want to feel the size of his hand over mine. He seems a little off-center, unsure of how to respond to my casual greeting.

"Good to meet you, Mrs. Broderick."

Even hearing myself addressed as Darry's other half doesn't save me from the feelings that have returned to my belly. Brad Fuller is politely dressed in a dark blue suit that I'd like to peel away from his skin.

The fact that I'm standing in the clinical foyer of an Olympia morgue does not make me want Brad any less.

It should. I know this as a basic truth. But it doesn't.

The desires that I'd managed to repress on the long drive up are soaring through my skin now, crashing into my borders, speeding up every breath.

I'm not letting go of Brad's hand.

"Mrs. Broderick?"

"Oh, sorry." I release my grip, feel the heat from his fingers slide off the thin skin on the back of my hand. "My first name's Elloise."

"Are you expecting any other family members to arrive before we view the body?"

"Um, no. It's just me. Darry's mom lives in Tennessee, and his Dad's passed on. So it's just me."

"Okay. We can proceed unless you'd like a moment for yourself."

"Aren't you closing soon?"

"Only technically. In our line of work, we can't assign any set hours to our responsibilities. So take your time if you need to. Chantel at the front desk has already prepared the required paperwork."

My pulse picks up, faster now, this time because of the confidence Brad Fuller has that I'm the right person to identify this body. He's willing to go through with this charade.

I can do this. I'm not afraid. Go in there, give my negative identification, and head across town to Darry's hotel. Surprise him with the best sex of his life. Behind my eyes, I'll be seeing Brad Fuller. Darry won't care. He won't know, and I'll make him feel so good.

"No, I'm ready to go now."

"Alright then... I'd like to let you know in advance, that once you've made the identification, you can request to spend time with the body, if you want to. If you believe that this is something you want, you just let me know and we can facilitate it. In this case, Darry's body will need to remain covered, due to the extent…"

"I won't want to spend time with the body."

"Okay. I'll take that into consideration. But you can still let me know, once you've seen him."

Darry's body. What the hell am I doing here? And I just checked out Brad's ass. Strong, if a bit high up on his back. I'd love to feel it, love to wrap my hands around it and pull him into me over and over again. If there was ever an apex of wrong place/wrong time, I'm shooting for it. Drowning in compulsion, surrounded by the dead, fantasizing about this stranger in a sharp suit.

I should be hungry, but I'm not. Should be sad, but I'm not. Should be scared…

I am scared. I stood by my car for twenty minutes before entering the morgue, and now I'm headed into what Brad's told me is the viewing room.

The viewing area is a carpeted closet with a window separating it from a tiled room. Two cheap chairs, a 10 gallon trash can with a fresh plastic bag in it, a small wooden table adorned with tissues and fake light blue flowers, and a wall-mounted microphone round out the décor.

Brad is in here with me, and his forehead shines with sweat even though the room sits at that clinical un-temperature. The sweat reads as discomfort. This is the part of the job he hates.

He flips a switch by the microphone and says, "Go ahead, Dale."

Dale, looking uncomfortable in a gray Sears bargain-bin suit too tight for his many pounds, wheels a polished silver cart into the room. An opaque black bag is resting on top. Dale is sweating, too, with moisture beading on his polished, bald head as he struggles to push the cart in a straight line to the center of the room. No one is looking forward to this.

The body on the cart, it's much shorter than my Darry. I take comfort in that.

The comfort lasts maybe half a second. I remember the words "under-ride."

Dale unzips the body bag and reaches into it with one hand, his fingers twitching like latex-coated spider legs.

I did not want to spend time with the body. I didn't want to stand next to it, or touch it, or hold it.

I did not want to spend another second in that low-ceilinged, piece-of-shit morgue.

I did not want to spend another moment looking at that tattoo of my name—Elloise—with nothing but torn flesh and empty space above it.

I know I didn't cry, although you could ask me until the end of time what look was on my face and I couldn't give you an honest answer. Can a face show nothing?

Paperwork was easy. I left Darry's mother's phone number with them so she could handle their questions about what to do with his body. I signed another sheet that let me have his effects, which turned out to be a wallet and some breath mints. His car keys were still in the wreckage.

I grabbed Brad's business card while at the front desk.

Through the whole process, I just sighed. Constant, shaking sighs—contents under pressure. No tears, and I still wanted to get off.

I'm sick and I've pinned a confirmation on alone. The widow, throbbing and numb.

So now I'm solo and sitting shocked in Room 202 at the Valu-Rest hotel off I-5. The key to the room was in Darry's wallet. It's one of those plastic cards that pops in and out of the lock and greenlights your entrance.

Darry had already been here a day. His toothpaste tube was uncapped, and a towel was sitting in a wet lump on the floor of the bathroom. One twin bed remained unmade—the Do Not Disturb sign was on display when I arrived—and his open suitcase rested on the other, the clothes from inside sprawled across the bedspread. I always admired Darry's tidiness at home so I'm a bit shocked by the disarray here.

By the bed stand there's a half-gone cup of tap water and Darry's alarm clock from home. He never trusted hotel alarm clocks. Press the over-sized snooze button on one of those and you miss the meeting you traveled so far to attend.

I can't ignore the thought—Darry should have hit snooze just one more time.

My mind flashes on Percy and SHIT HAPPENS but not even a twinge of smile follows.

Television makes me anxious. Not an option. I want distraction.

What would I do if today were a normal day? How much better would it feel to be at home now, in bed, drinking an iced coffee and reading one of Darry's Nabokov books and waiting for him to call?

But Darry won't be calling. Darry doesn't exist anymore. Jesus.

How alone am I now?

How hard do I have to deny this entire day to make it disappear?

I don't know. I don't. Stop thinking. Stay in motion.

I use the bathroom and smell Darry's musky cologne amidst the stronger smell of mildewing towels and the fermenting, hair-clogged tub drain.

It's easy to picture Darry running his morning routine, applying a spritz of cologne to each side of his neck before heading out for work.

Instead I picture rubber-gloved hands trembling under the weight of dead flesh, pressing into too-white skin beneath the black-ink scrawl of my name.

I picture myself, doing ninety down the interstate, looking for my own under-ride.

This is not the way. I may be sick, but I don't have to be alone. There's an army of men out there, lining up for me. They don't know it yet, but I'm available. And I want them all. Right now it might take a legion to fill me whole.

I'm a goddamned widow. Which isn't right. It isn't the way my life is supposed to be.

A mistake like this has happened to me.

Darry's clothes are quickly shoved off the made bed—I can't bring myself to touch the one he slept in—and I have a seat by the phone.

Eleven digits, a nine and Brad Fuller's cell phone number.

His voice comes through after the third ring. "Hello?"

Then, "Who is this?"

I almost hang up. Then I remember the width of his jaw, his broad shoulders.

"Brad, this is Elloise. Elloise, from earlier in the day. I need someone to talk to. I'm all alone, and I just… I'm thinking the wrong things and I can't…"

"Do you have any family in the area, even that you can talk to on the phone?"

"Nobody."

He's hesitating, looking for an out. This call is going beyond the boundaries of his job. I use his words against him.

"'In our line of work, we can't assign any set hours to our responsibilities.' You said that, right?"

"Well, yes I did, but…"

"Please, Brad, please come over. I can't sleep and I can't think straight and I'm afraid I might hurt myself."

He asks where I am. I tell him. He's ten minutes away, headed my direction.

I'm not wearing underwear, just a thin blue t-shirt and a pair of faded, soft khakis. My skin feels too hot, so I turn on the A/C and cool and wait.

I'm close enough to smell him now. No longer overwhelmed by the morgue, I can really take him in.

His cologne—Drakkar backed with a hint of formaldehyde, giving me fetal pig flashbacks. He's been chewing on breath mints, some sort of spearmint.

My perfume—Arden's Sunflowers, thinned by salty sweat, slightly undercut by the smell of sex on my right hand, which I hope he can detect.

He tries to talk to me from the doorway but I turn and walk into the room, sitting on the bed and leaving an obvious space for him next to me. He hesitates, but follows.

It's his responsibility to be sure I'm okay.

His right hand is holding a thin slip of something papery that looks almost like a grocery receipt against the span of his fingers.

Those hands… the idea of his hands underneath my shirt, wrapped around my ribs, forcing me down onto him, it's flooding through my brain and I can barely remember his name.

"Mrs. Broderick…"

"Elloise, please."

"Elloise, I brought you a short pamphlet about the grieving process that I think might help you to understand how you're feeling right now."

I doubt this pamphlet can tell me why I'm ready to tear the shirt off the man who showed me my husband's corpse today. Even if the person writing it understood, they wouldn't write about what I'm feeling in there. There are truths about this that will never make pamphlet-grade. But I don't want to understand this experience. I just want to smash it away.

"Brad, will you sit down by me?"

He sets the pamphlet down on the coffee-table to the side of the television hutch and has a seat.

Before he can say anything I shift my body right up next to his and put my head on his shoulder. He doesn't move away. I start to hitch my body and blow puffs of breath from my nose like I'm crying.

It works. He's got his arm around me now, and my body sinks into his. I let my left breast push against his ribs. My t-shirt's so thin he can't avoid feeling my nipple harden. He doesn't move away.

My left hand moves toward his neck, fingers drifting into his hairline. My right hand drops down and brushes the inside of his thigh.

With my head positioned like this I can actually watch him get stiff. Pavlov should have worked with men instead of dogs. They train easier.

Then his left hand reaches down and lifts up my chin.

His lips do not hesitate and mine are already open. This was a simple threshold to cross. Need is need. This is what people do. People that see death do this even more. A show of will, screaming at the ocean.

Soon we've got our shirts off and I'm kissing his chest when he picks me up and tries to set me down in the *other* bed.

The one Darry slept in last night.

I scream. Like I'm being stabbed. Like the knife is twisting and pulling back out at wrong angles.

I can't. I can't touch that bed. It's the last place *he* slept. It's the last place that I can picture Darry alive and peaceful and happy.

Reeling from my scream, Brad almost drops me. I probably blasted him deaf in his left ear. He sets me down and backs away.

"Jesus, Elloise. What's going on?"

Good question. And one with zero decent answers. I just shake my head from side to side, not acting upset anymore, but genuinely confused.

I mean, if I really love Darry, why is Brad the Coroner shirtless in my hotel room? What makes touching Darry's bed so wrong? Haven't I already proven how little Darry meant to me?

"Brad, my head's all twisted up, and I don't want you to go away, but I'd understand. I'm probably not a healthy person to be around, but I think I need someone to talk to, I mean, I'm sure I do. This has been the most messed-up day of my life… I'm not acting like myself and I'm not sure that I'd recognize who I am right now if I looked in the mirror. I can't… I mean, I'm just going to take a shower for a little bit. Try to calm down. You're welcome to stay… "

Before I finish the sentence he drops onto the bed where Darry's luggage used to sit and picks up the remote control.

He's still hard, biding his time. When he asks, "Are you sure you're okay to take a shower?" it seems like a courteous afterthought. Then I realize he's probably afraid I'm going to carve a y-section down my forearms.

"Yeah, I just need to relax for a moment. Sorry, this is weird. I'll be back in a sec."

I lock the bathroom door behind me, knowing the sound of the bolt clicking over will keep him around, wondering if I'm ever coming back out or if he'll be seeing me on his slab tomorrow.

The shower runs hot, near-scalding, to where the steam is hard to breathe. My face pushes into the water until the full force of the shower is focused on the spot where my hairline starts, dead-center. A wish floats through my mind, that the water would turn to white light and bore into my head and wash this whole day away. The wish goes un-granted, leaving me with the steady, pulsing streams of heat coursing down my face.

I wash myself with the credit card-sized bar of hotel soap that Darry had already unwrapped. The thought of his hands holding the same soap, rubbing it against his body, his warm, moving body, I can't bear it.

I block it out and turn the water temp up even hotter, to where my skin is turning beet-red on contact. The little fan in the ceiling can't keep up with the steam. There's a desert-hot fog bank in this bathroom I should never have known.

I sit down in the tub and curl up at the back of it, letting the water blast against my shins and the top of my feet. Somehow, I sleep for a couple of minutes like this.

I pop up out of my cat nap and for a second don't remember where I am. Then I see the little soap in the corner of the tub and try to fall back asleep.

No chance. Now I'm just bone-wet, and too hot, and ready to move past the reality of this day. Maybe Brad wants to lick me dry….

What? No, that doesn't sound right. Who am I now, without Darry?

I've got to get my head straight.

I grasp the shower curtain in my hand, the new hotel plastic squeaking against my skin. I pull the curtain back and almost scream for a second time tonight.

The steam on the mirror is not a steady sheet of moisture.

There are lines where the condensation is thinner. These are lines I recognize from a hundred mornings with Darry, evenly drawn letters on the mirror spelling out these words:

I Love Elloise.

Pavlov should have studied men. Darry's been writing the same thing on our bathroom mirror ever since we moved in together. He always left for work before me, always took a hot shower, always wrote this message.

Even hundreds of miles away, he wrote these words.

Even hundreds of miles away, I'm sure he meant them.

It's too much.

I wrap myself in a towel and rush out of the bathroom, steam twirling behind me. Then I'm yelling at Brad, who's watching music videos, probably unaware that he's stroking his crotch with the palm of his left hand.

"Get out. Get out. Go, please. Please get out of here."

"Are you okay?"

"No, but I don't want you here. I can't have you here right now. This isn't your place!" I hate my voice when it shakes like this.

"Listen, Elloise, you're obviously distraught. Maybe it's better if I stay here, just for the night, to make sure…"

He still wants to get laid. If he really cared he wouldn't have initiated that kiss, and right now he would be making eye contact, and he sure wouldn't still have his left hand on his dick.

"Fuck you, Brad. Get out."

He's putting his shirt on and moving toward the door. He stops and turns back toward me with his eyebrows scrunched together like he's never been so confused in his life. I know the look. I don't want to hear his voice.

"Go, Brad."

"I'm going, but I just want you to know… "

"Go." I don't want to hear this dejected little coroner telling me that I'm sick, or that I'm confused, or crazy, or anything. I just want to be alone. "Get out of here, Brad."

The spoiled bastard, he slams the door so hard that the corporate-approved watercolor painting by the entry falls off the wall. The frame breaks and there's shattered glass on the carpet.

I'm not cleaning it up. I hit the POWER button on the remote control by the bed stand and the television winks out.

When I feel truly lost, truly afraid, I try to fall asleep as quickly as possible. I have to do this now.

My towel drops to the floor. The A/C gives me instant goosebumps.

The bed Darry slept in last night is cold too, but I get in and pull the covers up to my shoulders and hope my body will warm the fabric.

The smell of Darry's skin is on the sheets, but each time I inhale it feels like the scent is fading.

I'm breathing him away.

And down below, between my legs, I can still feel my pulse.

I let my fingers seek out my heartbeat. I open myself up under the disheveled sheets and feel drips of water running from my skin to the bed beneath me.

I close my eyes, and now all I can see is Darry.

Thoughts of warm ointment, a still bleeding tattoo, and I'm moaning.

When I'm finished, I can feel tears tightening the skin of my face as they dry. The whole time, while my hips rolled and I remembered every sweet and every rough way Darry had ever touched me, I was crying and didn't know it.

I roll out of bed, slowly, and I've got hollow bones. I step around the shattered glass on the way to the bathroom.

I run the shower and the sink as hot as I can and fill the room with steam, sheathing the mirror and every other surface in tiny droplets of water.

Then there's just my finger, tracing trails on glass for longer than I'll ever remember.

The Parasite
B-Sides and Rarities

The following are mutant missives, separated from the bulk of the book due to their collaborative parentage, general excessiveness, or non-fiction nature.

"The Gravity of Benham Falls" was originally to be included in this section as it represents writing from the 1998-2004 era (most of which was collected for Angel Dust Apocalypse rather than the 2005-2011 stretch gathered for We Live Inside You). But once I looked at the primary line-up I realized that a traditional and somewhat sentimental ghost story might make the perfect mid-read break from all the surrounding intra-familial homicide.

This next story is my third collaboration with artist/writer extraordinaire Alan M. Clark. The first was the short story "Amniotic Shock in the Last Sacred Place" which was based on his series of Pain Doctors paintings. The second was the Bram Stoker Award nominated novel Siren Promised. And the following tale is the result of an experimental collaborative writing game of Clark's called The Bone-Grubber's Gamble (the results of which are featured in many splendorous forms in Clark's excellent collection Boneyard Babies). I don't know whether it was the nature of the game, or Clark's prodding to "really take this beast to outer space," but things kind of got out of hand. You'll see what I'm talking about.

The Musty Cow's Teat of Death

It was a snuffle-snort sort of situation, until blessedly it was snot, but that would take time. As cute as the dog was, I was going to slather and roast this creature and devour it with the help of my best friends while throwing whore's shoes in an outdoorsy, afternoony sort of setting. My neighbor, the pup's owner and master, a sweet fellow by the name of Ordwello, would be pissed.

But the social gods are fickle and demand offerings. I tried to appease my friends with a sack of rice, but it turns out I'd suffered an otic malfunction. Thus I was forced to proffer a blinding magnitude of blazing bunnies (which are a lot like kettle kittens and church dogs, but burn brighter and bluer). Even with this, I was threatened with a charge of Improper BBQ Etiquette, a crime that finds itself punished via the slickening sight of neighborly sickle-to-the-gut-coils. I was pre-unraveling inside my grey slop when I heard the familiar bark.

Of course! I'd burlapped Ordwello's pooch this morning when it attempted to landmine my lawn with noxious dog tootsie.

On presentation of the bagged canine my friends holstered their cursed sickles and the one filling out the citation put away his clipboard. They backed away as Ordwello burst through the fence to reclaim his pup, the cream inside his blue egg such a delicious odor it practically demanded a hatchet to the forehead.

But Neighbor Brains were a Sick-Maker, however delicious and piquant, and I hadn't the proper BBQ outfit to keep his meat blocks leaking an hour of sticky stew. Bad prep was no prep at all, and that's per the long-running President of BBQ Trackademy. Ordwello should have let the dog go, and let peace fall upon all of us via greased esophagus. Instead he invaded by means of yard-wounding fence-breakery and cries of, "Move the damn dog earthward, Dickface!"

The metal plates on his back opened wide and I was tempted to lob in a grenade of warm hospitality and festive cheer. My thought being, "Why kill your evil neighbor when maybe he could just join the party?" But the clot in my right temporal lobe had been on blood-thinners for weeks, its running regimen having remained dirigible, and it chose that moment to break through. The doctors later said the blood flow destroyed parts of my ventral prefrontal cortex, removing any constraints I might have had for anger.

Ordwello thought *he* was pissed, but when I was through with him he would be omicturated!

Only biting my tongue kept it from crawling out of Tooth Town, past the Vermillion Border, down my adrenaline-twitching torso, across the mixed fescue lawn, and up to Ordwello's throat. But using the Constrictor Feature I'd had newly installed in my mouth-meat would have ruined the show I'd planned for later, and I'd made too many hard-boiled eggs to let that agenda collapse.

Instead I crouched to the ground, crab-scuttled back a stretch to the garden, and grabbed a spiked philosopher's stone. Then, noticing that Ordwello's back plates had now extended above him in a three story V, I shouted, "Adulterer!" and gave the barbed boulder a mighty huck.

I'd heard that, against the wishes of his docphors, he'd had second tots on the eve of his third skelephant removal. It was a good thing for me he hadn't gone through with it, I thought, watching my mighty thought-bender pass between his second and third plate of beans (Why he carried his food around on his back was anyone's guess). As the stone slipped between his vertebrae and passed into the spinal fluid he normally filled his lighter with, my friends cowered in the pool to avoid the blast of reason when it went off.

I was not so lucky. Ordwello had told me of his voluntary Gumball Punctures before— all of those extra holes meant that the spinal fluid would be improperly pressurized. The explosion would be as vast and luminescent as a deep sea fish that learned to break-dance.

And, lo, it was! A personal-size purple mushroom crowd rose from his back. And I knew my only option was to tell it a clock-clock joke.

"How many clock-clocks does it take for a Zen Master to…"

"Woof!"

Shit! I was still holding his wriggly non-cooked pupkin, who had just startled the briefly mesmerized nuclear blast. And knocked over my iced tea! There would be hell to pay (or purgatory to rent, at a minimum) if I did not act fast.

These little nuclear crises do flair up from time to time and are usually not apocalyptic. I tried to reason with her. "Clearly, madam, I am an amalgam, much like what the dentist uses to fill your teeth." I was in a hurry and couldn't think of anything else to say, but she stopped expanding and I seemed to have her attention so I continued. "To indicate otherwise would trigger other whys you don't want answered. With that said, may I suggest that our friend Ordwello is not worth getting all hot and bothered over. Certainly not while there's a nice pool in which to cool your heels and refreshments to be had."

The great cloud hesitated, and so yes, I confess to raising public spirit at the point of a gun. With my non-pupkin-yielding extra sticky paste-hand I reached for the flare gun tucked away in the cottony wasteland of my E.T. Eliot brand waist-band.

One pull on the trigger unleashed a trolley of chugging Acquiescence Bullets.

"All aboard my positive suggestion!"

I flopped flat to the ground, semi-mindful of my fistful of pupkin as bullets knocked chunks out of the cloud's cheesecake smile. Twelve purple swirling death's heads nodded in agreement.

"A swim does sound lovely," they multi-phonically remarked.

My guests never predicted nuclear boiling annihilation, otherwise they surely would have posed in more pretty-making fashions, chasing the ever-present ambition to be the most becoming of the dead.

And so it was that the lobster-pot frenzy of hidden guest, chlorinated water, and pleasant atomic expansion met in a millisecond of accidental malice and made mist of prior problems.

With no one left to please, and no need to produce roast pupkin, Ordwello and I found ourselves death-quenched with little else to make of our evening. Noting the regrettable mess in my pool, I phoned the Queen's Service and employed several hirsute servants to fill the body bags.

After that, all was balmy evening and low-spoke words as we de-jawed the memories and made marionberry pies from our crumbling hearts.

"Woof!"

O, pupkin!

The symmetrina is an intriguing and challenging fixed form for prose narrative. Invented by Nebula/Bram Stoker/Pushcart/World Fantasy Award winning author Bruce Holland Rogers, this form follows so many complex rules that only a tax lawyer with a degree in physics can fully comprehend all of its facets.

Despite this challenge, I was honored to team with Bruce in creating an epic nine story meditation on ghosts and loss titled "Faded Into Impalpability" (a thematic Joyce reference added for bonus convolution!).

The following story is the centerpiece of the symmetrina and as such is the only story included which was written collaboratively. I hope you enjoy it, and that it points you toward Bruce's fantastic fiction (including his unique story-a-week service shortshortshort.com).

Mercy

Oscar worried about the dog. Bay Boy was thirteen years old, arthritic, and blind. Walking pained him. Even standing up was hard on him. But he was uncomfortable lying down, too, so his life was one of standing up, turning in a slow circle, and lying back down with low, resigned groan.

It was past time to put Bay Boy down, but Oscar couldn't face doing it. He told himself that it was because of his back. Bay Boy probably weighed sixty pounds, and Oscar didn't think he had the strength to lift him into the cab of the truck for one last drive to the veterinarian.

Bay Boy came into the living room where Oscar was reading and lay down with a sharp, high-pitched whine. Somehow the sound was more heartbreaking than anything a human could produce. Oscar understood why people started letter writing campaigns anytime a dog was hurt on television. They could stand hundreds of artificial human murders, but a dog's televised suffering, that was an abomination.

Bay Boy whimpered again, shifting one stiff leg out from under his substantial girth.

"You're having a hard night, aren't you?" Oscar said.

From the other end of the house, Evangeline called out, "You ought to just take that dog into the back yard and shoot him. Better for all of us."

All of us. Everything she wanted was always for the sake of "all of us." Oscar wondered how many of the millions that died under Stalin heard, "Better for all of us," before they caught their bullet. Oscar tried to picture himself putting his rifle to Bay Boy's head.

"Don't you worry," Oscar whispered to Bay Boy. "I'm not going to do that." He looked toward the darkened hallway. Years ago, Evangeline had insisted on getting every room of the house painted lemon yellow. When she watched TV, the lights had to be off in her room and in the hallway. Her end of the house glowed with the sour lemon light of the television flickering across those walls. "You ought to!" she said.

"She doesn't mean that," Oscar said.

"The hell I don't!" Evangeline shouted. "You ought to shoot him. Better for all of us."

He wanted to tell her that the neighbors would call the police. And there were so many security cameras, in the neighboring back yards, electronic eyes that would catch the muzzle flash. Although none of those was his real reason. He just wasn't ready to say goodbye.

It was better not to argue with Evangeline. Let her have her say, then ignore her. That was the way he had learned to handle things. Otherwise, there was no telling what she might do. Medicine or not, she was a little unbalanced.

When he argued with her about his cigar smoking, back in the days before he retired, he came home one day to find that she had cooked a full dinner: roast chicken, salad, corn on the cob. It was more effort than she usually made. For dessert, she brought out a pie. "What kind?" he said. She just smiled and served him a slice, let him see for himself. She had cut up all of his Ashton Double Magnums, soaked them in water, and baked them in a double crust.

He was almost too shocked to be angry. He stared at her abominable pie. Oscar's anger always took a while to rise. It emerged when he calculated the cost of her stunt. "That's almost two hundred dollars!"

"I know," she had said. "Disgusting waste of money, isn't it?"

He looked to his fork and for a split second he imagined it planted in her neck. Just as quickly he pictured his fork diving into the pie, bringing back a shovel-load of flaky pastry and limp tobacco to his mouth. He'd show her. He'd eat it!

But before he steeled himself to take a bite she headed back out to the kitchen and returned, smiling. She carried fresh corn muffins, his favorite, sans cigar filling. And later that night she kneaded his cramped shoulders in her hands and softly kissed the back of his neck. Always just enough honey to make her meanness slide down.

He never did smoke cigars again. When he'd walk by a neighbor's house and catch a sweet drift of smoke he'd hang his head low. It was like watching replays of a crucial game that he'd lost.

One by one, Evangeline had hounded the pleasures out of his life. He couldn't work on the car in the garage—she was disgusted by the sight of oil on his fingers. He couldn't go to the gym to relax with a pleasant swim—she hated the smell of chlorine in his hair. They'd been having sex in the exact same missionary position for over fifteen years now because any other variation gave her cramped calves and headaches. Finally, even that was too much for her.

One by one, Oscar's pleasures were removed to the kingdom of "Better for All of Us." Little by little, she reduced him to a ghost of himself.

Evangeline had been impressed by his rough-and-tumble take-charge attitude when they'd met at her parent's ranch so many years ago. He'd been a seasonal hand, bucking hay under hot sun and drinking away back pain in the cool evenings. One scorcher of an afternoon, the kind where you sweat so hard that you lose a couple of belt-sizes as the day rolls forward, Evangeline had brought out lemonade—great cool glasses of real fresh-juiced lemonade with big ice cubes and a mint leaf in each. Their casual flirting had started that day. And the way she'd looked at him then, the spark he'd put in her eye, he wished now that he'd seen it for what it was—the farm girl in her had spotted a horse worth breaking.

"But I'm not broken yet, Bay Boy. Not completely."

The dog didn't twitch an ear towards Oscar's whisper. Probably close to deaf by now, too, Oscar figured.

Evangeline hadn't always been so particular. But something happened when she hit menopause, something none of her doctors could pin down. She tried to take hormone replacement pills but her friend Clara told her about how they cull baby horses to harvest estrogen in the mama horse's urine, and that didn't stand with her. Shortly after she dropped the pills, she needed a hysterectomy. After that she changed. She went through a "dark time" and she could barely function until the doctors found the right combination of drugs. Nowadays certain smells gave her pounding headaches, certain colors made her nauseous. She always turned off the TV when there were children on the shows or commercials.

"Why are they always laughing?" she'd complain.

She complained about Bay Boy, even though Oscar took care of everything the dog needed. He stank, she said. He whined. Why was he always whining?

Oscar turned his gaze to Bay Boy again and was surprised to see the dog staring back at him through milky-blind eyes, his gray doggy-eyebrows squinted towards the center of his face in confusion, as if to say, "Where did the puddle underneath me come from?"

Oh dear, Oscar thought. That again. Well, he could clean the floor before Evangeline knew.

Bay Boy stood up with another grunt, still looking to Oscar for answers.

"Oscar! What in God's name is that awful smell? Do you smell that?" The voice from the end of jaundiced hall demanded answers, but Oscar couldn't let her know what was happening. Evangeline detested the smell of urine. Any urine. Oscar had to scrub the toilets with bleach on a daily basis. One time he'd even noticed her pinching her own nose shut while doing her business. Until that day he hadn't cried for three years, not since his brother Dale's funeral. But seeing her sitting there like that, so disgusted by herself, sent him out of the house to cry for both of them.

His tears were the sort of thing that somehow kept him close to her on the days when she demanded he give up another enjoyment for the sake of "all of us." He hated to call it martyrdom, but the thought had occurred before.

Oscar yelled back down the hall. "I don't smell anything. Maybe the neighbors forgot to seal the lid on their trash. You know how they are."

He cleaned the mess and put the piss-soaked towels out to the right of the back porch. He could launder them when she slept.

Bay Boy was harder to clean because Oscar had to get down on the floor and hand scrub the dog's belly and paws with a soapy towel. He couldn't risk taking the dog down that hall to the bathroom with the tub.

As Oscar scrubbed his dog's belly he was happy to hear Bay Boy's whine descend into a pleased panting. Once he dried the dog he rubbed behind the dog's ears and hoped the old mutt would slide into sleep.

Soon he heard Evangeline begin to snore. He laid his hand on his dog's soft warm fur and felt the chest slowly rise and fall.

There, alone in a house overcome by sleep, Oscar stared at the rifle sitting in his gun case and wondered about how to use it.

"What," he wondered, "would be best for all of us?"

Including a six thousand word second person crime story set in your hometown—and quite overtly displaying your James Ellroy obsession—takes some moxy in the first place. And putting it early in your collection where anti-second person readers are likely to be popped right out, that's pushing your luck.

But real hubris would be to include a twelve thousand word "Director's Cut" version of the same story, right?

Well, yeah.

But, for the folks who dug the first version, these are two different creatures. The first is pure STORY, trimmed as lean as I could take it, gunning for that Ellroy telegraphic prose style (and a length that would serve novella-shy readers). This latter takes a slightly more leisurely approach, including more character development, Portland flavor, Shaun Hutson references, a vagina dentata nightmare, and a smattering of prostitutes.

You know, the good stuff.

Persistence Hunting

Don't act surprised. Now is not the time for you to shake your bloody fists at the night sky.

You're the one who chased this down. Take a look at yourself. Figure out how this happened.

Help is coming—maybe a little reality check can keep you seething until it gets here. It's better than slipping into shock.

Face the facts.

You're laying there in the evening chill, broken and breathless and cold on the dewy suburban grass because of a basic truth:

You've always been a sucker for love.

And while you've also always been alert enough to know that about yourself, you've never quite been smart enough to do a goddamn thing about it.

Since day one, you little punk, you've had it in your genes.

Age seven: All Mary Ashford had to do was smile at you. You kicked over your chocolate milk. She skipped away and shared it with that red-headed oaf Mikey Vinson. They laughed. Held hands, even.

You rube.

Age fourteen: Sarah Miller actually asked you to the last dance of the year. Like a date, she said.

Why wouldn't you help her with her algebra homework? It was an easy down-payment on a guaranteed post-dance make-out session behind the modular buildings to the south of the school grounds. Maybe you'd finally have a reason to sniff your fingers on the ride home, in the back of Scotty's mom's mini-van.

You even gave Sarah your final exam answers, since she took the class later in the day. You were a huge help.

Sarah passed algebra.

Sarah passed on attending the dance.

Stomach flu—very sad. She even cried on the phone.

Two weeks later you hear she went to the final dance at a rival school across town. With Mikey Fucking Vinson. And the rumor mill pegs them as crossing the legendary fourth base in a hot tub.

You cursed Mikey Vinson, prayed to God for wolves to tear the lecherous bastard to pieces. You pictured it. The wolves always ate his cock first, then his face. It was important that his face went second, so he could watch, and you could see his agony. Sometimes the wolves disemboweled him in the hot tub—a steaming red bowl of rotten Vinson soup.

The revenge fantasies waned though. You knew the truth, even then. This was on you. Later you cried yourself to sleep, thinking Sarah Miller would probably be the last girl you'd ever truly fall for.

You chump.

Age fifteen: Love got blown right off the radar. And not because of some steely world-weary resolve on your part. No, you were still a mess of hormones and need and zero savvy charging headlong into the bayonets of the beauties that walked the school halls.

Love caught the boot that year because your parents burned to death on their eighteenth anniversary.

Each November, every anniversary weekend since you were born, your parents shipped you off to your Uncle Joshua's house in South East Portland.

This was fine by you since it got you the hell out of Salem—AKA Solame, Boregon—a city cursed by strip malls, bleach-toxic waterways, and virtues so minimal that to mention them as a counter-point to the city's greasiness actually made living there more painful.

Portland felt big and electric and Uncle Joshua had a cozy little bungalow just off Powell on 58th. At the back of this house you had your own appointed guest room. Your Uncle even put a wicker basket on your bed with towels and a washcloth and a tin-foil wrapped chocolate in it. He told you, "I knew you'd like that, you tidy little bastard" and then he laughed.

He liked to call you a bastard and a scallywag and a roustabout, and you liked it too. It kicked off your visits and let you know that things would be different, if only for a weekend.

Uncle Joshua did freelance cover design for a batch of different publishers, and his favorites adorned the single hallway that bisected his house. Most of these involved gorgeous, buxom women whose significant breasts had never known gravity. Inevitably these women were in peril, typically ape or tentacle or goblin-based.

"I'll never be Vallejo," he told you, "but I just love painting this shit."

It was great when he swore. You tried it on for size now and then but it sounded like you were pushing out the words, while your Uncle's profanity ran fluid.

There were other benefits to the Portland visits. Uncle Joshua didn't keep his Hustler mags that well hidden, so you found yourself in possession of glorious new jerk-off materials, finally getting a peek at what you'd so far been denied. The first time you saw a vagina spread wide open—"This is my sexy wife Roxy and she's been begging me to shoot her pic for Beaver Hunt!"—it was all pink and slick and deeper looking than you expected.

That night you dreamed you were having sex on your Uncle's couch and the woman's hole was gaping for a moment, a jet black maw, and then her snatch shot out like a sheath of wet intestine and wrapped around your penis and tried to swallow it whole.

It was not the last night you'd wake up sticky and scared at the same time. It was always the creepy dreams—the ones that skewed towards morally bereft or damnably weird or both—that guaranteed you'd lose your load.

You tried, on occasion, to talk to Uncle Joshua about girls, but it seemed a sore subject. He'd shift the conversation to what you'd been studying in school or reading about. His interest felt genuine, and when he said that something you were doing was cool it usually made you feel like your life was right on track and that maybe girls weren't ultimately a necessity for happiness.

Sure, your Uncle had women in his life, but you seldom saw them. They knocked at late hours and usually walked straight to his bedroom, sometimes leaving a trail of perfume in the foyer and living room that you secretly snorted up, like a horny little pig tracking hooker truffles.

You knew who these women were. You'd recognized one from her photo in the back of a Portland weekly paper that your Uncle kept on the laundry basket in the bathroom. The photo popped out because your Uncle had circled it in red Sharpie and jotted the word "TITS!" and a smiley face next to the phone number.

You pretended these women were the muses for his paintings, but you never saw him take brushes into his bedroom. And sometimes the noises coming from his visitors became a smidge too Discovery Channel, all animal grunts and squeals conveying feats of exertion that you couldn't even properly visualize, despite your Larry Flynt primers. On these nights you turned up your Walkman to eight and buried your nose in whatever book was on the bed-stand.

Your Uncle gave you great pulpy novels—mostly swag from the publishers he worked for—about rough-and-tumble detectives and man-eating slugs and serial killers. You were allowed to read them in bed, by flashlight, till any hour of the morning

The catch on the late nights was that you had to promise him you'd still wake up to go jogging with him every morning at seven sharp.

Conversation was part of that morning routine. Your Uncle liked to start running at a gradual "talking pace" and then accelerate through the rest of the run. And since initially his "talking pace" was your "Holy shit, I need more air pace" you mostly listened.

"The morning run blows the morning prayer out of the water, so far as I'm concerned," he told you. "Clears out the toxins. Gets you breathing. Gets you thinking, and thinking straight. And unlike prayer it really clears out transgressions. Mile one makes up for the greasy burger I slammed between lunch and dinner. Mile three makes up for that time I started shooting bourbon and then passed out on the couch. I still made my deadline for the painting, but..."

He'd use a word like "transgressions" with you and just assumed you got what he was talking about. And you did, though only in context at the time.

Half the time you were just trying to maintain speed with him as he spoke. Though each block of the city had its own set of sensory distractions, you always stayed tuned in to his voice.

"Don't get me wrong, kiddo. I'm not saying I consider running some kind of penance. God, that would be hideous. It's so far from a punishment. I'm just saying that it cleans everything out. The worry, the garbage, all of it. Now pick it up a little bit after this block."

He was always trying to get you to go a little faster.

Truthfully, you *were* a shit runner until after the weekend when you lost your parents, when it became all you wanted to do.

That was when running—as hard and fast and for as long as you were capable of—was all you *could* do, really. Any other scenario meant leaving a space open in your brain. Time to think and reflect.

Then you would have to picture your Uncle collapsed on the kitchen floor with the phone in his lap, saying, "I think this call was real. I think it was. Shit. Jesus. C'mere, kid." He reached out for you, hands shaking. You'd never seen him cry before.

You would have to remember the way your house in Salem looked when only a charred support post remained upright amid the ashes.

You would have to think about your parents in their bedroom, holding each other in slumber just moments before a combination of spilled champagne and dried rose petals and faulty electric blanket wiring caused the flash fire that consumed them before they even had a chance to escape their bed.

So you kept running. Your Uncle's house in Portland became your new home, the place where your morning prayer was the sound of left/right footfalls and your evening prayer was that you would not dream again of your parents trying to scream with smoke-filled lungs, like broken bellows that refused, at last, to compress.

It was about five years after the fire when love finally ran you down.

You were twenty-one years old and still a virgin. You'd decided to chase nobility and had never exploited your semi-orphan status for a cheap lay. Besides, that would have meant talking to someone. Maybe even getting to know someone. Not an option.

Your Uncle's route—female companionship as commodity—never quite seemed like the right tack.

You'd become fairly confident that chasing the cat was for suckers anyway. You had transcended that status because you had a *new* kick, and it was something you'd guessed was much, much better than pussy: THEFT.

You weren't stealing for the money—your parents' life insurance and allotments from a nice little trust kept you financially sound—so much as you were stealing because you'd recognized a great opportunity.

Portland was a runner's city, and while it was impossible during the day to hit the waterfront on either side of the river without seeing a jogger or two, it was also fairly common to run into different crews at night. OHSU medical researchers training for the Portland Marathon at two in the morning. A pair of cabbies whom you always spotted jogging through the streets of the overdeveloped condo blight near the Pearl District. Running zealots like you, who absolutely had to run and were thus forced into the night shift.

You kept your morning jaunts with your Uncle going, of course, but he was seldom interested in cracking open more than a three-to-five miler. So the evenings were your time for the long hauls. The air was cooler; the minimized traffic meant sucking down less exhaust. And the further you traveled, the easier it was to black out from exhaustion after you got back to your house, hit the shower, and hobbled to your bed. Less time staring at the ceiling, thinking about who you were, what your life meant, just how truly alone you might be.

Most nights you spent a few hours on the streets, tearing up one of your three rotating pairs of Nikes. And what you started to notice was that Portland's runner omni-presence rendered you invisible to the cops. Or if not invisible, then negligible—a non-threat. Just another fitness junkie trotting around in fancy gear. Garmin GPS runners watch—Check. CamelBak water backpack with enough H2O for the long slogs—Check. Yellow reflective vest—Check. Short shorts designed to hug your junk for minimum shift and emulate that 70's basketball player style—Check.

Sure, you looked like a douche-bag, but this wasn't about attracting girls with your NASA-approved space gear or Kenyan physique. It was about the act itself. It was about going further when you could, letting your legs burn a little more, trying to push the dreaded "wall" —that utter vacuum of energy that forced you to stop and walk—out another mile or two. Sometimes you got lucky and accidentally ran yourself into a runner's high and found yourself soaring over miles of terrain, the air tinted with a slight taste of cotton candy as it surged in and out of your chest. Other times you fought for every stride, side knotted up, thighs burning, guts liquefying. But you always loved it.

It cleared things out, and it gave you your own space to carve through the night, temporary and unseen.

You actually thought that the cops might be ignoring you because you reminded them of what they should be doing off shift. These guys, with their proto-fascist moustaches and Krispy Kreme-endorsed lard rolls rubbing raw against their belts, they couldn't catch a running criminal without a K-9 unit or a bullet.

You always waved at them, or gave them a nod that said, "Hey, boys, here we are. Upstanding citizens keeping things safe, sound, and healthy on this fine and muggy evening."

Sometimes they waved back. Some of those times you were running right by them with a thousand dollars worth of pinched jewelry jammed into the inner pockets of your CamelBak.

Never did they think to turn around and question you. What self-respecting thief would run right by a cop car while rocking reflective gear meant to call attention? Hell, what self-respecting human being would wear little nylon hot pants like that if they weren't a die-hard running fanatic?

To them you were just another night runner fading in the rearview.

And in fairness to them, you were pretty minor shit at first. No better than your standard jockey-boxing meth-head menace.

It all seemed so easy and made you feel clever and dangerous. You used that feeling to try and squash old jealousies that you knew were worthless but couldn't keep from harboring. You thought, "I bet Mikey

Vinson never had the stones to pull of this sort of thing."

You were most familiar with the suburban streets of your South East neighborhood, but it didn't feel right to jack the low income starter families and Russian and Vietnamese immigrants that called it home. The ritzier region of the North West hills seemed like a better target. You'd frequently run near the NW 23rd (AKA Trendy Third) street shopping district, an upscale consumer rat's nest where surgeons and lawyers parked their Harley's out front of the Starbucks. You believed that one day the 1960's Sonny Barger would magically materialize and beat these men with a length of chain, but it never happened. Despite your dismay over this lack of justice, 23rd remained a decent through-street to Thurman, where you always turned to head up to Forest Park and the Leif Erickson trail.

The neighborhoods on the way up to the trail were beautiful and the streets were strewn with easy targets. Suburbans and BMW's and Jaguars (and a smattering of Portland's ubiquitous Subarus and Priuses). You started to spend less time running the trail and more time learning the surrounding territory. You memorized the location of older vehicles—hoping they'd be less likely to have alarms—and as you ran sidewalks you looked to see who had a habit of leaving small valuables in their ride.

You scanned purses, cell phones, MP3 players, laptop computers, PDA's, you name it.

You acquired gear for the job. The LifeHammer tool was designed for drivers who found their vehicle suddenly submerged in water. It was lightweight and one side featured a razor which the driver was supposed to use to cut their seatbelt loose. The other side was the real gem—a small metallic hammer specifically designed to make shattering tempered vehicle window glass a breeze. Ostensibly created as an exit tool, it also worked great for entrances.

So one evening, around two thirty in the morning when you guessed cops would be even busier nabbing drunks, you LifeHammered your way through the triangular rear window section of a jet black Escape, reached in and popped the lock, and then grabbed a pale blue iPod Nano. You accidentally hit the control wheel and the light flooding from the player caused a temporary panic—Is it a flashlight? A cop's floodlight?—quickly abated as you recognized the glow and stuffed the player into your backpack.

You got out of there fast, hands sweating but mouth parchment-dry. Your shorts felt extra tight and you realized you were half-way to a raging hard-on. You could still smell the mixture of stale air and over-sweet cologne which had floated in the cab of the rig.

It was glorious. Without intending it, you tracked a new record pace on the run back to your house.

This was beyond a runner's high, and the kick had a momentum you couldn't contain. You hit twelve more cars in the next two weeks, sometimes scoring nothing, sometimes taking a worthless object just to have a totem from the night. Your spree temporarily upped the patrol presence in the area, giving you your first chance to wave hello to the five-oh and clueing you in on the idea that it might be better to strike more randomly. Your territory shifted between the hills on the North and South West side and the richer South East neighborhoods near Laurelhurst Park.

Each evening's loot got stashed in a cardboard box in your closet, which you picked through during the day, deciphering what you could about the people you had taken from. You fell asleep to other people's play-lists (you loved it when you accidentally scored the player of another hip hop fanatic) and studied the smiles of strangers in digital photos.

Your Uncle Joshua stopped you one morning, before your mutual run, and asked you why you seemed so happy. Why the little smiles during breakfast?

You said you didn't know, and that was enough for him. Your shared loss had kept you close, but quiet, as if speaking too much might bring you each nearer to what had happened. It was years ago but still floated under the ice of every conversation. Each word shared threatened to chip away at the agreeable distance. Unless, of course, you were talking about movies or music.

You gave him one of your best iPod's later that day and showed him how to operate it. He spent that night uploading King Crimson albums and painting a pirate lassie with sea-spray gleaming on her treasure chest.

You spent that night taking your brief career in burglary to the next level.

After all, any tweaker can crack a couple of car windows. The vehicular smash-and-grab felt like the definition of inelegant crime, and the buzz was starting to dwindle.

Breaking into houses seemed like a logical next step. You started to smile just thinking about it, but killed the grin in case Uncle Joshua was watching. You laced your shoes double tight before leaving the house that night. The rain was thick to the point of sheeting as you began your run, but you barely noticed.

You came so close to bailing out.

You'd done your research, been by the place—a beautiful art deco rip-off in the NW hills—enough times to notice the owners almost always left the sliding glass door on the side of their house open. But as you moved quietly through their yard you heard the wet grass squeaking under your shoes and you felt too conspicuous. Would your sopping shoes leave prints on their floor that would sell you out? Only one of their three cars was out front, and the lights were off, but what if one of the owners was sitting home right now, polishing a rifle in the dark? Was it worth it?

You backed off. You were taking this too far.

You opted for an auto break-in instead. They still had an older model Infiniti sitting in the driveway, no alarm light blinking near the dash. The front right window crumbled under the LifeHammer. You reached in, popped the locks, ran around to the driver's side.

You didn't even know if there was anything valuable in there. It was a desperation move. But you got lucky—you opened the glove compartment and found a receipt. Franzetti Jewellers—$6,000. Dated that day. You scrambled the rest of the car for the jewelry box but came up with zero.

Was it in the home? Earrings, a necklace, a ring—any of those would fit into your backpack so easily. And something like that was so much more intimate than an iPod. A purchase like that represented a history between two people, a choice, a serious debt. It had gravity, and it pulled you towards the house.

You walked right up to the open side entrance. You knocked on the edge of the door frame at the entrance to their kitchen and said, "Hello?" as loudly as possible. You figured that if anyone answered, you had an easy out. Feign injury, start to limp, say you rolled your ankle coming down from Forest Park and heard a crunch, that you were so sorry to impose but really needed a cab so you could head to the hospital in case it was broken. The neighborhood was swarming with runners. It wouldn't seem implausible.

No one answered back. After your third "Hello" echoed back from nothing, you crossed the threshold.

It took you five minutes, the longest and most exhilarating five minutes of your life, to find the jewelry box. Bedroom dresser, third drawer down, under a pile of gold toe socks.

It was a square cut rock mounted on a platinum setting that seemed to strain to hold the gumball size gem. How many carats, you had no idea. It seemed an engagement must be in the cards.

Just for a second you thought about leaving the stone there. But then you remembered Mary Ashford. You remembered Sarah Miller. You remembered where marriage ultimately led your parents.

You had to save the guy from becoming another sucker, so you hit the streets with the box tucked away behind the plastic bag of water in your CamelBak.

The jewelry went into the box in your closet. You knew you wouldn't be able to sleep once you got home, so you reviewed all your swag, these tiny pieces of other lives. About every ten seconds your attention returned to the ring.

You were shaking in the shower that night, laughing quietly to yourself, occasionally whispering, "Holy shit, I fucking did it."

Your life sped up. You couldn't keep your brain off the B & E's. You kept it to one a week at first, spending Monday through Thursday on casual jog recon, with weekends dedicated to the break-ins. People were out on the weekends, traveling or hitting the nightlife while you prowled their houses. You were no safe-cracker, but you did a fair job of sniffing out where people kept their valuables. Jewels were your favorite. They spent time close to other people, had a sentimental value and memories associated with them. Seemed like they'd be easy to pawn off, though you never did. You'd take cash when discovered, but never credit cards. You wore thin white runner's gloves and hoped they'd be enough to keep the oily prints of your fingers from being left behind.

One house a week became "whenever the coast looked clear." Your record was three break-ins in one night. You started prying back window screens and using the LifeHammer. You had to be more careful with the non-tempered glass. Couldn't catch a cut and leave blood behind.

You pushed yourself to stay in houses longer and longer each time, until the tension and paranoia became unbearable. You would look at photos but never take them. You'd read notes left on the fridge and kitchen counter. Most read as a variant on the standard "Hey, babe, went to the market, be right back" refrain, but occasionally they were more interesting. You found a post-it note stuck to a bathroom mirror in a SW hills McMansion that read, "William, I know about the other account. I've gone to Lisa's. Don't call, please. I still love you. Just need time."

You kept that note.

You carried tiny steak-flavored dog treats but never had the guts to break into a house after you'd heard a dog start to bark. You petted cats when they'd allow you to.

If a whole pack of cigarettes was left out you'd take one smoke, but only one. You'd save it for the morning and puff on it at sunrise.

Sometimes you went to hip hop shows before your evening run. It was easy to stay low key and enjoy a show solo. You kept your hood up during each show and felt like an anonymous gangster among all the dudes fronting around you. They could talk up the criminal life, but you were *living* it.

You tried to maintain the morning runs with Uncle Joshua, but he noticed your owl eyes and lagging pace and was beginning to look concerned.

For the first time in years, you dropped the routine. The nights were just too long.

It was in this mental state—harried, sleep-deprived, lead-legged, junkie-hungry for more break-ins—that you let everything fall apart.

You were coming back from the hills via Burnside that night, as you often did, maneuvering lightly around the sleeping bag bum-clusters near the river. An old toothless alky with a piece of corn in his beard gave you a one handed wave and slurred out, "Hey, runner guy." You returned the greeting with a head nod and a "Good evening."

You were fucking high out of your mind off a twenty minute break-in session. All the jewels had been on lock down, but you scored a homemade mix CD with a bow wrapped around the case. It had just called to you. The entire house smelled like summer lilac and you wondered if they'd paid to have that piped in at all hours.

That sweet smell is what you were thinking about at the moment the little black car took a no-look right turn at 10th and Burnside, just past Union Jack's. You saw a bright flash out of your left peripheral, heard a thump that you later ID'd as your body hitting the hood of the ride, and within seconds you were rolling on the pavement.

The car came to a rapid stop about ten feet later. The brake lights made the scene run red. You were able to figure out the model of the car but couldn't get your eyes to focus on the license plate. Shit.

This is one of the many dangers of running on a major street after all the last-call closeout boozers hit the road. You'd accepted that and tried to watch for it. You just couldn't accept the fact that you might have had your life ended by a fucking Jetta with a butterfly sticker on the rear window.

You saw a pair of gorgeous legs in camouflage fishnets emerge from the driver's side. The girl stood, giraffe-tall in five inch heels. She was crouched by your side in a second, and though you couldn't quite focus on her face, you caught her wide hazel eyes, tiny flecks of gold floating in the green.

You mark—you might have been in love before you even lost consciousness.

She danced under the name Avarice, and said that when she told a guy he could call her Ava it guaranteed extra tips. Up the false intimacy, amplify the fantasy. When boys pointed out the fitting nature of her name she called them clever. That pulled more tips, too.

She was irresponsible, taking you to her apartment instead of the hospital, but her license was already suspended for another offense (she had a drinking habit, passed down from her dad). Ava had freaked out at the idea of real jail time and was strong enough to get you into her back seat and then her first floor apartment. She had watched you sleep on her couch for a few hours, making sure you kept breathing, and gave you an ice compress for your head. You asked for some Advil and she came back with two Valium and a Xanax, delivered by shaking hands with chipped black polish on the fingernails. The pills were what she had at the moment, though she hinted she could get you some better stuff if you really needed it. Like morphine better.

She asked you why you were running so late at night, with a slight tone of accusation. You told her you worked a day job and preferred to run when it was cooler out. She asked what you did. You said roofing. It seemed tough.

She asked you running questions and caught your excitement about the topic. Played up to it. You could see her game—ingratiate until she knew any charges would be dropped—but you didn't want to stop playing. You liked the way she was tending to you. It stirred something you hadn't felt in years.

It also didn't hurt that she was, as your Uncle would say in grinning understatement, easy on the eyes. Heart-shaped pale face framed with short black hair. Decent lips made more charming by a crooked smile. Legs that seemed to be two thirds of her frame. She was wearing grey shorts with pink trim piping and a thin green cotton t-shirt that showed off the curves on each side of her small breasts.

You knew most men didn't get to see her like this, so casual and relaxed and gracious. She knew you knew it and rode the vibe. She showed you her tattoos—two thin stripes, one running up the back of each leg, meant to mimic the back seam of a pair of pin-up stockings. As she got closer you saw that each seam was actually composed of slender cursive words.

She bent forward and touched her toes so you could see the entirety of each line. You did your best to conceal a burgeoning hard-on.

The right leg said: …I asked him with my eyes to ask again yes and then he asked me would I yes to say yes my mountain flower and first I put my arms around him

The left leg continued: yes and drew him down to me so he could feel my breasts all perfume yes and his heart was going like mad and yes I said yes I will Yes.

"It's from Ulysses," she said. "James Joyce."

She admitted that every time she read that last chapter she felt like "rubbing one out." She made a circling motion in the sky with her index finger and closed her eyes. Then she smiled at you, full blaze.

You were already prepared to die for this girl and she hadn't even kissed you.

You never had a chance. It all happened so quickly.

If you had a concussion it was minor and never really manifested itself. More disconcerting was the new gimpy sensation in your right leg. When you tried to run the IT band next to your knee felt tight and sharp, like a white-hot poker was being dragged across the tissue.

Though it made you anxious, you decided to drop running for a week of so. If something in your leg was on the verge of tearing it was better to let it rest.

Ava had been an Olympic-level tease. When she dropped you off at your Uncle's house, after you seemed properly enraptured, she leaned in close to your face and said she wanted to look at your pupils to be sure you didn't have any brain damage. She locked you in at the eyes and let her lips float a hair's-breadth from yours, the heat from her face mixing nicely with your Valium/brain damage buzz.

She whispered in your ear, "I think you'll be just fine." Then she told you what nights she worked at which clubs and invited you to come.

She didn't seem surprised that you were there every night. You dipped into the box in your closet and swapped jewels for cash at pawn shops out on 82nd. You loved the idea of spending your ill-gotten gains on Ava.

You bought every lap dance you reasonably could, and when anyone else got too close to her they looked like Mikey Vinson. You boiled but tried to stay cool in case she looked your way.

You turned creepazoid one night and crawled her apartment when you knew she was at the beginning of her dance shifts down at Sassy's. You were pro at climbing in through windows, and the summer heat had everyone's open. It seemed she barely lived there aside from her disheveled futon and the explosion of clothes scattered throughout the house. You threw two pairs of her underwear in your CamelBak and bailed home for an epic stroke-fest. You tied off her lacy yellow G-string around the base of your cock and huffed the blue cotton pair and pounded yourself into exhaustion. You never ran short on fantasies about her, though your favorites involved her sneaking into houses with you and violating every room.

If it wasn't obsession, it was pretty damn close.

Things seemed fine, spectacular really, until the night she invited you over for coffee at her place. You accepted, secretly ecstatic of course, but caught the heebie jeebies when you noticed she kept looking over her shoulder and wasn't talking to you on the way back to her place.

Once you were at her apartment she brought you into the loop—She liked you, more than she expected to, but she already had a man, on the low, and he was insanely jealous, sometimes to the point where he got rough with her. She didn't know how to leave him, and she didn't want to endanger you. The guy never came down to her clubs, but his friends sometimes did, and they'd noticed you. How could they not?

You puffed up your chest. "Who is this guy?" you asked.

"Have you ever heard of Stump Lo?"

Shit. You had. You un-puffed your chest.

Stump Lo was a Portland rapper who'd been struggling for years to try and pimp his pseudo-Cali-gangster-style hip hop to a general populace more interested in commercial hits or backpacker rap. He was the dude that you always had to sit through while you waited for the good rappers to come on—tolerated but not truly loved, and you could feel his resentment on stage. Word was he'd shifted to coke sales a year or two back—he wanted the cred and his album sales weren't churning out the royalties—and had worked his way to the upper echelons of Snortland suppliers.

This moment, right here, is where you should have made a run for it, gimped leg and all.

Instead you looked into Ava's eyes and decided to tell her about who you really thought you were. It was the best sales pitch you had to try and keep her in your life. You had to give her an alternative to this Stump Lo dude, somebody just as bad-ass that wouldn't trap her in a web of jealousy.

You told her you weren't a roofer, you were a fucking roughneck criminal, and at the top of your game you were probably Portland's best cat burglar. You also broke your code and exploited your parents' death, saying you'd even had to see their bodies. You told her you hadn't felt fear since that day. If she didn't want to stay with this guy, she could roll with you and things would be just fine.

All of this shit just came flying out of your mouth, and as you escalated your bravado with each detail you noticed a spark in her eyes.

She wanted to hear more about your break-ins. You told her about all but one of them. She called you crazy.

She loved your runner's scheme for evading the law. She called you clever, and you believed you really were.

You did feel more powerful. You'd averted an awkward break-off from the most dazzling girl you'd ever met.

You realized that you were really, at last, taking control of your life. She leaned over, put her hand on your face, and told you that she thought she had an idea.

You were all ears. You sorry Rescue Ronnie Captain Save-a-Ho motherfucker.

You sold the rest of your stolen swag, which meant going to about every pawn shop in Portland. Moving one item seemed reasonable. Offering a box of Blackberries put you on a suspect list.

You were back out on 82nd hustling your wares and you recognized strip clubs that Ava said were closer to brothels. She said twenty extra bucks turned a lap dance to a backseat blowjob, maybe more depending on the club and the girl. They're whores, she said, not dancers. You contemplated buying a prostitute so you wouldn't be a virgin when you were finally with Ava, but what would happen if you got burnt? Giving Ava herpes wasn't part of the master plan.

You liquidated your trust and cashed out your swollen checking account. Ava had found a great place in the Caymans online, and you'd always wanted to see the islands. You knew you'd miss your Uncle, but you had no other ties and figured that Ava's legs wrapped around your back could ease pretty much any type of pain.

Ava told you she'd already bought the tickets.

She also confirmed she'd found a buyer for Friday night—she knew plenty of dealers who liked to show off their cash in the clubs—so now it was just a matter of making sure that you acquired the blow.

Stump Lo was going to be kicking off a show for Keak da Sneak that night. It was a small opening, maybe a few hours, but after you made the acquisition all that was left was a short shot up the interstate to meet with Ava's connection, then on to PDX airport and to paradise.

You met up with Ava after her shift on Wednesday night to give her a surprise. You wanted her to have your best diamond ring. It was from your first big break-in, and you couldn't bring yourself to hock it. You waited near her car, not wanting to risk any of Stump Lo's friends seeing you in the club.

She ate it up. Even got a little teary-eyed—no one had ever given her anything that nice before. She put her hands on your hips and pressed her cheek against yours and said, quietly, "I think I might be falling in love with you."

She smelled like sweat and cigarettes and too much perfume and you loved it. As she pulled away from you she had a look on her face that read, "Can something this great really be happening to us?"

You wanted to lean in and kiss her but she was already gesturing you towards her car. You got in the passenger side, thinking that now was your time, that she couldn't contain her need for you anymore and was going to fuck you right here in the parking lot.

Instead she wanted to review the details for Friday night. She would be at Stump's place a few hours before the show, to wish him luck. She would make sure that his Rottweiler—named Scarface, of course—was kenneled. You would watch for Stump to leave and once he did you would run around back and disconnect the air conditioning unit running into his office. That was your access point. After that it was as simple as grabbing the coke and getting out. A quick quarter mile jog would take you to your meeting point with Ava. You'd roll in her car, make your quick sale, and then get into costume for the airport.

She'd been inspired by your adventures in social camouflage and figured it could work to her advantage too. You would enter PDX as proud parents-to-be and her prosthetic belly-bump and draping maternity gear would conceal your collected cash nest egg as well as a half a brick of coke.

You didn't want to seem soft, but you had to question the wisdom of bringing the drugs. Carrying all that cash was already highly suspect, but the coke turned your trip into trafficking. Why risk it?

"The US dollar is on the decline, but coke is universal tender. We can turn it into more money, connections, favors, more coke even. I think it will help us, big time, and I've never seen a pregnant chick getting searched at the airport. Have you?"

You hadn't.

"Besides, with this rock on my finger we'll look like we're engaged. It's perfect."

You considered proposing. Make it real right then and there. But it might spook her, and you knew that even better times were to come. Wouldn't it be better to propose at sunset, in the sand, with a light buzz kicking from some tropical fruit bullshit cocktail? Yes it would.

Besides, you hadn't even kissed yet. For all you knew, as much as you tried to exterminate the thought from your mind, she might still be fucking Stump Lo. But if she was it was just to perfect her cover and keep things smooth until you could begin your life together. Right? You squashed the question, the thought, the images. You focused on her face.

She pinned you down with her eyes and asked you if you thought you were ready for Friday night.

The version of yourself that you were selling could only answer Yes.

Getting in was simple. You saw those window-mounted A/C units as a big sign reading, "Not only do I not give a shit about the environment, I really don't mind if you come inside my house." You'd brought your LifeHammer as a back-up, but all you'd needed to access the Stump Lo residence was a small screwdriver and the ability to disconnect a plug. Easy peasy.

You were halfway up the stairs to the upper bathroom where the stash was supposed to be hidden, and feeling like the air had been replaced with a Dexedrine mist. Your mouth was dry but your face was a constant cooling sheet of sweat.

You noticed a drop of sweat fall from the tip of your nose to the carpeted stair underfoot, and you were wondering if anyone would be able to detect that or use it as evidence.

You were bent over using your runner's glove to try and swab up the sweat droplet, thinking of yourself as a thorough criminal mastermind, when Scarface caught your left calf in his jaws.

For a split second you thought it was a severe and sudden cramp. Maybe you'd been favoring your left leg to go easy on your fragile right and the imbalance caught up with you.

Even when you heard the growl and felt his teeth sinking in you couldn't quite believe it. After all, you'd received Ava's text: DG KNNLD, STMP LVG ½ HR.

What neither of you'd thought of was that Stump might decide to remove Scarface from the kennel prior to leaving.

Call it an oversight.

An oversight that was quickly turning your left leg into a chunk of shredded meat.

You collapsed forward on the staircase as Scarface dug in deeper and swung his head from side to side.

Agony, and you'd stopped thinking. You tried to kick out at him with your other foot but couldn't land more than a glancing blow. You wished you'd started running in steel-shanked boots instead of lightweight sneaks.

You tried to speak, to say, "Hi doggy good doggy it's me your friend please let go" but when you opened your mouth to assuage the hound all that came out was, "AAAAAAA! SHITSHITSHIT! OH JESUS!" It seemed to rile him up; he clamped down harder.

You found the beefy treats you always carried in your pocket for just such an occasion. You tried to extend your arms backwards with the snacks so Scarface could catch the scent.

No interest. So you did your best to wing the snacks at him.

A yelp! Sweet mother of mercy—his jaws cut loose for a second. You rotated, looking back, bracing for the next assault.

Scarface was pawing at the right side of his face, whining. One of the stale old snacks must have clipped him dead in the eye.

For one tiny moment you felt bad for him. Then you saw his head start to drop below his shoulders and you realized he was about to pounce again. You kicked out in desperation, eyes closed, and felt both of your feet make contact.

Scarface thumped to the bottom of the staircase and lay still on the floor.

Shit! You felt terrible—instantly cursed. Steal a man's coke and his girl and he might just move on with his life. But kill his dog and he'd probably hunt you to the ends of the Earth.

Without thinking you were walking back down the stairs, towards the dog, to see if you'd actually killed it. Then you heard a growl, low but increasing in volume.

Scarface popped back up in full bristle, teeth bared and bloody.

Your blood. It took you a split second to recognize that.

You leapt up the stairs, four at a time. You had to lean more weight on your right and felt the tightness there turn to razor-wire. Then you were in the upper hallway and running, bounding, trying to remember what she'd said.

Third door on the left. Guest bathroom.

You collapsed into the third room, not caring if it was even the bathroom, just wanting to kick the door closed and shut out the beast.

You heard the door click shut and pressed your right foot against the wood, hoping to brace it, as if Scarface had become a battering ram with teeth.

You could tell he was out there, hear him gnawing at the door with the side of his mouth but finding no purchase. You reached up and locked the door. Gnashing turned to barking, furious guttural eruptions.

You worried about the neighbors being alerted but remembered what Ava had told you—the whole joint was supposed to be soundproofed since they used to get complaints about the studio bumping beats at all hours. You hoped it was true.

You flipped the light switch and caught yourself in the mirror, bloody and shaking, in track gear. The image ran surreal, like you'd been smacked down when a riot popped off in the middle of the Portland Marathon. But at least you had landed in the bathroom.

You were glad that the mirror had to come down—seeing yourself in that moment brought in a rush of feelings and questions that were better not contemplated. At this point it was action required, not thought.

You grabbed each side of the framed mirror, lifted up and pulled it back off its mounting screws.

The hole in the drywall was there, as she'd described. You reached in and found the plastic loop, pulled it off the nail in the stud. The loop was attached to a vinyl cord, and it strained your shoulders to reel in the compressed leather duffel bag at its far end.

Seeing the bag gave you new confidence. You'd found your grail, and your princess was waiting for your return. You re-mounted the mirror. You used a towel to clean your blood off the floor and then wrapped it around your leg to staunch further bleeding.

You heard Scarface's paws thump against the door, nails scraping. He was not calming down, far from it. You scanned the bathroom for a weapon and found nothing that would allow you to confront the hound with confidence.

That left you with one point of exit—a small sliding window mounted above the shower.

You slid the window open and popped out the screen. You tied off the duffel bag to your CamelBak and used the vinyl cord to lower them both to the ground below.

The drop from the second floor was unfriendly no matter how you went about it, but you managed to hang and exit feet first. Both legs felt equally savaged so you couldn't pick one to bear the brunt of the fall. Instead you tried to let your legs collapse and shift your weight to your back so you could somersault out of it.

This did not work.

Instead your left leg hit first and before you could shift your weight your knee was driven into your jaw. It was a world class uppercut delivered by yourself, and it had the added benefit of forcing your teeth to crunch together. A tiny piece of the side of your tongue was severed clean and before you could register what you were doing you had swallowed it. For a moment everything was fireworks and copper and dust, and then your brain cleared out and you realized that you had made it.

Your contraband was to your left, Scarface was a distant (if still voluble) threat, and you were only a quarter mile from an angel in waiting.

What you didn't expect was… well… any of it. Not really.

Ava was at the meeting spot, a dusty trailhead near the Wildwood hiking areas. So that part matched up with how you'd pictured it.

She'd stepped out of the car and closed the door. She'd left the headlights off and you couldn't see her that well. You'd taken longer than expected to reach her, moving along with a pretty decent limping trot, and you began to apologize.

"Hey, baby, I know I'm running a little behind but you won't believe…"

And then she hit you with the Tazer.

You were already on the gravel before you recognized the crackling sound and felt the fire where the darts had pierced your belly.

For a moment you thought that you'd been shot. That Stump Lo had found the pair of you and you were dead for sure. Soon Scarface would be gnawing the marrow from your bones.

But it was Ava holding the Tazer, and she wasn't letting up on the volts.

Your right leg was folded underneath your body, and with the next blast of juice you felt your calf pull too tight. Your fragile IT band finally gave with an audible snapping sound. You would have screamed with this new agony if your jaw wasn't clenched shut.

Ava let up on the trigger. She said, "Bag!"

You gestured towards your pack and the duffel bag, thrown three feet to your side when you were zapped.

What the fuck was happening? "Ava…"

She turned the juice back on and grabbed the duffel. Clearly, she was not interested in conversation. She stepped closer to you and said, "I'm going to release the trigger, but if you start to talk I'll Taze you until your hair starts on fire. Got me?"

You made your best effort at a nod.

She crouched closer to you. "You're not coming with me, but you should still run. You probably didn't even think of this, but Stump has a shit-ton of cameras in his house. Doesn't really need them, not at his level, but they make him feel gangster. You're definitely on tape. He's no killer, but the people who supply him will not be pleased."

She'd been rehearsing this. You could hear the exactitude in her voice. She was leaving no room for emotion. Maybe she really loved you. Maybe this was some kind of test…

She continued. "You've probably killed me. This is what people will think. They will find a letter at Union Jack's, talking about how you'd been planning to rob Stump, how you threatened to kill me if I didn't go along with it. You'd even joked about burying me right out here in Forest Park and keeping the drugs for yourself. The girls I worked with last night think I'm scared of you. I really sold it. There are plenty of strip club employees and patrons who've seen you staring at me for hours. It will read as stalker behavior after the letter gets out."

"But Ava…"

ZZZZRNT! You seized up. Too much pressure behind your eyes.

She was not trigger-shy on the Tazer.

"Don't try to find me."

Another long jolt with the Tazer and then she was kneeling by your side, properly pegging you as too jellied to lash out. Even in the dark, you could sense she was smiling. She was back at your ear again, whispering, "I did love the ring, by the way, but I had to sell it today. Easier to send off the struggling single mother vibe without it."

Then she was above you, and her breath smelled like black licorice, and she leaned in to kiss you on the lips.

And you, you sorry son of a bitch, you still wanted it, and when her lips met yours you closed your eyes and prayed for time to slow, so that it would never finish.

But it ended, and too fast, and she was up and the Tazer was left behind in the dirt.

"You're smart enough to know I'm right. Get the fuck out of Portland."

"Ava…"

"Good luck."

Her car door slammed. Headlights slapped you blind and then she was gone.

You alternately dragged and hobbled yourself about three miles before you realized that you couldn't go any further, that dawn would come and that you were far too savaged for your runner's ruse to help you.

You made it to a house which looked un-occupied and then found and memorized the street address. You crawled to the backyard to keep from being spotted on the streets.

You drained the water from your CamelBak but still felt Death Valley thirsty. All that electricity…

There was one stroke of luck in all of this. Ava had left you with your cell phone.

Call it an oversight.

Your first phone call was to your Uncle Joshua. He slurred a groggy "Hello?" upon answering, but was alert after hearing your voice. You gave him the address. Said to come to the backyard of the house. Don't ask why.

He didn't. You'd run with him as best you could this last Thursday, knowing it might be the only remaining time you'd be able to do that together. He'd started to ask you questions, wondering about your late nights and your hitchy right leg. You'd cut him off and said, "Things are just kind of crazy right now. I met this girl…"

Uncle Joshua had started to laugh and let out a slow and knowing "Oh." You'd worked hard to ignore your leg and pick up the pace. He got the message.

You hoped he'd pick up the pace this morning. You'd lost a lot of blood. How long did you have before Stump Lo figured out he'd been jacked? How long before Ava's friends would have the cops scanning Forest Park for a body they'd never find?

A light turned on over the patio at the rear of the house. Could be on a timer, but you weren't taking any chances. You crawled across the grass and spotted a large dog house at the rear left corner. From ten feet back you could see it was empty. It would have to work.

You crawled in and found it surprisingly plush. You figured this might be a figment of your shock and delirium, but you could swear the west wall had an on-switch for a tiny A/C unit. Even the *dogs* up in the hills were living easy.

You leaned up against the rear wall and set your CamelBak on your burnt belly. You unzipped the pack and pulled out your accidental insurance policy.

You'd broken in to Ava's place on Thursday night, knowing she was working at Devil's Point, to bring her underwear back. Ever since you'd stolen them you'd felt weird about it. They turned you on, without a doubt, but you wanted to move past that part of your life, past connecting to people through their things. You had a chance to be with the real flesh and blood girl, and starting out on such a psychotic note just felt wrong.

But once you were in her place, you couldn't help looking around.

You rifled the bag she had packed for your trip, wanting to see what kind of swimsuits she'd be wearing when she was laying next to you on the beach. What she might be wearing for you at night.

You'd been living with compulsion so long you didn't even question it when you pocketed the thing. She was going to need it with her anyway, and this way you'd be certain that she wouldn't forget it.

But you could have left it in the bag. It was already packed. She wasn't going to forget it. Maybe, deep down in the recesses of your memory, you were thinking of Mary Ashford and Sarah Miller, and that twinge of pain kept her passport in your pocket.

Your second call was to Information. They automatically connected you through to a Customs agent at the Portland Airport.

It was getting harder to breathe inside the dog house, and you noticed tiny silver sparkles in your vision that couldn't mean anything good, but zoning on the photo in the passport made it easier to focus.

God, she *was* easy on the eyes. Too bad she was murder on the rest of you.

You told the man on the phone what she looked like, and what kind of uniquely marketable baby she was carrying. You told him that the woman's birth name was Jean Christenson, but that she preferred to be called Ava, which was short for Avarice.

He noted that the name seemed appropriate.

"More than you'll ever know, pal." You closed the cell and thought of her last words to you.

Good luck.

Your chest began to shake.

You were still laughing when your Uncle Joshua had arrived and spotted your running shoes sticking out of the tiny house in the stranger's yard. He crouched down and looked you over.

"Jesus! Are you okay?"

In between gusts of mad laughter you managed to say, "No. Nope. I'm in a bad place. I'm going to have to run."

"Alright then. We'll get to that. First, let's get you out of that fucking dog house so somebody can take a look at you."

It was hard work, but he managed to get you upright, with your arm around his shoulder and as much weight as you could bear on your dog-mauled leg.

Once he started the car he looked over at you, seemingly relieved that you'd stopped laughing. You couldn't help it—the pain of moving had killed the chuckles.

Your Uncle had a hundred questions on his face. He asked one.

"The girl?"

You nodded in the affirmative then, over and over again, knowing that somehow he would understand: Yes she pulled me into this and yes I was a sucker and now I'm in real trouble and yes I thought it was love and yes I'm so glad you're here because you're the only person that really cares for me and the only thing keeping me from falling permanently into hate and yes I sold her out but only because that's where she'd taken our game and yes I'm still remembering her kiss and yes the very worst part is that if you ask me if I am still in love with Ava gorgeous terrible amazing vicious Ava I might say yes oh yes despite it all Yes.

You began to shake but kept yourself from crying. Your Uncle could tell you'd just dropped over the threshold of what your mind could handle. You kept nodding, locked in. You started to mumble: OhGodohGodohGodohGodohGod....

"Okay, okay. Take it easy. Trust me, you've just hit the wall, and you know that's as bad as it gets. I'm with you and you're gonna get fixed up. You've got to tell me enough to keep you safe, but that's it. We'll go where we need to. And soon as you can foot it, soon as you get past this wall, the morning runs are back. And this time there's no dropping it. No goddamn way. Whatever's got itself inside of you, kiddo, we're going to hit the streets and clear it the fuck out."

He sounded angry, more with himself than with you.

He twisted his grip on the steering wheel and gunned his car down slender curving roads on the way to the hospital. Dawn was approaching and it was likely to be another beautiful grey-green morning in Portland. Could your Uncle really be willing to leave his home behind just to protect your mangled love-junkie carcass?

You wondered at your luck, knowing this man.

He approached a red light, started to hesitate, took one look at you, and then pushed right through.

And you, you love-sick bastard, you finally let shock take hold.

When I write I always have The Mars Volta in the mix. Large chunks of Angel Dust Apocalypse were written with their brilliant Frances the Mute blasting. I've made no secret of my love for their work. So when their manager contacted me about working with them to tell the story behind their upcoming album, I spent a few days grilling my most devious friends in order to confirm it wasn't a cruel prank.

A month later I'd listened to The Bedlam in Goliath over one hundred times, had several halfway insane discussions about the album with Cedric, and spent so much time in the world of the project that I was infected with its potent paranoia.

The end result was...what? A band bio? A press release? A study in hype and hoax? A ghost story? A true story about the creation of art in the form of bizarre (non)-fiction?

The Volta make complex albums and employ ambiguity and mystery to great effect. I tried to honor that.

But if you were to take a shovel to the soil in front of the small apple tree in my back yard, is it possible that you'd really find an "interred" copy of the symmetrina that I wrote to close the curse's influence on my house?

Who knows? The line between art and madness is vapor-thin, and the worms are always hungry...

The Mars Volta's Descent Into Bedlam

A Rhapsody in Three Parts

The genesis of The Mars Volta's new album The Bedlam in Goliath is one of the weirdest stories in the history of modern music, a tale of long-buried murder victims and their otherworldly influence, of strife and near collapse, of the long hard fight to push "the record that did not want to be born" out into the world. And I swear we'll get to all of that in a second.

But right now, before we drag any new passengers on the Volta Express into the lunacy of The Bedlam in Goliath, we've got to bring them up to speed. And so I present "A Very Brief History of The Mars Volta":

Back at the turn of the century guitarist/producer Omar Rodriguez-Lopez and lyricist/vocalist Cedric Bixler-Zavala decided to form a musical partnership called The Mars Volta. They grabbed a few other intrepid musicians and recorded The Tremulant EP, which was incredible and weird and proved these guys were trailblazing far from the paths tread by their prior band, At the Drive-In.

Then they released De-Loused In The Comatorium, an astonishing album that served as both an elegy for and celebration of their friend Julio Venegas (as told through the fictional character Cerpin Taxt whose life-and-death travails are chronicled via the songs). The album was huge in terms of exposure, influence, and raw momentum.

Next came Frances the Mute, an album with a central plot, based, sadly, on the loss of another friend (this time fellow musician and bandmate Jeremy Ward). An equally bizarre and powerful album. For this record and the remainder since, Omar has produced solo, dropping some of the pop sheen that Rick Rubin brought to the first album in favor of more experimental textures and structures. If De-Loused... was a dark album, this thing is obsidian. And also inspiring. And majestic.

Most recently they released Amputechture, their first album with no central concept (aside from stretching the boundaries of their prior musical achievements). Omar worked as a director/conductor/visionary, writing all the music and providing motivation, while Cedric stretched his vocals and lyrics around multi-tiered songs about things like modern witch-burnings, cultural oppression, and madness. The soaring intensity of the single Viscera Eyes alone is worth the admission.

The tours supporting each of these albums have proven that The Mars Volta is an endlessly ambitious group intent on turning a standard concert into something transformative that can best be described as an aural blitzkrieg. Saul Williams, no slouch when it comes to rocking a stage, once joked that he rushed through his opening sets just so he could watch the Volta sooner.

Point Being: If you don't have these albums, you need them. If you do have them then you know exactly what I'm talking about and you're anticipating The Bedlam in Goliath more than any other record this year. And you know, as I do, that if the Volta comes to your town for a show that you *have to* be there or a little bit of your soul dies. That's a science fact.

Which brings us to the now, on the eve of the release of The Mars Volta's stunning new recording. Which brings us to The Story.

Perhaps it's best to insert a prologue for this tale stating that some (cynics, pragmatists, people who would like their life to be more boring) may instantly respond with rolled-eyes and disbelief. And that's okay. But others are willing to acknowledge that most metaphysics may just be the elements of physics our brains can't quite comprehend yet, and that there is a great power in words, and in belief.

Quotes from two Volta compatriots offer a relevant lead-in:

"The things you speak to can shape your world. Look at Biggie. 'Ready to Die.' Dead. Word."

—Saul Williams (again)

"This is the sound of what you don't know killing you. This is the sound of what you don't believe, still true. This is the sound of what you don't want, still in you."

—El-P

And so, all that being said, here is The Story (and various annotations): Omar was in a curio shop in Jerusalem when he found the Soothsayer. It seemed to him an ideal gift for Cedric, this archaic Ouija-style "talking board." So it was then and there, in a city where the air swims with religious fervor, in a shop that might as well have carried monkey's paws and Mogwais, that Omar changed the fate of The Mars Volta forever.

Had he known at that moment that the board's history stretched far beyond its novelty appearance, that its very fibers were soaked through with something terribly other, that the choral death and desire of a multi-headed Goliath was waiting behind its gates… well, he might have left it at rest there on the dusty shelves.

The Upside of That Choice: No bad mojo unleashed. Erase the madness that followed. Erase the bizarre connection to a love/lust/murder triangle that threatened to spill out into the present every time the band let its fingers drift over the board.

The Downside: No Soothsayer means The Bedlam in Goliath never would have existed. And it turns out that this demented spiritual black hole of a muse has driven The Mars Volta to produce a crowning moment in their already stellar career.

So if Omar hadn't given in to his curiosity and brought the Soothsayer home to Cedric then the band would probably have been happier, healthier, less haunted.

But you and I, Lucky Listener, we would have been robbed of one fucking *amazing* album.

More on that in a moment.

Back up to the last big tour. The Volta and the Red Hot Chili Peppers are tearing venues in half, retreating to their busses, rolling through the night. But instead of the normal Rock God routines the guys are sitting around Cedric's new Ouija board, which they've dubbed the Soothsayer. And they love it—it's the new post-show addiction.

The Soothsayer offers them names: Goliath, Mr. Mugs, Patience Worth, Tourniquet Man.

The Soothsayer offers them a story: It's always about a man, a woman, and her mother. About the lust floating between them. About seduction and infidelity. And pain. And eventually, murder. Entrails and absence and curses and oblivion. Exactly the kind of spooky shit you'd want from your Ouija.

Now here comes the rub.

The Soothsayer starts asking the band what *they* have to offer. This connection that's set up runs both ways, and the invisible voices begin to speak of their appetites.

They threaten oblivion and dissolution, or offer it as seduction. The voices merge as Goliath, a metaphysical quagmire and unfed saint whose hunger to return to the real world grows more urgent with each connection.

There are proper ways to close this union, but The Mars Volta have never been anything if not adventurous. They stay in contact—even taking phrases from the board and inserting them as song lyrics—but never offer themselves as surrogates. And so the starving Goliath extends its influence.

Inexplicable equipment issues abound while on tour.

Conflict with the existing drummer escalates and results in a change of guard.

Ritual gives way to injury and Cedric is laid low by a randomly (and severely) gimped foot.

A completely reliable engineer's mental composure cracks, pushing him from the project. The tracks he leaves behind are desperately tangled.

Omar's music studio floods, threatening to send him right over the same precipice as the engineer.

Long-term album delays hit and people aren't sleeping well.

Nonsensical words and phrases the board had previously spoken begin to pop up in things like documentaries about mass suicide.

The Soothsayer keeps telling the same story but the details are becoming more brutal.

One day the label on the board peels back revealing pre-Aramaic lingo written across weird cone shapes.

It's bad mojo writ large, and things are crumbling quickly.

Worst of all, the board has shifted from pleas to demands.

To threats.

So they buried the fucking thing.

There are many ways to close a spiritual connection. Wear white for a whole year. Surround yourself with salt. Close a board and ask someone else to open it, thus transferring the ownership. Break the board into seven pieces and sprinkle it with holy water. Or bury it.

Omar wrapped the Soothsayer in cloth and found a proper place for it in the soil. Cedric asked that he never be made aware of its location.

And then their album found a new, more urgent purpose.

The Bedlam in Goliath is here to consecrate the grounds where the Soothsayer lies in wait. It's metaphor vs. metaphysics. Its story will be told to you and I, Lucky Listener, and we're the ones re-opening the board. Taking on the ownership.

Perhaps if Goliath is spread between us all its hunger will dissipate. Or, as it threatened, it could become our epidemic.

So there's the story, up to today, but it's not over. Because this thing is about to enter the hearts and minds of countless listeners. My hope is that the album will do exactly as The Mars Volta have engineered it to do, and lift the unseen burden that hangs over them.

When they first sent me The Bedlam in Goliath and asked me to write this, I was nervous. What if the music itself was somehow cursed, a sort of audio Macbeth?

But after over one hundred listens I can tell you with confidence that I'd risk a little spiritual vengeance for this album.

From the opening surge of Aberinkula to the Brobdingnagian blast of Goliath to the frenzy and near escape of Conjugal Burns, The Bedlam in Goliath is the sound of a band transformed. The Volta have never been what any sane person would call restrained, but in the heat of this bedlam, in their teeth-baring cornered animal response to an invisible entropy, they've created a truly relentless musical juggernaut.

The returning roster (Omar Rodriguez-Lopez on guitar and production, Cedric Bixler-Zavala on vocals and lyrics, Isaiah Ikey Owens on keys, Juan Alderete de la Pena on bass, Adrian Terrazas-Gonzalez on horns, Marcel Rodriguez-Lopez on percussion, Paul Hinojos on guitar and soundboard, Thomas "Holy Fucking Shit This New Guy is Incredible" Pridgen on drums, and Red Hot Chili Pepper/regular-Volta-album-contributor John Frusciante rounding out the guitar armada) have crafted a record that manages to contain the echoes of their considerable prior work and merge them with their uncompromising desire to carve out new territory in the musical landscape.

Wax Simulacra carries with it the energy of De-Loused's This Apparatus Must Be Unearthed and elevates the tone with frantic looped vocals and a swirling mix of horns and drum rolls. The mind-melting freak-out crescendos of tracks like Frances the Mute's Cassandra Geminni or Amputechture's Viscera Eyes have always given the Volta's albums and shows an air of transcendence, and there are moments on new tracks like Goliath and Cavelettas and Ouroboros that guarantee escalating listener paroxysms, if not Scanners-style exploding heads. The more relaxed new tracks, like Ilyena or Tourniquet Man, manage to encapsulate the strange lamentation of other Volta slow-burners while adding an eerie sense of menace. The entire Volta crew is pushing themselves further than ever before. And to anyone concerned about the arrival of a new drummer, rest at ease. The Bedlam in Goliath unveils Mr. Pridgen as a drum-pummeling berserker mainlining cheetah blood and snorting dusted mastodon bones, proving masterful with the elaborate and the explosive (and often melding both at the same time).

It's worth noting, amidst all of this rhapsodic praise, how Omar and a crew of dedicated musicians have managed to breathe thrumming life into what was almost a stillborn album. The audio that the first engineer (who, on an up note, is now on the mend and feeling much better) had left behind was close to unworkably snarled. In his absence it became a scramble to rebuild what the band knew they had been creating in the studio. Robert Carranza kicked in heavy on the engineering, sinking himself into the whole project with an added focus on the drum sonics. Lars Stalfors and Isaiah Abolin were also called in, and along with Omar they dodged daylight for too-long stretches and slaved to rework each track. Shawn Michael Sullivan and Claudius Mittendorfer did their best as editors to keep the band from having to start all over again. The ever-reliable Volta-mixer Rich Costey tried to keep things positive and helped Omar battle what he called Goliath's "quantum entanglement" (which even Rich saw evidenced by things like randomly disappearing drum tracks).

The depth of that entanglement becomes apparent when you realize that Omar, always at the center of these struggles, almost gave up on this record. The same Omar Rodriguez-Lopez that moved to Amsterdam and cut four solo albums while also working on Amputechture and a soundtrack for the Jorge Hernandez film El Bufalo de la Noche. The same guy that's probably working on a DVD, his own film, and 10 new albums right now. But at certain points during work on Bedlam his nearly incandescent creative force was on the verge of being snuffed out. And he was sure Goliath was behind the chaos. After his studio flooded, Omar even banned all mention of the Ouija board for fear that simply acknowledging its existence might bring down some fatal blow. Despite the disallowance, he remained haunted. He'd wake to fits of late night inspiration only to find that there was a power blackout (but only in his loft), or that the parts he'd crafted in the midnight hour would later vaporize. Production work became so nightmarish and Sisyphean that he'd occasionally check on the Soothsayer's burial site, to see if it had been exhumed and "reactivated."

Knowing about the immense challenges faced in the creation of The Bedlam in Goliath only elevates my appreciation for Omar's production. With this record he has laid out a blueprint for anyone else seeking to combine the complex with the primeval and make it all hit you where it counts. This is an album that's electric for both the 3:00 AM headphone listener and the guy doing 90 on the interstate with the windows down. This is an album with an immense level of control *and* experimentation on display; for every section with intricately panning gut-punching drums and shimmering horn sounds and scorching guitars there's another where you can sense a mischievous musical mind at play (e.g. the fuzzed out bass tones at the end of Ilyena or the real inserted recordings from Jerusalem or the sound of a live jack switching between demo and final versions on Askepios). As a filmic analog, picture Kubrick or Fincher working in tandem with Bunuel or Jodorowsky.

Actually, similar analogs could be extended to the whole of the album itself. The Volta have acknowledged the immense influence of surrealism and film on their work. In relation just to Jodorowsky, The

Bedlam in Goliath manages to evoke the languid madness of Fando y Lis, the infidelity and murder and worship of Santa Sangre, the broad-spectrum religious imagery of Holy Mountain, the sheer guts-on-the-table awe of El Topo. Throw in the identity confusion head-fuckery of Lynch's strangest films, Werner Herzog's sense of obsession, a few dollops of Jonestown: The Life and Death of Peoples Temple, and pinches of The Exorcist and Don't Look Now and you're starting to get the right idea.

On the lyrical front, you should be warned: This is an unsettling piece of work. You're welcome to take Cedric's vocals at surface level—he sounds incredible, his range broader than ever, his energy and emotion undeniable.

Or you can begin to translate. Cedric Bixler-Zavala, like fellow musical mavericks Bjork and Ghostface Killah, uses primarily English words but speaks his own lyrical language. If you examine the meaning behind his shrapnel-burst imagery, his obsessions with the grotesque and the profoundly sacred, you begin to realize he's created a complex associative tapestry that's designed with spider-web precision. And before you know it you're trapped.

The more you read the story he's laid out (an intricate meta-fictional narrative reminiscent of Danielewski's House Of Leaves, involving both the transgressions of the past and the desire of the Goliath parasite to infest the Ouija-using host), the more you research his allusions and the history of the spirit board, the more uncanny connections you are bound to make. You start to recognize a tie between certain vocal effects and messages from the board. You wonder if focusing on this story too much might invite Goliath into *your* world. Soon you're jumping at shadows, shopping for salt and all-white outfits, surrounding yourself with graphs and counting words and letters and looking for codes, creating your own primordial cymatics using the album, feeling phantom tendrils in your bones. You begin to hope that all the positive elements Cedric covertly slid into the songs (a legion of religious references including snippets of Santeria-derived prayers, classic fables, the hidden name of a regal actress he holds in high regard, an underlying reverence for creation/menstruation, vague hints of redemption) really are helping to balance out and maybe even negate the darkness that has infested the album.

You're bound to have questions. What exactly transpired in the tragic triangle? Who was really in control and who were the victims? Was *anyone* innocent? How did they die and what happened to the bodies? How did they come to rest within the Soothsayer? If they return to our world, what will they do?

Those answers (and more) are in there, fused at every level to songs of equal complexity and gravity. And the closer you listen, the further you voyage into The Bedlam in Goliath, the more disquieting and compelling the Volta's brilliant audiocelluloid epic becomes.

This album is the sound of a band playing—magnificently—for its life. And it is a recording of such strange power that I believe the Goliath that haunts them will be forever struck down.

Word.

—Jeremy Robert Johnson, October 27th, 2007, Portland, Oregon

The Zayin Division—A Second Stage Burial

I. I am the simian martyr's bullet-borne deliverance.

II. Ideomotor effect. Forced cryptomnesia. Your shroud returns stale whispers. Ropes tighten at each limb.

III. He half-woke to a wild leopard, to blood-pregnant air, the smell of his courted collapse. Laurel twigs crossed her hidden tools.

IV. The holy glyph floats close, its gray light angles suffuse the bones now dust, flesh now jelly. Every cell shakes loose its viral code. *Supernus pacta sunt servanda.*

V. Its hands swept through in the crooked mandible, the chemical lobotomy swung blind, the monoxide possessions. All of it annelid territory.

VI. Sandover light shone symbiotic until you saw it swallow-shift. Your retractions granted final grace.

VII. I will not follow your collapsing oblivion.

—JRJ, October 28th, 2007, Portland, Oregon (First print copy interment)

Author's Notes

The Oarsman— Written for the Fractal 10 conference, based on their event theme: Reinventing the world. The result is a bit grim, I admit, but the organizers knew my work and were pragmatists about the result. Step on a rattlesnake, he bites you. Ask me for a story based on themes of ingenuity, creation, hope and rebirth, and I give you Buddhist empathy bombs and stranded sociopaths. (Thanks are due to event artist Oscar Montoya, who allowed his wonderful art for the story to appear with the story's US publication in Dark Discoveries.)

When Susurrus Stirs— There might be a list on the wall beyond my laptop, and that list might include the names of several parasites I find endlessly revolting/fascinating. So if I do, on occasion, produce a story about a mutant variation on the parasitic wasp/bot fly/candiru/guinea worm/liver fluke/etc., please permit me my obsession and attempted exorcisms. And for anyone who thinks I'm going for the "gross-out" here, spend about five minutes looking up the above creatures on YouTube and you'll see I've been rather gentle in relating their methods.

Persistence Hunting— Just prior to the release of Angel Dust Apocalypse I had shifted to a mostly nocturnal writer's schedule, and I was also training for my first go at the Portland Marathon. Chugging down the road in a black stocking cap and baggy gear at 3:00 AM in the morning, and the cops never gave me a second glance. The bum camp that popped up beneath the underpass at 17th and Powell gave me plenty of grief for running through their temporary bedrooms, but I think I would have had to bring along a chainsaw to catch a cop's interest.

The Witness at Dawn— The first of the four fixed form stories that made up my contribution to the symmetrina "Faded Into Impalpability." I've always found it intriguing how people are more accepting of vigilante justice if it stems from a paranormal source. Charles Bronson shoots a murderer, and you've got yourself a moral gray area. Ghost kills the same murderer; the world is back in balance. Ghosts are so obsessed with accountability. And ominous plate throwing.

Consumerism— Yes, this is the same Ron from "Priapism" in ADA, and I originally intended to write a trilogy of his father's one-sided "dialogues," ultimately allowing Ron some kind of revenge. But then this idea landed and it wouldn't go away, and I don't know if the ending constitutes "revenge" or is just one more fundamental life changing abuse that further ruins Ron's life.

Trigger Variation— Every rat finds a button to press. Even self-flagellating ascetic monks are trying to flip a switch. Some rats are just more self-righteous about their particular button.

The Gravity of Benham Falls— The original version of this story included a very pornographic scene beneath the waterfall, with all kinds of intimately described oral and breath control play, and I read that version to a number of elderly folks at a Boy Scout camp site. By candle light. And despite the number of times I have wished otherwise, this story remains true. (Scene altered for pace/gratuitousness and in an effort to erase the memory.)

Cathedral Mother— Did I mention the list on my wall? Two Richards are owed for this tale. The first debt is to Richard Selzer, whose essay "The Exact Location of the Soul" sparked in me an early fascination with infestation and parasitism (human and otherwise). The second debt is to Richard Preston, whose wonderful non-fiction book The Wild Trees chronicles the alien environment of the giant redwoods and the brave explorers who venture there.

The Brilliant Idea— The second of the "Faded..." stories. All of it—the tense, the precise word count, even the content of the allusions—dictated by the laws of the symmetrina. I recommend this form to every writer I know. The restrictions and obstacles in place create challenges which leave you with new tools, and the form can drive you to create a story outside of your normal mode. I don't normally play with "fun" or "quirky" but I think I skirted both for this flash.

Simple Equations— Written for an anthology of horror stories set during WWII. I was initially hesitant to participate because of the sheer pre-existing quantity of stories set in that environment, and the danger of writing Wolfenstein-style stock Nazis. But after watching Trinity and Beyond I researched the way scientific communities in Germany, Japan, and the States all acquiesced to the military (out of fear, for funding, or due to a "pure" desire for knowledge outside of moral bounds). Those scientists who are still alive almost uniformly state that their efforts were about saving lives and making future wars so destructive they'd become untenable for the human race. But as McNamara pointed out in The Fog of War, when addressing the Cuban Missile Crisis, rationality won't save us.

Cortical Reorganization— The third of the "Faded..." stories. Portland has its share of corner "spangers" and I have a history of coughing up for those who have dogs with them or are missing limbs. I once spotted a "spanger" in Eugene who I thought was exploiting people by wearing a baby doll in a harness on her chest. It looked very real and she pretended to rock it and concealed the plastic face from you as the traffic light turned green. I was pissed every time I saw her, until I had a conversation with a mental health professional who told me that they frequently provided such dolls to folks with mental illnesses, as it gave them a companion and someone to care for. So this lady was either a con artist (she raked it in) or a very sick woman whose only friend had a tiny plastic head and plush body. Due to the ambiguity I had to remove her from my Things to Pointlessly Seethe About list. (On the flipside I once tried to give a spanger a Taco Bell Ten Pack and he replied, "What the fuck am I supposed to do with that?" Which says something about Taco Bell Ten Packs. He acted like I'd tried to pass him a box of diarrhea, and I guess that if you follow the process all the way down the line, he was kind of correct.)

A Flood of Harriers— When I was younger and my family would travel up the I5 corridor, I would beg for a visit to a corner bookstore in Eugene that carried Cemetery Dance and Fangoria, both of which had proven more difficult to cop in Bend. So when this story appeared in Cemetery Dance so many years later, it meant a great deal to me. I was *very* surprised when the story sparked controversy and debate with some readers radically misinterpreting the piece as racist anti-Native American propaganda. When someone earnestly (if absurdly) equates you with Goebbels, it's a bad time. I wondered if they'd even read through to the end, which seems to embrace the idea of genocidal blowback (a sort of Re-Manifested Destiny) as a terrible return to karmic balance. The fact that the opening scene is a barely fictionalized version of an actual conflict my then girlfriend and I had at a rest stop in Warm Springs made the issue even more complicated. However, the editor at CD stood behind the story's publication, and in the end I was introduced to a large and appreciative horror readership and given some great advice by Nick

Mamatas: Not everyone is going to "get it." Always be true to your vision for the story and write with your ideal reader in mind. (Thanks are due to all the folks who helped me through the exciting/wildly stressful time after this story's release.)

The Encore— The last of the "Faded…" stories. Probably the most "quiet" story I've written in some time. Which is weird since it was inspired by my repair of a busted vacuum, an event which was far from quiet and almost cost me a finger. Before you rush in to mend a smoking piece of machinery, no matter how bedraggled and rushed you are, UNPLUG IT. That's sound advice.

Laws of Virulence— That parasite list on my wall sits right next to some inspirational quotes from Mailer and Ellroy (I know—Muy Macho). I'd always wanted to attempt a story told through transcript, as Ellroy did with a lot of the transitional and buffering "documents" in American Tabloid. I was originally going to mirror an actual CDC outbreak report, but they leave little room for the human aspects of the story. Plus, the formatting, with all of those little boxes, was a bitch.

States of Glass— I now have difficulty, having done the research on under rides and having seen some awful photos, driving even fifty yards behind a semi truck trailer. Most have protective bars extending below the bed of the trailer, per regulations, but I'm not sure those things would hold up at decapitation velocity.

About the Author

Jeremy Robert Johnson is the author of the cult hit ANGEL DUST APOCALYPSE, the Stoker Nominated novel SIREN PROMISED (w/ Alan M. Clark), and the end-of-the-world freak-out EXTINCTION JOURNALS. His fiction has been acclaimed by Fight Club author Chuck Palahniuk and has appeared internationally in numerous anthologies and magazines. In 2007 he worked with The Mars Volta to tell the story behind their Grammy Winning album The Bedlam in Goliath. In 2010 he spoke about weirdness and metaphor as a survival tool at the Fractal 10 conference in Medellin, Colombia (where fellow speakers included DJ Spooky, an MIT bio-engineer, and a doctor who explained the neurological aspirations of a sponge). He is working on a number of new books. You'll just have to trust him on this.

www.jeremyrobertjohnson.com

www.swallowdownpress.com

About the Artist

Alex Pardee (born February 5, 1976) is a freelance artist, apparel designer, and writer born in Antioch, California, USA. In addition to having his fine art exhibited in galleries all over the globe, Alex has acted as art director for numerous musical, animated, and film projects. Most notably, for the bands THE USED, IN FLAMES, and hip hop artist CAGE, and for the TV/film projects CHADAM & Zack Snyder's SUCKER PUNCH, for which he created art for the film as well as for the marketing campaign. In 2007, Alex also co-founded a successful art and apparel company called ZEROFRIENDS, which acts as a marketable extension of his artwork and storytelling.

www.zerofriends.com

www.eyesuckink.com

CPSIA information can be obtained at www.ICGtesting.com
Printed in the USA
LVOW060717060713

341354LV00004B/448/P